WHISPERS FROM THE ABYSS
2

WHISPERS FROM THE ABYSS 2
A collection of H.P. Lovecraft inspired short fiction.
Copyright © 2016 by 01Publishing
All Rights Reserved.
Cover Art by Patrick McEvoy
Internal Artwork by Patrick McEvoy
Graphic Design by Josh Finney

All stories are copyrighted to their respective authors, and used here with their permission.

01Publishing
www.01Publishing.com

This book is a work of fiction. All characters, names, and events portrayed are fictional or are used in an imaginary manner to entertain. Any resemblance to any real persons or dead is purely intentional for the purposes of satire. This book contains no safe spaces.

No portion of this book may be reproduced by any means, mechanically, electronically, or otherwise, without first obtaining the permission of the copyright holder.

Edited by Kat Rocha
Co-Edited by Josh Finney
Copy Editors: Kat Rocha, Melissa Hofelich, Marcia Finney, Lee Finney

ISBN-10: 0983923086
ISBN-13: 978-0-9839230-8-4

Printed in Taiwan by KrakenPrint

ACCLAIM FOR
–WHISPERS FROM THE ABYSS–

"Anthologies like *Whispers From The Abyss* don't come around as often as they should... Here, horror is shown as a terrifying whisper, and anyone who enjoys readable, accessible collections should pick this one up."

–*Adventures in Sci-Fi Publishing*

"*Whispers From The Abyss* is an impressive collection of short stories that are inspired by the Cthulu Mythos...the stories contained within vary widely in tone, with each writer approaching the mythology from
a distinctly different angle." –*SFFWorld.com*

"4½ STARS" –*Amazon.com*

"...a fresh perspective rising above Lovecraft fan fiction. The best of the bunch carve their own path through the mythos to great effect."

– *Jaffalog*

"...the stories contained within vary widely in tone, with each writer approaching the mythology from a distinctly different angle."

–*Good Reads*

"*Whispers of the Abyss Volume 2* is successful at delivering Lovecraft-inspired stories on a short scale. The intended audience may be folks on the go, but a wider audience will definitely appreciate them."

–*Fanbase Press*

This tome of sacred knowledge was
made possible by...

High Librarian of Pnakotus
-RAVEN DONOHUE-

Cosmic Decoders of Yith
-SHAHEENA KHAN-

-MICHAEL DI SALVO-

-MIKE STINE-

WHISPERS FROM THE ABYSS 2
The Horrors That Were & Shall Be

A collection of H.P. Lovecraft inspired short fiction.

-EDITED BY KAT ROCHA-

CONTENTS

Introduction by Michele Brittany..09
We Are Not These Bodies, Strung
Between The Stars, *A.C. Wise*..11
His Carnivorous Regard, *John C. Foster*..................................23
The Labyrinth Of Sleep, *Orrin Grey*..37
Death May Die, *Nathan Wunner*...47
The Knot, *Dennis Detwiller*..55
Skoptsy, *Jonathan Sharp*..61
Red Americans, *Cody Goodfellow*..69
Shadow Transit, *Ferrett Steinmetz*..83
Baby Rhyme Time: Youngsters Enjoy Initiation
At Innsmouth Public Library, *Deborah Walker*.....................95
Nyarlathotep's Way, *Tom Pinchuk*..99
Strident Caller, *Laird Barron*...113
Lucky Chuck Takes The Sunshine
Express, *John Palisano*...125

CONTENTS

Notebook Concerning The Class Struggle In Dunwich, Found In The Ruins Of A Construction Site, *Kevin Wetmore*...................141

Five Minutes Or Less, *Michael Hudson*..155

The Baby Downstairs, *Chad Fifer*...163

Gifts, *Robert Stahl*..165

Now We Are Nine, *Joel Enos*..169

The Thing In The Fridge, *Samuel Poots*...175

God Does Damn The Mind, *Marc E. Fitch*....................................185

I Saw The Light, *Greg Stolze*..193

Kickstarter, *Richard Lee Byers*...203

The Vindication Of Y'ha-Nthlei, *David Busboom*,,,.......................209

Echoes In Porcelain, *Konstantine Paradias*...................................217

Shadows Of The Darkest Jade, *Sarah Hans*,,,................................227

The Dreadful Machine, *Martin James Hunter*...............................239

About The Authors...247

Devoted Cultists...256

"The Sacrifice" by Patrick McEvoy

INTRODUCTION
By Michele Brittany

The 1920s reflected a fascinating period of time: the hustle and bustle of streets—electric trolley cars, horses and buggies, foot traffic, street merchants, automobiles. Skyscrapers pierced the sky, becoming an iconic image of modern civilization. Electric lights extended day into night as people sought relaxation and amusement in this new urbanity of illuminated signs and brightly lit department stores. Lively, decadent, without rest, the city of this time represented new cultural standards, which clashed with traditional ideals of agrarian conservatism and vied for attention, radically transforming the individual's relationship to nature and society. Mechanization created feelings of both wonderment and trepidation: this was the time of H.P. Lovecraft. It was a world he was not altogether comfortable with—modernity with its positive and negative connotations—became one of his themes that he wove into the fabric of his short stories.

H.P. Lovecraft had a rampant imagination, coupled with a stifling, narrow view towards modernity, especially in relation to the diversity of cultures coalescing into a preverbal mixing pot of the American experience of the early 20th century. He struggled as a writer and editor, and he spent most of his short life in near poverty. After his death, his writing laid in obscurity for decades; his stories making brief appearances in dark library corners and old used bookstores, discarded like a loose thread. However, the seed was planted in the creative minds of individuals who found inspiration in Lovecraft's often stilted, meandering prose that uniquely tantalized the reader's imagination to fill in the gaps of suspense and horror, just around the corner. With technology – probably much to his chagrin – Lovecraft's brand of horror gained further traction in the collective psyche, of course it has not been without ruffling feathers when mediating the disagreeable beliefs, namely racism, that were unfortunately common place at the time of Lovecraft's life. In spite of the controversies, his stories have continued to be influential.

This year marks the 125th anniversary of Lovecraft's birth in Providence, Rhode Island, however he has been commemorated for several years with NecronomiCon Providence, H.P. Lovecraft Film Festivals in Portland, Oregon and San Pedro, California, and was even the subject of a panel at this year's San Diego International Comic Con – the granddaddy of popular culture! His stories have influenced a great many films, comic books, graphic novels, video games, music, and even Cthulhu plushies. However widespread his influence has been over the intervening decades since his death, Lovecraft's roots are in the written word.

For the second time, editor Kat Rocha brilliantly edits together a collection of short stories that accommodate our modern life – a life on the go. Among these pages, each writer finds their respective Lovecraftian thread and weaves a balance between suspense and simmering madness in the vein of *The Case of Charles Dexter Ward*, *The Dream-Quest of Unknown Kadath*, *Azathoth*, *The Color Out of Space*, to name a few. Each story represents our early 21st century mores, such as the use of Kickstarter to raise money, the spirit-breaking status quo of the mundane life, sacrifices for love, desires to experience all and live forever, class struggles, and prejudice against others. In addition, the use of humor is fascinating because while not necessarily creating a somber tone, these writers have demonstrated their cleverness to spin a yarn that taps their breath of knowledge of Lovecraft's mythos and locales. These stories are a reflection of our time and may they prove their place in the rich tapestry of literature inspired by Lovecraft.

Michele Brittany
September, 2015

WE ARE NOT THESE BODIES, STRUNG BETWEEN THE STARS
By A.C. Wise

I'm one of the ones who remembers what it was like before R'lyeh rose. Before New Orleans sank. Before Venice burned. When Mi Go first screamed through the space between the stars, and when Shoggoths last in the dooryard bloomed. For the record, it doesn't make me one of the lucky ones.

Like right now, I'm slogging through a water-filled lobby, all greenish and faintly luminescent. If I look too close, I'll see indistinct shapes moving just beneath the surface, so I make a habit of not looking. The floor is canted, just enough to remind me that the Baltimore, once one of the art deco "Grand Old Dames" of the city, is now either sinking or rising. No one's quite sure which. There's a fish tank behind what used to be the reservation desk, a cruel joke now. Things that aren't quite starfish cling to the remains of the shattered, dusty glass, opening and closing their eyes just to remind us they can.

The elevator hasn't worked in years. Probably since before all this started. The gold filigree cage is rusted halfway open; the outer doors with their ornate friezes mercifully wedged all the way into the walls. One less depiction of the nautical scenes—the stylized waves and curling tentacles—is a good thing. They're bad enough outside the building, the brackish growth furring them gives them unwanted depth during the day, and makes them shine faintly at night.

My hip-waders squelch, trailing water as I climb toward the Baltimore's top floor. Nothing but the best for us, by God. A few propped open doors remind me we're not utterly alone. A face with thin, down-turned lips and bulbous eyes peers out suspiciously before a webbed hand slams the door. From another, strains of what might be music, or keening loss, or both, drift into the hall.

At the top of the stairs, I pause for a deep, wracking cough. A smoker's cough, though I haven't been able to get my hands on anything like a real cigarette in years. Just another legacy of the bad old days. I knock once on the penthouse door, not expecting an answer, and enter.

The curtains are drawn. The room is murky-dim, redolent with decay, but betraying hints of former glory. The previous occupant was in a bad way when I discovered the place, gasping for air through slit gills, but refusing to go into the water. It was an act of mercy, really.

Zee lies on the couch. Their head back, their eyes closed. All the shit that's going down, is still going down—will go down? time is slippery these days—and Zee is dying from good old-fashioned cancer. And there's not a goddamned thing I can do about it.

"Hey." I touch Zee's brow, smooth their hair back.

When I take my hand away, the hair sticks up in sweaty spikes. I suppose that's one advantage of not having access to chemotherapy—Zee gets to keep their hair. They always were proud of it; used to do it up in a real cock-of-the-walk Elvis pompadour back in the day.

"Here." I push a bottle into Zee's hand; after a moment, their fingers close.

We gave up on miracle pills, vitamins, and New Age homeopathic bullshit a long time ago. But the hormones, no. Some things are too important to lose. If Zee is going to die anyway, they are going to die with dignity in the body they chose.

Because the alternative...The alternative is too horrible, and I pray Zee won't ask me again. But I know they will. They'll ask, because they've been asking since the day we came back to that stinking underground tunnel after being stretched across the stars.

Zee finds my hand, grips surprisingly hard. "Did you find a way? We have to go back, John. We have to."

"What do you remember?" Zee's voice comes from a million miles away. "It's important. Please, tell me what you remember."

The words are thick, clumsy, but filled with desperation. My lids crack half open. My mouth tastes like—what? Iron. Violets. Broken glass. Rock candy. Bitter weeds.

A flame flickers, inches from my face. The heat singes my lashes. Light. I focus on it. My lighter, a cheap plastic thing bought at a gas station a lifetime ago. Of all the stupid, bloody things to survive...

A ragged gasp. Turning into a laugh, digging and clawing deeper than the worst of my coughs. Tastes like tar. Like honey. Like...

"What do you remember? Please." Zee shaking me.

And oh God.

I remember. Too many limbs. Or not enough. In the wrong places. They are clicking. We are clicking. I am me and them and us.

Enormous, vaulted chambers. Round windows. Globes of luminous crystal. Looking out on gardens filled with mad, geometric blooming. Vast metal shelves and the memory of a thousand, thousand races scattered across the stars. It is the past and the future and the eternal now. Time is broken. And it is being broken at home, in my home, on my earth. Am I causing this? No. This always happened. Is always happening. And Zee is there with me and...

And.

"What do you remember?"

The flame is inches from my face, casting strange shadows under Zee's eyes, across their cheeks. My neck is at an odd angle, and I can't pull away. We're in a different part of the tunnels than we were before. We were gone, and our bodies moved. I push with a hand that is and isn't mine. Zee tumbles into the brackish water. The light goes out. I flail, beating my hands against the sludge. Panicked, because my body isn't right. We've been gone a million years and only a day.

The city is sinking. We've been gone a million years and only a day, and we've come back to our doom.

"What do you think?" Zee splays photographs across my desk, grainy and showing the graffiti-strewn walls of an abandoned building.

"I think it's time for lunch." I start to stand, but Zee presses me back to into my chair with two fingers in the center of my chest.

"I'm serious, John."

"So am I." I look away from Zee, their high cheekbones, slicked-up pompadour hair, but keep them in my peripheral vision.

With one hand, Zee toys with their suspenders, over a shirt with rolled up sleeves. It looks like something Charlie Chaplin might wear. Zee has always been unstuck in time, mashing up the 50s, the 70s, the 1800s, and somehow they pull it all off. The other hand, nails worried ragged and short, taps the pictures.

"Okay, what am I looking at?" I say.

This could be any abandoned building; the city's infected with them. There's nothing goddamned special about the one in Zee's pictures. Across the street, however, at Tina's Diner there is a very special smoked meat sandwich that has my name on it. Literally. Tina named it after me, sweet old gal.

"These markings." Zee taps the picture again, and I look closer.

I wish I hadn't. In the dim light of our shared office, the markings crawl. It's brief, but definite, and the motion puts an ache behind my eyes.

"Where were these taken?"

"The old station at 33rd Street."

Zee watches me, waiting for my reaction. I rub the bridge of my nose, pinch it hard, but the ache doesn't go away. Behind my temporarily closed eyes, there's a gutted body strung up by its ankles. Why is it that these cultists always think their gods want bloody sacrifices? Why would anything aeons old possibly give a shit about petty human lives? Might as well send them a box of chocolates and a dozen roses as a ritual killing for all they care.

I want to ignore it. I want to push it off on beat cops, say it isn't my problem. But Zee's got that look in their eyes. Zee and I found the first body, not the drained and strung up one, but the one laid out across the altar. Another abandoned station. It was clear even then. Something about this case makes Zee want to worry at it like a dog with a bone.

I don't know much about Zee's past. They've never said, and I've never asked. As far as I know, Zee didn't exist until the moment they walked into my office, offering information and wanting a job. We work well together. What else do I need to know? If Zee has scars, if they are running from something, that's their business, not mine. I only investigate things that want investigating, need investigating. There are pieces of my past I'm not exactly proud of, things I wouldn't share unless under duress. Everyone is entitled to their privacy. Bottom line: I trust Zee with my life. And I would do anything to save theirs.

"So, the station?" I stand.

"We can stop for a sandwich on the way." Zee offers a half-smile by way of apology.

"Let's go." I nod toward the door. After a moment, Zee follows.

Except really, I'm the one following. Into the graffiti choked station, down and under the ground. Wherever Zee goes, I will be right there on their heels. Always.

The cube is sticky, a cross between tar and spirit gum, its shade somewhere between pitch and honey. Except bees died out a long time ago.

"Zee wants to go back," I'd told Sam.

"This is almost as good as," Sam had replied, declining to tell me exactly what the sometimes-black-sometimes-gold substance was.

Back in the drowned apartment, I study it in the dim, watery light. Zee is asleep in the other room. Zee sleeps a lot these days.

For the fifth, the thirteenth, the hundredth time, I consider giving in. "You can find anything, John. That's what makes you so good at your job. You can find things that don't exist, things that don't want to be found."

And what about things I don't want to find?

I still have the damned lighter. The damned, cheap plastic lighter that was on me when we went down into the dark, and was there in Zee's hand when we returned. I place the tarry substance in an old Snapple cap and hold the lighter underneath until it bubbles. I have no idea if that's the way this stuff works, but I can't give it to Zee untested. Sam said something about it being different for each person. Sounds familiar.

Zee remembers it differently than I do. That place where we went without actually going. Vast, soaring walkways. Glittering subterranean caverns lit by tiny star-shaped blossoms that were also starfish—glowing, living creatures clustered on the walls and flying wingless through the air. And shelves upon shelves of books. All the scientific and artistic knowledge of ages. The thoughts and dreams of a thousand lost races, stretching into the past and the future.

The Yith are a peaceful race. They never wanted war until those... things brought it to them. They're librarians. Seekers of knowledge. They're victims, fleeing endlessly into the past and the future, trading bodies at a whim in order to stay alive. And if those bodies happen to be occupied when they need them... If they have to pry the knowledge they seek out through skin and muscle and fat and bone...

That's the part Zee doesn't remember. Or chooses to forget. Or maybe Zee just doesn't care, because they understand.

What the hell. Bottom's up.

The not-quite-liquid sears going down. My lips blister and it scrapes my throat raw, gums up my mouth so I can't even scream. I fall, curling my legs against my chest, shuddering on the floor.

What will I see? The memory of a scoured desert filled with the bones of things that have no skeletons? Empty carapaces, wind-hollowed and playing a terrible music? The ruins of Carcosa? Or R'lyeh rising everywhen and everywhere? The bloody heat death of the universe. The last, thin light the color of skim milk and cold ash going out, out, out.

No.

I see a cement block shed, eight feet by eight, lit by a single naked bulb. There's a man tied to a chair, and each time the light moves, it drags his shadow across the floor. There's a drain. A rusted tap connected to a length of hose. Old stains slash the walls with once-color, like organic graffiti. There's a tray with careful instruments laid out all cruel and sparkling, and bright. They're mostly for show. The only sounds in the room are ragged breath, the meaty connection between fist and flesh and bone, and wet, ugly sobbing.

I wish to God I was the man in the chair.

I wake gasping, clawing at my skin. Trying to skitter away from my body, I crash into a lamp that hasn't worked in ages. It goes over, and the dead bulb dies further with a soft pop. What the shit did Sam sell me? I scrub hands over my face. From the other room, Zee softly calls my name.

When Zee is sleeping again, after they finally agreed to take something from our small store of pain meds, I creep downstairs. I try not to think about the bruised look of Zee's flesh. The shadows that aren't shadows under their eyes. I tap on our neighbor's door.

I'm running out of options. How much longer before I give in?

There's a scent like the withdrawn-tide, leaving beach and stone garlanded with slick wetness, stripped bones, and creatures with too many eyes, gasping outside the salt-blood of the waves. The door opens a crack. A yellowish eye rolls in a face that no longer fits it. Fingers, joined by translucent membrane, undo the lock and my neighbor shuffles back to let me in.

I call her Mama, though I don't know if she ever had children, or if she was even a she before everything changed. She doesn't seem to mind.

"Brewing tea," she says as I close the door behind me.

There's a small camp stove on the crooked table that was an executive meeting space in a former life. Mama lives in the adjoining suite. The door between the two rooms was torn down long ago; ragged fabric hangs in its place.

I take one of the worn chairs. It creaks in protest as I try to swivel it around. Mama pours tea, and takes the chair catty-corner to mine. She doesn't exactly sit, more squats, her joints awkward and painful-looking. She wraps long-fingered hands with one too many knuckles around her mug. Her translucent inner eyelids nictate, waiting for me to speak.

"What do you know about Yith, Mama?" I say it like a place.

In my mind, it is, the people—the race—inextricably linked with wherever, whenever, we went when we were ripped from our bodies and stretched out like cat's-cradle string between the stars.

"Long time ago," Mama says. One shoulder rolls, not exactly a shrug.

The tea has a briny tang. I don't ask how it's made.

"Are you sure?" I gesture to the window.

The building across the street pulses, great ropes of muscle, or sinew, wrap it from foot to crown—devouring it, loving it, keeping it safe? I can't tell. The sky is purple, flickering with strange lightning. A rift opened there, or will open there, or was always open. Hard to keep things straight.

From what I've heard, it's actually better here than most places. The streets are generally in the same configuration as before the world ripped itself apart. Only some of the statues weep; only a few of the pigeons coo tekeli-li, tekeli-li. The degenerate things huddled in doorways, wrapped in rags and stinking, might as well be the same bums we had begging for change in the good old days. Except they want less from us.

"Why?" Mama says.

She's asking why I want to know, and she already has the answer. But just in case I'm too blind, too stupid to see it for myself, she grabs my hand and turns it palm up. Her skin is warm from her mug, and surprisingly dry for all that it glistens. She traces one finger—not over the life lines and heart lines— over the veins knotted like old yarn underneath. She doesn't stop with my hand, tapping her fingertips over my wrist, up my arm to the crook of my elbow, and at last to my chest. She taps twice over my heart, and says "hmpf".

It's as much of an answer as I'll get.

"Thanks for the tea, Mama," I say.

She makes that rolling motion that passes for a shrug, but is more like the grey-green heaving of waves—here long before me, and there long after I'm gone.

When did I first realize I was in love with Zee? Before my first marriage crumbled? After my second? Was it the moment they walked in my door asking for a job? Too cliché. Was it in Pnakotus, the Great Library, trapped in our cone-bodies, all claws and eyes and too-long limbs? Where I knew more definitively than ever that I didn't give a fuck what kind of body either of us was in?

No. It's not even that simple.

Time is broken. And because it is broken, it has always been broken. So I have always been in love with Zee. I will always be in love with Zee. Every moment of every day, I am falling in love with Zee.

When did I first realize Zee would never love me in return? Yeah. Each and every one of those moments too.

"Are you sure about this?" My foot slips, a chunk of brick giving way, dropping me down two steps.

I catch myself, but the flashlight slips, bouncing ahead of me, cracking on the remaining steps and splashing at the bottom.

"Shit. It smells worse in here than a normal subway, and that's saying a lot. Couldn't you have found us a nice sewer to crawl around in instead?"

"Relax, John." Zee swings their flashlight around, blinding me temporarily.

I bring my hand up to shield my eyes. When the beam swings away, I'm left blinking at after-images of Zee, haloed behind the light. Down here, in the dark, Zee is bright. I can't explain it. Maybe it's just the sense of kinetic energy barely contained by Zee's sharp angles. Whatever it is, I can scarcely stand to look at them.

I can't look away either.

I watch the shape of them ahead of me; their brightness crushes the air from my lungs. Would it be so bad, just once, to say "I love you" out loud? Fuck embarrassment. Fuck not hearing it in return. What could it hurt for Zee to know one more person cares about them more than anything in the world? The knowledge could be like a smooth stone to take out of their pocket and look at and think, "well there's that: I am loved".

But every time I open my mouth, my tongue trips on the image of Zee looking at me like I've put an incredible burden on their shoulders. It's a look of pity, and one that says "Why would you tell me this thing when you know you can't possibly hear it in return? Why would you make me feel like a guilty sack of shit for hurting my best friend?"

Zee reaches the bottom of the stairs, splashing into the muck where my flashlight disappeared. I swallow my words again and wade after them.

I don't notice the precise moment the graffiti turns from the usual slurs, tags, and graphic description of who put what body part where and when, to something deeper and far older. But when I do notice the signs, they shudder and buzz and crawl at the edge of my vision. I don't look straight on. I know better.

"Here." Zee grabs my wrist, sudden in the dark, and I let out a yelp.

They pull me to duck through an access tunnel, then crawl, Zee following whatever sense guides them. Behind the walls of the abandoned subway line, there are older walls still—brick, almost lovely, furred as they are in decay. It's drier here. But the shiver-hum is worse, the symbols denser. Almost a song. If I listen long enough, I might understand it.

Zee drops from sight, and my heart lurches into my throat. I scramble forward. There's a hatch; peering through, Zee is unharmed, playing their light over the walls of a space scarcely bigger than a broom closet. I lower myself cautiously; close enough to touch, but not touching. Our breath is loud, echoy. The word nest comes to mind. And tomb. Both seem accurate.

But there's none of the buzzy, fly-gnawed darkness we encountered around the gutted body, or the one draped over the altar. The close space smells like dust, not blood, and the symbols on the walls, while they shiver, are only paint. Could there be two cults at work? More?

A canister leans up against the wall, half-buried in a drift of rubble. The metal shines dull, even when Zee's beam isn't directed straight at it. It looks old, and something about it makes me think of screaming brains traveling between the stars. I kneel, not quite touching, but holding my hand over the surface. Cold radiates, and I pull my palm away before it burns.

"John, look at this."

I'm not sure what I'm looking at when I turn towards the spot illuminated by Zee's flashlight. It's a carving. Or a machine. I can't quiet tell. It might also be a living thing. Strangely grown, twisting and doubling back on itself. Or maybe it's a door. Or a...

"No!"

But it's too late, because Zee is already reaching. I'm reaching too, diving in the too-small space to knock their hand aside. But instead, our hands touch down at the same moment; Zee's and then mine, one on top of the other, fingers almost laced. The markings on the—pyramid? cone? what the fuck is this thing?—are incised into it, and rising out of it.

I'm screaming. I think I am. I try to pull my hand away, but it's seared to Zee's, seared to the stone, tacky strands of skin like pulled taffy melting and bubbling and godohgodicant.

We are flying, falling, hurled though the universe. We are wound and woven, thread between the bright points of the stars. We're everywhere and everywhen. And there are things wearing our bodies and questioning the nature of the universe by watching the cataclysm that is earth when everything changes, when R'lyeh rises and everything else falls and the stars are so wrong and so right.

The Yith are always there at the end. Fleeing a thousand, thousand times, from past to future, civilization to civilization. Always escaping death by a hairsbreadth. Immortal, but never resting, with no place to call home.

They are. We are. Prisoners. Here but not. Knowledge, all of it, at our fingertips. But we have no fingers. We have claws, speak by clacking, a rapid-fire sound I don't understand. I blink too many eyes. Reach out for. What? Everything.

"What do you remember?" The words drum. A clicking, heartbeat rhythm. They want to know not just about human history, but my history, what I have seen, what I've tasted, what I know.

I don't know how to give it to them. Will they tear the knowledge out of me? Fist cracked to bone and arcane symbols painted in the splash of my blood against cold cement walls?

But it isn't like that here. Even though my mind insists otherwise. Keeps breaking the picture of vast libraries and soaring archways into something else, something brutal, something violent. Something human that I can understand.

"What do you remember?"

I try to give them what they want.

I give them Zee.

If I could travel to any point in time, like the Yith, where would I go? To a moment when Zee was bright and not dying, grinning and shining and wanting to drink the world whole? Would I put myself in a body Zee could love?

Or would I go back to a time before I met Zee? Rewrite everything so I left the office early, locked the door and wasn't there when they walked in?

It doesn't matter. I suspect there isn't a before or after now. Maybe there never was. Maybe that's the secret, the key, and if so, then what Zee has been asking me all along isn't to take them back, it's to let them go to the place where they've always been.

Maybe there are other things I need to learn to let go, too.

The penthouse is dark, as always. A crack of light slides through the hairline gap in the curtains. Zee lies on the couch. Their breath shallow, pulse a scant flicker beneath bruised skin. When I lift them, they are feather and ash between hollow bones, wrapped in paper-light skin.

I don't bother with my waders this time, sloshing through the lobby with its tilted floor and shattered fish tank, with the softly piping things clinging to its sides. Out, in, down. Into the ruins of the city. It's not too late. It can't be too late, because this is where we've always been, seared to the stone and stretched between the stars.

Lightning gashes the purple sky, bleeds it black. By the flicker, I walk Zee down another set of stairs. Deeper. I keep my gaze straight ahead. Don't look down. Don't check if Zee is still breathing. It is not too late.

A keening rises to meet me from the tunnels, a soft, wild cry. Maybe it's me, already down there, still down there, hand pressed to the stone-metal grown-sculpted machine. My body is a strange organ of skin and bone, skeleton hollowed to flutes and pipes, lungs and heart the bellows to sing me.

I splash into the water. Kick the flashlight I dropped just a minute ago. The symbols glow and crawl and shiver around me.

Zee is ahead of me. Oh so bright in the darkness. I cling to the bundle in my arms, crush is tight against the erratic beat of my heart.

"Hold on, Zee. We're going home."

HIS CARNIVOROUS REGARD
By John C. Foster

"So you're going to cover all my meals?"

"You'll never eat the same thing twice. Henry VIII didn't eat like you'll eat."

"Who?"

"Not important. And then there's the sex."

"This sounds too good to be true. I can do anything I want?"

"With as many women as you can handle."

"Kinky shit?"

"We want you to explore everything."

"This sounds too good to be true."

"You'll be exposed to art. You'll sky dive. You'll wrestle an alligator and scuba in a shark cage. You'll get drunk on the finest wines and the cheapest vodka. You'll trip the light fantastic on psilocybin and LSD. You'll sit by quiet seashores and run with the bulls in Pamplona. You'll experience everything."

"And you're gonna put something in my head?"

"The device will monitor your brain's reaction to each experience. We're creating a map, a guidebook, a lexicon of how you experience things."

"So you'll record it if I wanted to, you know, fuck someone in the ass?"

"We want you to fuck them in the ass. We want them to fuck you in the ass."

"I dunno about—"

"And don't forget the money. Mr. Machen will provide one hundred million dollars to whomever you choose."

"This sounds too good to be true. I have to go up in the ship and—tell me again what exactly I do up there? I didn't follow everything the first time you explained it. You know, the space stuff."

The man in the charcoal gray suit explained it to the candidate, whose look of confusion rapidly devolved into anger.

"You're outta your mind. Count me out."

The potential candidate stormed out with a gratuitous door slam and the man in the charcoal gray suit sighed, drawing a line through the twenty-third interview subject. He took a moment to line up the papers on his desk and tapped the intercom next to an obsidian nameplate reading CHALMERS.

"Next."

There was an axe buried in a wall speaker. Maxwell was still trying to sort things out so he left it where it was.

He leaned back in the leather and brass captain's chair of the derelict craft and let his eyes wander over the screens where a small, olive-skinned man was eating, fencing, swimming, sodomizing, and otherwise experiencing every measurable activity Etan Machen's researchers could dream up. Pop-up boxes on each screen showed three-dimensional images of the candidate's brain, tracking the activity resulting from each experience. Sights, sounds, smells, pain, pleasure, anticipation, fear, ecstasy.

The ozone stink of an electrical fire still lingered, but most of the equipment had been repaired before Maxwell docked with the ship. Tools had been scattered about the floor, ready for his use.

There were terabytes of data on the olive-skinned man and his experiences. Newer data, data closer to the time of the incident, required some reassembly.

The ship's lights were down, power run in from GALILEO Station enough to restart life support and the computers, and in the dimness lit only by flickering screens, Maxwell let his gaze linger on the candidate frolicking in a hot tub with two nubile things. He felt himself stiffen but had already been infected by a slight strain of paranoia from the candidate's journal—the man's awareness that everything he thought and felt during his last year of life was being recorded and analyzed, his inner workings deciphered for mass consumption—and Maxwell felt himself under some sort of existential observation, a paranoid secularist's idea of *God is watching you*.

He slid over the deck in a low-G walk and lowered the volume until the grunts and cries of the grappling threesome were no more than a whisper, his gaze wandering around the hemisphere of the observation dome overhead, silently damning whoever had applied a haphazard coat of spray paint. He wondered which of the five crew members had done it and if it was the same person who had painted over the mirrors in the lavatory. Perhaps the same wit whose finger painted OBJECTS IN MIRROR ARE CLOSER THAN THEY APPEAR over the airlock.

There was no one to ask, of course, because Machen's ship had been recovered with no crew, no indication in the captain's log or computer log as to where—and how—they had gone. The airlock had its own tracking system for comings and goings and the only person on board who had been outside the ship was the candidate.

The candidate who never returned.

The crew had simply vanished.

As he passed through the airlock to the Spartan confines of GALILEO station, Maxwell shivered. His job as investigator meant countless routine explorations, the forensic analysis of every possible bit of evidence. So he had spectrum analyzed a small scraping from the painted words over the lock.

The words were written in blood.

From the Commonwealth Dictionary, Fifth Edition: "Dark Matter" – (n) – non-luminous material postulated to exist in space including weakly interacting particles – known as cold dark matter – or randomly moving high-energy particles created soon after the Big Bang – hot dark matter – postulated to account for gravitational forces observed on astronomical objects.

As much as 96% of the universe is made up of dark matter.

From the Icarus Journal: The theory that X-ray signals originating from dark matter in the Perseus Galaxy cluster are a form of sentient communication has been widely discredited.

The candidate swirled the cabernet in his glass and sniffed audibly before taking a small sip and rolling it around his mouth.

"Blackberry and tannins, big tannins. Chocolate, plum and maybe...cedar," he said.

Chalmers nodded and made a note on his tablet. He observed the concurrent brain activity and made another note as he said, "Your palate is growing more refined."

"So is my sense of smell," the candidate said.

"Excellent, excellent."

During the 45 minute flight across the Atlantic the Lear Hyperjet suffered a loss of power and rapidly descended some twenty thousand feet. The candidate screamed and nearly fainted before power was restored.

His brain activity was noted.

Maxwell sat up in bed and shuddered, releasing a breath as his head swiveled, looking for the tall shadow man who had watched him sleep.

"GALILEO, lights please," he said and an ambient glow issued from the ceiling. "Brighter," he said and the lights adjusted accordingly.

"Your heart rate is accelerated, Max," his wife's disembodied voice said. "Would you like to visit the infirmary?"

"Just a nightmare," he said. He weighed (again) the comfort he took in programming the computer to speak with his wife's voice against the eeriness of a machine co-opting that part of her. "Infirmary isn't necessary."

"Alright, Max."

He stood and staggered on feet that felt as if they had been stripped of flesh, bare bones against the floor tiles, and winced as he tottered to the circular window. "Retract," he said and the protective shield irised open.
Bracing his hands on either side of the window, Maxwell leaned into the glass, looking up and down, right and left, beholding the pinprick glow of a billion stars in the Deep.

He wished he wasn't alone.

By the eleventh month of his last year on Earth, the candidate became more contemplative and not wildly hedonistic, as might have been expected.

He was lifted to orbit along with Chalmers, the erstwhile man in gray, where they were transferred to Etan Machen's personal ship.

Chalmers asked: "Why are you so quiet?"

The candidate said: "I'm tired."

They chuckled for different reasons.

The candidate said: "Will I be aware of what's happening?"

Chalmers said: "For an infinitesimal fraction of a moment. So brief that you will not be able to consciously process it. But we will be able to record every micro-reaction and slow them down so that we might understand what you are experiencing."

The candidate put aside the book on Zoroastrianism that he had been reading and it bounced off the side table, floating to the floor.

The candidate said: "This takes some getting used to."

Chalmers said: "Low gravity?"

The candidate said: "Everything."

Chalmers regarded him, pleased that his consciousness seemed to have expanded so much over the year.

The candidate said: "Machen's dying, isn't he?"

Chalmers did not answer.

Maxwell secured a collapsible stepladder to the floor of the flight deck of Machen's craft before affixing a mask and ascending. He alternated between wiping the newly manufactured paint thinner along the interior of the observation dome and scraping away the resulting mess. It seemed an unacceptably gauche act to commit in the luxury craft, but he felt an overpowering need to see outside.

He had recently attempted to relay a hyperburst transmission via the Earth-sat network to his superiors in D.C. and was unsuccessful, which was unusual but not unheard of. After several tries, he attempted to reach his wife in Portland and established a link lasting 37.3 seconds. The link froze as soon as he began to express his concerns about the current investigation. He stared at his wife's awkwardly immobilized face, her expression stretched and cadaverous in mid-word, and felt a searing moment of loneliness.

Eventually he had dispatched a spider swarm ostensibly designed to track sunspot interference, with a secondary objective of circumventing the Earth-sat network.

Both were feints.

Maxwell had cleared much of the dome before estimating enough time had passed. He hesitated, staring out of the great swipes of flickering galaxy he had revealed. Had the crew been afraid to look out?

He returned to GALILEO station and checked on his spiders, sitting with a grunt to interpret the results.

At the end of a complex chain of corporations and shadow holdings owning various elements of the Earth-sat network was a single name.

Machen.

Maxwell knew—everyone knew—that Etan Machen was the wealthiest individual on Earth, but his secretive control of the Earth-sat network indicated influence several magnitudes beyond what the public suspected.

Machen was a single man with the financial might of a superpower. Six people had already died to satisfy his mad curiosity.

"I will complete the report," Maxwell said to the empty room. He had no intention of being the seventh.

The candidate sat in lotus at the bottom of the mold as the gelatin glubbed and splattered in from three wall mounted tubes.

"The gelatin will last five minutes once you are jettisoned from the ship, at which point it will rapidly degrade, an eye blink's time, and you will experience direct and unvarnished contact with the universe," Chalmers said to the quietly breathing man as the yellowish substance rose above his nipples. "You are mankind's first necronaut. The explorer for a new age."

The candidate spoke so quietly that Chalmers could only just make out, "I wonder what I'll—," before the gelatin rose over the candidate's head.

The candidate felt no acceleration but knew he had been hurled at tremendous speed into space. He was a glowing meteor soaring among giants, marveling at them, and wondering if they, in turn, marveled at him.

Glorious.

He thought of Thoreau's idea of living deliberately and abstracted it into the great step he was about to take.

He wanted to experience the ultimate.

He wanted to see.

Chalmers scratched at three days growth of beard and turned to see who had entered the flight deck.

No one was there.

The only other crewmember on the flight deck was Tarkenian, head and shoulders buried beneath a command console.

Three days ago they had fired their necronaut from the airlock. Five minutes later, the moment of truth after a year of preparation, the culmination of decades of research and development, the ship's computer suffered a catastrophic crash as the result of an impossible data surge.

"Stinks in here," Tarkenian said, pushing himself out from beneath the console and sitting up on the scorched carpet. He scratched under his arm and shot a glance at the obscured dome overhead. "Fucking Royal. I hope you reported her."

"It was noted," Chalmers said.

Clarice Royal had been restrained and sedated after suffering from a psychotic break during which she painted the interior of the dome. "He sees me. He sees me." All she would say in response to Chalmers' questioning. "Is it the candidate? Can he see you?"

"He sees me."

Chalmers had shoved his face within inches of hers, trying to hold her eyes with his, but she looked right through him.

Following an impulse, Chalmers had carried a small, shaving mirror into Royal's room and sat on the edge of her bed. He held the mirror out over her face and repeated her name until she opened her eyes.

She batted the mirror out of his hand. He was forced to summon Simon, the crew medic, to increase her dosage.

The next day Tarkenian chewed off the end of his fingers and painted OBJECTS IN MIRROR ARE CLOSER THAN THEY APPEAR over the airlock before trying to depressurize the ship.

They carried the raving man to his room where Simon put him under.

Two days after that, Chalmers was forced to render Simon unconscious with a blow from the coffeepot. He bandaged the newly bearded medic's wound and sedated him. With Simon out of commission and the computers impaired, Chalmers was forced to guess at the dosage.

Ship's medic Simon ceased respiration three minutes after that and failed to respond to CPR.

Ship's pilot Komi methodically smashed every mirror on the ship before retreating to her cabin to ingest an overdose of sleeping pills. She was dead by the time Chalmers forced her door. Close examination revealed that she had scratched bloody furrows in her scalp, beneath her hair.

Wincing at the sharp tang of his own body odor—showering was out of the question even with the bathroom mirror broken—Chalmers completed as much of Tarkenian's repairs as he could and sat in the captain's chair to decipher meaning from the candidate's last millisecond of brain activity. The task was enormous for the damaged system, so he asked the computer to model the man's final facial expression.

A three dimensional wire frame image appeared on screen, quickly filling in as a perfect replica of the candidate's skull, over which pink layers of muscle and fat were forming. Ultimately the skin and hair was layered on as eyes grew in their sockets and Chalmers found himself staring at the expression of a man in his very last instant of life.

He sagged in the chair as ice water filled his middle.

What he saw on the man's face was undiluted terror.

After five minute staring into the mirror with the water running, Maxwell put down the unused razor and washed the depilatory cream from his cheeks. Even this last, simple task was challenging as his gaze strayed from his own reflection to see what the mirror might show lurking behind him.

"You have an incoming call, Max," his wife's voice said, and he padded on bare feet down gray hallways until he reached the command deck and sat down in his molded plastic chair. He rubbed his shoulders against the chair back, addressing an itch.

The screen activated before he consented to the call, which wasn't supposed to happen, but Maxwell already understood he was in the grip of something much greater than he.

"Chief Investigator, I am Etan Machen," said a well-modulated voice. It filled the air around him, transmitting in via GALILEO Station's public address system rather than the normal comm system. A cheap tactic, as blatant as greeting supplicants from behind an elevated desk.

Cheap but effective. Maxwell fought the urge to squirm in his seat as an image resolved on the screen.

"Mr. Machen," Maxwell said, forcing himself to look at the wrinkled ancient coated in an oxygen permeable polymer that gave his exposed skin a yellow sheen, as if he had been varnished in a thin coat of amber.

"Where is my crew?" Machen's voice writhed but his mouth did not move as the words were transmitted. Maxwell doubted the man's throat was capable of producing anything more than a dry croak without enhancement.

"Unknown. Not on board your ship."

"Where is my report?"

"The computers were damaged following the launch of—"

"My necronaut."

Maxwell swallowed bile. "Yes sir, your necronaut. I am piecing together what I can with the aid of GALILEO Station and your onboard cameras. The behavior of your crew became erratic after the launch. In some cases, destructive."

The bloodless worms of Machen's lips slithered into a smile beneath the amber sheen. "Ah, then we have contact."

"Contact, sir?"

"The message has been speaking to me since 2009, but we believed we lacked the technology to understand it."

"Sir?"

"We are the technology, Chief Inspector, our consciousness the key," Machen said. "My necronaut was an organic translator. We must have the data from his contact so that we may interpret it and build our dictionary."

"To understand what happened to the crew?"

"It has spoken." An arthritic claw corded with blue veins flapped at the camera in dismissal. "Now I will speak to it."

The skeletal face abruptly contorted and Machen was consumed by racking coughs. He spat a gob of mucus laced with red veins, which was processed out through the polymer to slide down his chin. A female hand reached in from off screen and wiped the smear from He Who Would Speak to the Cosmos.

"Continue your investigation and report directly to me. Time grows short."

"Are you alright, sir?"

"I have no concern about how I am, only about what I will become," the trillionaire said, milky eyes rolling. A gray tongue poked between his lips as he grinned again. "By the way, your wife..."

The tonal quality shifted mid-word until the air was filled with the familiar female sound. "...has a lovely voice."

The screen went black and Maxwell ground his teeth.

Thirty minutes later he returned to Machen's ship.

Chalmers sat in a stained pair of pants, his shirt discarded. In his filth he felt his skin crawling with mites and his greasy beard swarming with lice. A sharp smell of ozone was the only relief from the putrid cloud surrounding him.

He had not eaten or consumed liquid in nearly thirty six hours. He had not left the captain's chair even to relieve himself.

During that time, the four other crewmembers ceased to be aboard the ship.

During that time, Chalmers sat in his chair and listened to the primordial sound waves pulsing over the comm system. They were growing and as they grew, he had the sense of meaning not quite forming from the sounds, but passing through them. A whale surfacing beneath a tiny boat. But a thousand times larger. A million.

A fire axe jutted from the console. At hour twelve of his vigil Chalmers briefly entertained the idea of stopping the signal by destroying yet more equipment. He was unsuccessful. The data, which had been so unfathomably vast that it had overloaded the system arrogantly attempting to record it, had ultimately determined that the system itself was unnecessary.

And so he, microbe, listened to the shifting of tectonic plates and the groan of ice shelves calving as he read from the candidate's book on Zoroaster.

Mankind's proto-religion provided no comfort.

The shadow man said: "You will see, you are seeing, you have seen."

The book told him: "Time is a circle."

The shadow man stood behind him, he knew this without turning his head, and he saw the figure's shape in a dozen dead screens before him. The reflection of his own face was superimposed over that of the shadow man's.

He watched the reflection of the shadow man as it leaned down and whispered in his ear. Instead of warm breath he felt the cryogenic chill of space.

Something in his chest broke and he sobbed.

Blood ran from his tear ducts, nostrils and ears. His tongue swam in coppery, red warmth. When he cocked his head as if to hear a faint call, a red tide spilled from his lips and splashed in his lap.

He wrote quickly, dipping his index finger in his own hot ichor and defiling several pages of the book before he tossed it aside and spoke to a functioning surveillance camera.

When he could put it off no longer he tilted his head back and beheld the painted dome overhead.

"You have to eat, Max," GALILEO station said.

Maxwell squeezed the tube and swallowed the protein shake despite his lack of appetite. He scratched at the back of his neck, barely noting the red crust beneath his fingernails when he finished.

"You've lost several pounds since we docked with the derelict craft, Max. Do you want to visit the infirmary?"

"I'm fine," Maxwell said, because that's what people said when they were most definitely not fine. He had tried to reach his wife again, this time via spider swarm, the most elaborate he had ever dispatched. He received not a single return, his swarm swallowed in toto by cyberspace.

By Etan Machen.

He prodded the sticky book with his finger and it slid an inch across the white cafeteria table. He had discovered it resting on his pillow.

"Are you sure there was no one at all in my room?"

"Only you, Max. You put the book on your pillow and left, only to return and retrieve the book."

"How did I look?"

"You looked like you, Max."

"I mean did I look the same both times? Was I wearing the same clothes?"

"I...my files have been damaged. The video file has decayed. I took the liberty of checking your vitals on both visits to match brainwave and heart signatures but only the second trip is registering. The first trip did not record properly."

"GALILEO?"

"Yes?"

"Can we disengage from the derelict craft?"

"I'm sorry, Max. I have been subjected to an inhibitor."

Maxwell leaned back in his plastic chair and glanced around the pristine, white space. GALILEO scheduled the cafeteria and small kitchen to an auto-clean every twenty four hours.

He opened the book and began flipping through it, frowning until he realized it was the book the candidate had been reading near the end.

He almost put it aside there, but several pages were partially stuck together and he worried at them until he could tug them apart.

The words had been finger painted in blood dried to a cabernet brown and covered several pages. He had to flip back and forth several times before he understood the message.

"The Devourer sits athwart the track of time, sweeping us into his infinite maw with both hands."

He tossed the book across the room and it landed face down, bending several pages.

"GALILEO, are you aware of the energy signal described by Machen?"

"Yes, Max. I have always been aware of the signal. I detected it the very first moment my systems went online."

"What did you think it was?"

"Noise."

"Can you play it for me?"

He felt a vibration in the soles of his feet before he heard the long, groaning pulses. It reminded him of deep sea dives during his time with the oceanic navy. Plasteel dentistry picked up the vibration and his jaw ached.

"Can you interpret the signal?"

"No, Max. It is simply the natural noise of open space. The vibration of collapsing stars and emerging worlds and infinite cosmic collisions."

"Poetic."

GALILEO had no response and Maxwell expected none. He considered the video message Chalmers had left in the wake of his bloody penmanship.

"He lies; there is no inevitability without recognition. Do not look upon him. To see is to be seen. To be seen is to be consumed."

There had come a tremendous gout of blood from Chalmers' mouth at that point, but his eyes were clear when they returned to the camera.

"Good luck to you, whoever you are," Chalmers said and signed off.

A brave effort, Maxwell thought, albeit futile.

He wept for awhile in the empty kitchen without decoration or the scent of herbs or the presence of his wife. Eventually he made his way to the command deck.

"I'm in a sharing mood, GALILEO," he said. "Open a channel to Etan Machen."

The screen before him went to static for several minutes before resolving into the hideous face of Machen.

"Chief Inspector, I take it you have made progress," the wealthiest man in the world showed visible excitement despite the near immobility of his gleaming face. "Tell me."

"He sees you," Maxwell said.

"What does that mean? Make sense—"

"He sees you," Maxwell interrupted, surprising himself by laughing. "He sees you and there's not a damned thing you can do about it."

He lunged forward and struck the screen repeatedly, feeling his knuckles break even as the screen erupted with sparks.

He stood and sucked at his bleeding hand, nostrils widening at the smell of smoke.

"I love you, Beth," he said to the wife he would never see again. "GALILEO, tell me you love me."

"I love you, Max," his wife's voice filled the air and his heart.

"Repeat the phrase at varied intervals until I leave GALILEO Station."

"I love you, Max."

He considered and discarded attempting to activate the self-destruct sequence. Whatever inhibitors had been placed on GALILEO would undoubtedly prevent it. He held to the tenuous hope that Machen's control of GALILEO Station at the end was so overt that no attempt would be made to reach it without his consent. That no one else would ever be exposed to what they had found.

"Max, someone is attempting to access my files."

"Deny them."

"I can't."

"Run a complete anti-viral diagnostic with rolling shut downs."

"I will."

That would delay access long enough, he hoped.

"I love you, Max."

"Thanks, hon," he said, making for the airlock.

"Max, don't leave GALILEO Station."

He stopped, glancing at the nearest surveillance camera. "I have to see."

He crossed through the airlock into the dim space aboard the derelict craft's flight deck and stood behind the captain's chair, bracing his hands on the back as he felt the impossible weight of cosmic regard and imagined a great eye stretching from star to star, staring down at his tiny form.

"I love you, Max."

He heard his wife's distant voice and determined he was ready, and in so determining, lifted his chin and looked up.

He was not ready.

His hands slapped against his face, nails digging red furrows down his cheeks as his eyes bulged from their sockets.

He saw.

"I love—"

He screamed.

THE LABYRINTH OF SLEEP
By Orrin Grey

Beyond the wall, the first moon has already risen. Kendrick stands still for a while, getting used to the changes to the air, to gravity. He can still taste the last bitter dregs of the cigarette he stubbed out just before hooking up to the machine. Can still smell the antiseptic tinge of the room he's left behind, as a breeze perfumed by distant and unnamed glades carries it away.

Down below him, at the bottom of the hill, is a forest of tall white trees, and beyond that the beginning of the Labyrinth. He's been here before, maybe not *right* here, but near enough. He's seen this moon before, stood under its light. He's been in that forest, even if maybe some other part of it. He's seen the split-headed giants that live there; the doors that they build in the ground, the men with cloven hooves and the heads of dogs, the black shapes that occasionally flit in front of the moon. All of this is familiar to him, but something about the night, *this* night, feels different. A smell in the air, like the ozone smell before a storm. Something…

Maybe it's because this trip is different. Not some hapless dreamer he's riding in this time but another rider, another professional. McCabe, lying in a drugged coma in his hotel room. McCabe, a few milligrams of noxitol short of dead, lying there on his bed, hooked up to monitors and IVs and to the machine. McCabe, waiting somewhere in the Labyrinth for Kendrick to come in and find him to learn why he'd gone to the needle instead of his oldest friend.

The company is paying for the hotel room now, for the monitors, and paying Kendrick double his usual rate, but this one he'd do for free. He has to know what happened, what changed. Or, the worse answer, if nothing has, if this was always what waited at the end of McCabe's street and he's just been blind to it until now.

One way or the other, he has to know, and so he starts down the hill, toward the Labyrinth.

It probably started with the drugs; the new kinds of sleep aids to help a world full of light and motion find the time to dream. But it was the machine that ultimately did the job that brought the wall of sleep crashing down. And what we found on the other side wasn't what we had expected, not at all. Not a changing jungle of Freudian symbols, not personal, not subjective. An actual place, the Labyrinth and the lands that surrounded it.

It took the machine to find it. The dreamers themselves never remembered somehow that they all went to the same place. On their trips back to consciousness the details of the dream world were lost, their minds replacing them with the minutiae of their memories and their own imaginations, the things that they remembered as their dreams. Always keyed to events in the Labyrinth, but never identical to it.

The machine was the silver key. With it, another person, a rider, could piggyback in on the dreamer's trip to that secret world. Not asleep, not really, and therefore not subject to the forgetfulness that true dreaming entailed.

It became a fad, a drug, an industry. In the waking world, there were dream parlors in every mall, where you could hook into someone's sleeping mind and take a ride to the Labyrinth. But most people were nothing more than tourists in the dreamlands, children stumbling along the turns of the Labyrinth. Kendrick and McCabe, they were professionals.

Or they had been, before McCabe tried to make himself sleep forever.

The walls of the Labyrinth are always black. Basalt, or something that can pass for it, the dreamland equivalent. They always rise up too high to scale, too high to jump. Once you're in the Labyrinth, you're in it, submerged, blind to anything except the next corner, and then the next.

Countless efforts have been made to map it. Kendrick has never known a professional who didn't have at least one in-progress map tacked up somewhere. But no one has ever managed. You can't see the Labyrinth from anywhere except the top of the hill, near the wall, and from there it all looks the same, and once you're in it, well...

There are landmarks. Some have been seen by more than one person. He and McCabe had compared their lists late one night. They'd both seen the fountain choked with moss. They'd both seen the doorway in the middle of the courtyard, the ground on the other side of it darker than on this side, but neither of them had been brave or stupid enough to step through. Kendrick had once seen a river, miles down, that cut a roaring chasm through the midst of the Labyrinth. McCabe claimed to have found a building that looked like an abandoned mosque, with no one inside but an altar set in the back with some kind of mummy in an alcove behind it, one he couldn't quite make out without getting closer than he suddenly found himself wanting to.

Some people say that the Labyrinth changes, and certainly Kendrick has never known two pros whose maps ever really lined up. Most people have an opinion on the subject, once they've put a few beers in themselves at the end of the day, but Kendrick never really thought about it before. To him, the Labyrinth was what it was. It was always there, on the other side of the wall, and it was always the same, really. Even if the paths changed, its nature never did, and that was enough for him.

He stands at one of the gates to the Labyrinth. All the gates he's ever seen looked identical. No horn or ivory, just unadorned clefts in the sides of the Labyrinth. Others have tried to mark them, he knows, but the markings were always gone when they came back. Either that, or no one has ever gone to the same gate twice.

It should be impossible, what he's doing. Going into a place that can't be mapped, to find someone who's been lost there already. It should be, but it never is. Something's different about the dreamers, maybe, or about the pros. Something in how they approach the Labyrinth, or in how it approaches them, but he's never gone in after a dreamer, never once, and not found them.

It isn't by any conscious art that he does it, though, at the same time, he knows it's not something everyone can do. He walks the Labyrinth as blind as if he were a dreamer himself. No one really knows how the professionals do it, the dream hounds, the *Oneiroi*, as some in the industry have tried to dub them, though the name never stuck. Kendrick has this theories, all the pros do. To him, it's all in the thinking. Dreamers don't think while they're in the Labyrinth, not really. They can't. They're caught up in the black, forgetful rivers of sleep. But the riders, those who follow them in, *can* think, and, by thinking, by keeping their minds on their quarry, they can track them down, whether that's by changing the turnings of the Labyrinth itself, or simply by knowing which way to turn their own steps, Kendrick doesn't know, and has never bothered to care.

Though time has no meaning here, still he knows that this is the longest he's ever been under. Out of the corners of his eyes, he sees what might be landmarks down curving paths, but already his feet are carrying him in another direction. He wonders how much time has passed out there in the waking world. It could be hours, minutes, days. They were prepared before he went under. IVs to feed and hydrate him, so that he could stay down no matter how long it took.

How long will they let him stay? How long before they pull the plug, before they decide that this errand is costing more than it's worth? He wills himself to hurry.

There are things that live in the Labyrinth. He's always known it. Not the giants or the dog-headed men or any of the other things that live outside. These are different, he knows, even though he's never seen them. He hears them sometimes, their hopping, shuffling gait just on the other side of a wall, just a few turns away. Sometimes in the waking world he tries to picture them, to imagine them as he goes about his day. He always sees them as pale, eyeless things, adapted to a life lived deep underground, though, of course, the Labyrinth is always open to the perpetual twilight of the dreamlands' sky.

When he's here, in the Labyrinth, he tries not to think of them at all, because he believes that thinking here has power. Even now, as he hears them behind him, he tries to think only of putting the next foot in front of him, then the next. Of going faster, not of why. Even when they sound like they are right behind him, just around the next turn, not even that far. That if he turned his head he would see them, see them at last as they are and not as he imagines. Even then he keeps his eyes forward, keeps his thoughts only on McCabe, McCabe, McCabe.

And then he turns a corner and he's somewhere he's never been before. Normally in the Labyrinth he can't say that, not with certainty. Most of it looks the same, excepting the occasional landmarks. But this is something else entirely. More than a landmark. This is *the* landmark. He knows it without even having to look around, knows even before his mind has processed what he's seen, knows with the faultless logic that is sometimes the province of the dreamlands, that this is the center of the Labyrinth.

The things behind him are forgotten, and, as if they are driven back by some invisible barrier, or as if it really has been his attention, however indirect, that held them here, the sounds of their pursuit cease. Or, was it ever really pursuit? Were they herding him here?

What would he call the structure that he sees before him, this extruded building of green stone with its soaring towers and many gaping windows, if he saw it in the waking world? A castle, a tower, a house?

There have been countless attempts to map the Labyrinth, and even more to explain it. Is it the first step of an afterlife, a tiny taste of death that we get each night when we close our eyes? Is it a representation of something from the collective unconscious, an enormous symbol housed in all our psyches? Is it a literally just the maze of our own neurons? These were things Kendrick never thought about, not outside the Labyrinth and certainly not within it, but he thinks about them now.

What does it mean, this structure? No map of the Labyrinth has ever found its center. No rider, no dream hound has ever come this far and returned, at least, not that he's ever heard of. In the mind of every sleeping man and woman, a maze, and in the center of the maze, this place. And inside this building, he knows with that same faultless logic, McCabe.

Without hesitating any further, he goes through the front door.

Inside, the house is *like* a castle, though strangely sparse and unfurnished. There are no guttering torches in sconces on the wall, but it isn't dark, either. The green stone seems to provide its own illumination.

When he passes windows and looks outside, what he sees isn't the Labyrinth, and that doesn't surprise him. Out one window massive storm clouds gather into an anvil-shaped thunderhead, crackling with multihued lightning. Out another, he looks down upon a misty valley, where golden statues nestled in peaks watch some kind of gladiatorial game on the distant floor below.

He walks here as he walked in the Labyrinth, one foot in front of the other, keeping his mind focused always on McCabe. This house isn't separate from the Labyrinth, he knows. It's part of it, maybe the greatest part, and here, more than ever, he must be very careful.

He tries to clear his mind of expectations, and so he is surprised when he suddenly stops walking. He's standing in the doorway to a room. At first glance it's no different than any of the other rooms he's passed, but then it is. It's furnished, with a fireplace and a single high-backed chair, and the window in the far wall is covered with a thick, velvet curtain. Kendrick stands in the doorway for a long moment, holding his breath, and then he steps inside.

"McCabe," he says, because he knows that McCabe is sitting in the chair, turned away from him, facing the window. He knows in the same way he's known all along which way to turn his feet to find this place.

There's no answer, not right away. Instead, the figure in the chair stands slowly and turns to face him.

In the waking world, Kendrick isn't a handsome man. He was once, when he was young, but a poorly-healed job of plastic surgery done to repair a face mangled by a broken bottle left him much the worse for wear. In the dreamland, though, he has greater control over his features, and he always looks as he did when he was a young man, the way he still sometimes sees himself in his own dreams.

Kendrick has never seen McCabe in the Labyrinth before, and he had never thought to ask what the other man looked like here. He's surprised to see his friend looking old, worn, tired beyond his years. His hair, which is still black in the waking world, is gray here, and wrinkles of worry mar his eyes. He looks, Kendrick thinks without being able to stop himself, like a man who might welcome death.

"I had hoped they wouldn't send you," McCabe finally says, when they're facing each other across the suddenly small room. "Though I knew they would. And, to be honest, once I failed the job myself, I needed them to, because I knew there was no one else I could trust."

Kendrick hasn't rehearsed the lines he'll say now. He's kept them out of his mind, just as he keeps everything out when he's inside the Labyrinth, everything except the thought of his quarry. "Why?" he asks, and he's surprised himself by the notes he hears in his voice, the betrayal, the hurt.

"I'm sorry," McCabe says. He doesn't step forward, he stays standing by the chair, and Kendrick can see the effort it takes him not to turn his eyes back toward the curtains. "I suppose I should have come to you first, but I wanted to spare you. I see now that I couldn't, that no matter what I did you'd have found your way here sooner or later. I wish I could have, though, that there'd been a way. Now, more than ever. Now that I know what you would do for me, how far you'd go."

Kendrick feels like he should be confused by what McCabe is saying, but it makes a strange kind of sense. McCabe learned something. Of course he did. Something that he wanted to keep secret. But men like he and Kendrick were in the business of finding secrets, of running them to the ground, even in places like this, places *made* of secrets. So he tried to hide in the one place he knew that no one, not even dream hounds, could track him: death.

"You should have told me," Kendrick says, taking a step forward. "I could have helped. I could've protected you."

McCabe shakes his head, takes a step back to match the one that Kendrick has taken forward, which makes him freeze. He's made a mistake, he realizes. He's misunderstood something.

"I'm not protecting the secret, Kendrick," McCabe says sadly, and Kendrick can see that there are tears in his eyes, this man who he's seen shot, who he's seen kill, and never seen shed a tear. "I was protecting you. But I can't, not anymore. You're here now, and even if I could make you leave without explaining, without showing you, you'd come back. Again and again, until you found out. Wouldn't you? Even if I asked you to leave it alone? Even if I asked you to walk away?"

"I'd try," Kendrick says, softly.

"But you'd fail, yes?"

A nod.

"I know. I would, too, if our places were reversed. I'd come here, eventually, to see what it was that had taken you from me. So I'll show you, I will, but you have to promise me something first."

Kendrick nods again, knowing already that he's lost somehow. Lost a friend and more than that. "Anything," Kendrick says, and McCabe tells him the secret, and then he pulls down the curtains and shows him.

The men guarding the two bodies are bored. It's been three hours since

Kendrick plugged into the machine and dropped away from the waking world, and since then they've had nothing to do but stand and wait. There's nothing here to guard, not really, but their jobs depend on them staying, so they stay. The technician who monitors the readouts on the dozens of screens connected to McCabe and Kendrick is asleep in a chair. One of the guards stares out the big picture window, the other plays solitaire on his phone. Neither is prepared when Kendrick suddenly wakes up.

Normally, riders coming back from the Labyrinth are sluggish, half-drunk from the things they've seen, their senses still attuned to the dreamland. But Kendrick is a professional, one of the best, and he's gotten accustomed to acclimating quickly. He's on his feet before the machines can give their warning beep, and he's crossed the room before the guard has even looked up from his phone. Before the technician has come awake, Kendrick has the first guard's gun out of his shoulder holster and is using it to kill the second guard, whose phone drops to the floor and shatters. The first guard tries to elbow him, but Kendrick steps back, faster than he looks, and shoots the guard twice, once in the back and once in the side.

If the technician hadn't been asleep, he might have had time to run. Might have made it as far as the door of the hotel room. But as it is, by the time he's gathered his wits enough to be afraid, Kendrick is already standing over him, his finger already squeezing the trigger. Then he walks over to McCabe and begins unplugging machines. McCabe will die on his own, given time, without the machines to keep him alive, but there will already be more men coming, and neither of them has that much time. Kendrick touches his friend's cheek, puts the gun under his chin, and pulls the trigger.

The door of the hotel room is already locked, but he pushes a chair under the handle to slow the men who'll be coming to break it down. Then he walks over to the window and looks out and down, down all those many stories to the street below. He could do for himself the same way he did for McCabe, and he will, if he has to, but he wants a few more minutes first. He can hear the men out in the hallway already; hear their muffled shouts and the banging on the door. It won't be long until they're inside. He looks down at the gun in his hand.

Three shots are enough to shatter the window, and then he steps out. For a moment, he's flying, flying as he sometimes does in his own dreams, and then he stops dreaming for good.

"We're so goddamned arrogant," McCabe had said in that room in the heart of the Labyrinth. "We think we're the masters of his place, the makers of it, that it sits out here for our entertainment, our enlightenment, our edification. But we're fools, and we're wrong. That's the secret, Kendrick, just that.

"Look at this place. Look around. It doesn't seem familiar, does it? This isn't something we made with our thoughts, our wishes, our prayers. This place is a dream, of course it is, what else could it be? But it's not our dream." And here he had pulled down the curtain, torn it from the wall, and Kendrick had felt himself carried to the window to look out across a vast expanse, like an alien planet, with hillocks that darted at the movement of the eyes beneath, and vistas that rose and fell with gigantic breath. He had seen the great, dreaming, cyclopean thing, and he had finally understood.

DEATH MAY DIE
By Nathan Wunner

From the log of Cpt. Randall Skinner, aboard the e-class cargo transport Nautilus, just outside the orbit of the planet Pharos:

A merchant once asked me how I could live with myself doing what I do for a living. Defiling the resting place of corpses to turn a profit. When the day of judgment came, they asked, and I had to stand before God and recount my sins, how would I defend my actions?

I laughed at him. Friend, I said, I've seen every corner of the "heavens". There's no God floating around out there. And if there is, he doesn't give a shit about you and me.

Then I took a long swig of whiskey, and I said "Do me a favor. Bury your son with as much gold and as many jewels as you did your wife."

I got socked on the jaw for my trouble, and I'm banned from the city of Rerra indefinitely, but I've got to say, the look on that merchant's face was worth it.

1.

It was like something from a dream. A shape like a coil of barbed wire wrapped around a metal spike, floating against a backdrop of frothing storm clouds and violent flashes of lightning.

A mausoleum ship. My next payday.

"Neura. Info dump."

Neura's tinny computer voice came through my earpiece. "Point of origin: Unknown. Construction: Unknown metal-matrix composite. Current destination: Un…"

"Skip to what you *do* know, please."

"Architectural design elements and size of the craft are consistent with vessels designated 'mausoleum ships', which came into common use after the intergalactic war to house the massive numbers of deceased…"

"I can see that much with my own eyes. Is that all you've got?"

"That's all I've got, boss."

That was Neura for you. Best argument I'd ever seen for not buying your data-cubes second-hand.

Still, space gets quiet. It's nice to hear a voice other than your own from time to time, even if it happened to be the voice of an idiot. "Neura, auto-dock. Wake me up when we get there. I've got a hangover to sleep off."

2.

Abandoned space ships always reminded me of the carnival spookhouses we used to have back in the colonies. Flickering lights, the hiss of static from a black screen, frayed wires spitting sparks onto the floor, and a thousand moving shadows that lingered in the eaves and vanished when you glimpsed them from the corner of your eye.

Mausoleum ships have this same atmosphere dialed up to eleven. They're often built like mazes, designed to keep you from ever reaching the heart of labyrinth. Full of booby traps and dead ends.

And why, you might ask, would anyone ever want to explore one of these death traps?

Because there's money in it.

I operate on the fringe systems. Colonists are superstitious out here. They don't poke around in ships full of dead people. Less competition means less gunfights with other looters and more time to properly pillage my find. Of course, being out in these remote areas means less ships come floating by; but I make the best of what's offered to me.

I exited my ship, the Nautilus, with Neura in hand. The docking bay doors snapped shut behind us.

Locked in the tomb, with all of the other corpses. Heh.

"Neura. Is the air breathable?"

"Affirmative, boss."

I ditched my helmet. Space suits always made me feel itchy.

The docking bay only had one exit; a narrow door leading to an unlit hallway. But one way forward was all I needed.

3.

Neura switched to black light mode. I marked the walls with phosphorescent chalk to keep track of which halls I'd already been down.

I was always good at mazes. My father used to build a haystack maze each fall, back in the colonies. Every year I'd race in and be the first one through.

Progress was slow. Out of boredom I caught myself trying to find a pattern in the symbols etched into the walls. Grave robbing is pretty common in the core systems; so words of warning and gruesome images carved into the walls, or even the hull, of mausoleum ships was not uncommon. What was strange about this ship was that I wasn't seeing symbols repeated very often. The text here looked more like an ongoing narrative than a re-iteration of a warning.

"Neura. Any idea what language this is written all over the walls?"

"Unknown. Similarities to Caravian. Rylian. I can attempt to translate, if you'd like?"

"Please do."

The images all blurred together after a while. My eyes started to hurt looking at them. I turned my attention back to the task at hand; navigating the maze.

I rounded a corner, and with no warning or fanfare whatsoever, I spotted a corpse lying on the ground.

Not an uncommon sight in my line of work. I just wasn't used to seeing them up and out of their coffins. Or defiled quite so gruesomely.

The body was completely mutilated. Its limbs were twisted or bent backwards, and its broken jaw hung loosely from its skull. Despite the body's condition my first thought was to check its pockets for anything of value. Habit of being a grave-robber. I'd feel guilty about the thought if I hadn't done worse.

There wasn't enough light for me to tell what species it might be. Its skin was waxen like a candle, translucent. "Neura." I whispered. "What is it?"

I heard little clicks and bloops as Neura searched through her memory. "Biologically it's no different from you. It's human."

I cast Neura's light over the corpse again. It couldn't be human. I could see its organs through its skin. It looked like something that had spent its life in a cave and had never seen the light of day.

A trail of blood lead from the corpse down the hall and around the bend. The blood was dried, almost orange in color. "How long has it been dead?" I asked.

"Without doing a thorough analysis, I'd guess several days."

I approached that corner slowly, straining my ears for any hint of a sound. And I kept my hand on my sidearm. "Neura. Confirm for me one more time. You detect no life signs on board?"

"Affirmative, boss."

I rounded the corner. Nothing there.

Whatever killed that person, I guess it didn't survive the encounter either.

4.

The heart of the labyrinth. I'm used to seeing catacombs with corpses numbering in the thousands; each decked out in funeral garb and jeweled trinkets, laid to rest in velvet lined coffins laced with gold trim. That or the mass graves, full of soldiers hastily heaped one on top of the other; still clutching their weapons.

But this? This was the first time I'd ever seen a mausoleum ship built to house just one corpse.

The interior of the modestly sized room was stark compared to the rest of the ship. No writing on the walls. A plain black coffin sat upon an elevated platform at the center of the room, lid slightly ajar. There was nothing inside.

I rubbed my temples with my forefingers. This couldn't be it. I couldn't have come all of this way for nothing.

"Boss?" Neura said. "I've partially translated some of the writings outside."

"Anything useful?"

"The warnings in this ship are distinct in that they don't seem aimed at protecting what lies inside the ship, but in protecting others from it."

"What?" I said.

"Translation:" Neura began, "'The devil dabbled in dark arts. Many grew mad just listening to it. Sickness fell upon our people. It spoke blasphemies in languages never heard by the elders. Even after we removed its tongue it spoke these bizarre curses. It would die neither by drowning nor decapitation. We burned it to ashes and it laughed as it reassembled itself out of the dust. We had to exile it. To freeze it, and let it drift in the unending dark of space.'"

I looked down at the empty coffin. "So much for that."

That corpse I'd seen back in the maze, the human; perhaps it came with others. They turned on life support, woke up whatever this thing was, and had to put it down. Or maybe it was the other way around.

Either way, if there was ever anything of value to be found here it was likely long gone. I'd shown up to the party too late. And if there was some kind of space-zombie walking the halls, then all the more reason to make a quick exit.

"Boss?" Neura said. "Alarming news. Someone just boarded the Nautilus. I'm receiving a transmission."

The voice that came through Neura's speakers sounded like a hive of bees drowning in water. "You have no idea how long I've slept, dreaming of returning home." It said. "How long I've drifted, lost. The others awoke me and escaped. But here you are with your navigation charts, and your maps of the stars. I should thank you. Perhaps I'll take you back with me." The voice went silent.

Neura began to flicker and fade in my palm. "Boss? The lights. . ." Her voice trailed off into nothing.

The room was plunged into darkness. And in the darkness, I felt the unusual sensation of breath on the back of my neck.

5.

I awoke to find myself strapped to a chair, staring out a window. The stars were growing distant. All of them. Faint pinpricks, their light so weak it might as well have not been there at all. Ahead of us was nothing but a void.

It was freezing cold in that room. I couldn't feel my fingers. I heard a terrible noise, like the piping of a hundred broken flutes playing out a rhythmless melody.

The sound wasn't coming from inside the ship. It was from out there, in the black of space.

I heard something enter the room. It took a spot just to my left. Even craning my neck I could see only glimpses of it in the corner of my eye; pale, paper-thin skin stretched over sharp bones, and a pair of dark eyes sunken deep within its elongated skull.

The alien's insect-like voice managed a slurred, mangled approximation of human speech, and its cadence was as awkward as that shrill music coming from outside. "My people have a theory regarding the creation of life in the universe." The alien said. "Would you care to hear it?"

The creature loomed over me, face still obscured in shadow. I saw protruding from its back a thin limb, long and sharp like a spider-leg. It dangled in the air, glistening and shaking like a wet dog. "Our theory goes something like this: life wasn't created at all. It was an accident. One tiny cosmic amoeba, a mindless thing with all the intelligence of a rock, it split into two, and the two became four, and on and on it went, for millennia, this mindless expansion; though we tried to create systems and dogma to explain this expansive impulse."

"Why are you telling me this?" I tried to get up, but the straps held me firmly in place.

The alien leaned over and caressed my chin. Its hand reeked of rot. "My people, ages ago, set off into the void in search of a God. Our maker. Like your kind, we wondered about our origins."

I felt its fingernails digging into my cheeks, splitting the skin. "Do you know what we found?"

There was a pressure at the top of my head, and then behind my eyes, as that spider-leg appendage chiseled its way into my head. I heard myself screaming, but the sound felt like it was coming from miles away. My skull cracked and eventually give way beneath that piercing limb; and then came the maddening sensation of it moving around inside my head and slicing away chunks of my own brain.

Blood seeped from the open wound in my scalp and stained my vision red. I felt something in my mind, some pressure that clawed its way up my spine and made my teeth grind against each other.

A flood of information poured into my mind. I saw sights that weren't pulled from my own memory, even though they came with sensations of smell and touch. In my mind's eye I glimpsed unlit shores and empty skies. I saw waters teeming with life that thrived not from the light of a sun, but the heat from a collapsed star. I watched pale forms pull themselves out the murky waters and take up residence in caves; and there they resided in multitudes, a legion of blind creatures wandering in the dark, scratching words into the stone with jagged fingernails.

The alien towered over me, leering.

My head was turned back towards the window. Out in the black of space I saw a frenzy of movement. There were shapes in the dark; fangs and twitching millipede legs and a thousand lidless, glassy eyes. It was impossible to tell where one of these creatures ended and the next began. Or if there were such things as beginnings and endings.

The piping I'd first heard when I awoke, that choir of broken flutes, grew louder in my ears. Absent any cadence or rhythm, but continuing on just the same; as though whatever was playing was desperate to keep up some pretense of purpose. I could now see that the sound emanated from several tumorous protuberances within its mass.

"This is what we found, in our quest for God." The alien resumed his story. His voice was inside my head now, echoing off of the hollow walls of my own skull. I saw him gesture towards the window, at the things that dwelt in the darkness outside.

"Some of my people gave this chaos a name. Azathoth. But as you will soon see, names are of no consequence. What you are seeing is not an entity. Not an intelligence with a will to enact. It is a representation of the truth of all existence."

The thing outside throbbed like a beating heart. My eyes reluctantly traced it's multitudes of limbs all the way out to far reaches of space, where the stars trembled and shied away. Its tendrils seemed to spread and touch every point of creation, every soul; filling them with festering disease.

"A disease of consciousness." The alien said. "Awareness. Ego." And as it said this, the amorphous beast outside laughed from a thousand gaping mouth-wounds.

At the heart of the chaos I saw an eye, massive in scale, grey and filmy like that of a dead fish. This eye reflected the writhing void like a mirror held up to a mirror, projecting it's horrors out into the infinite.

Behind me my captor whispered, "Behold. The Garden of Eden."

I closed my eyes, only to find them forced open again. "Don't be afraid." I was told. "Your eyes will adjust to the dark."

I felt Azathoth's eye on me, its mindless idiot gaze, no matter how I tried to twist and squirm.

The straps holding me down were pulled loose. My body was thrust violently against the window. Once, and again, and again; until my bones crumbled and my organs were mashed to jelly. I absently wondered how I could still be alive. An answer came from inside my own mind, even if the voice that gave it was not my own. "You will be alive for quite some time to come."

The glass shattered, and I felt the icy grip of deep space gnaw at me. I tried to draw a breath and found that there was nothing to breathe in except the writhing meat of Azathoth itself; filling my lungs, caressing me as it dragged me into its depths.

As I felt consciousness leave me I looked up and saw Azathoth's glassy eye still looking on. Uncaring. Unknowing.

Our creator, just as it had always been.

THE KNOT
By Dennis Detwiller

No human will ever read this message.

I saw the man with translucent skin, like that of a newborn, at the mall in Richmond in 1992. The pale man saw me, seeing him, and he nodded, then considered the sky through the lattice work of cheap, Plexiglas. I walked on, shaking.

It was the same man.

In 1945, I arrived at the Jornada del Muerto, just in time to watch the detonation of TRINITY. I was twenty-four, and an expert—or as expert as you could be in those days—in radioactive isotopes. I was there to look at what came after, if there was an after. The Y-1561 device, the gadget, I got to see it, twice. Once to measure the surrounding structure, and second, in heavy edited blueprints. I did my math and waited at the ranch with the others.

I never saw Oppenheimer, though I know he was present. And we all know what happened. I did my job. My early math became the guideline for what would become Air Force fallout rate calculations. But that's not important right now.

I saw the pale man first, there (or the first in a series of pale men), the night before the detonation. Emilio Segrè was yelling at someone about some math, and this odd man stepped from the shadow of the ranch and quietly said something to him. The other man stepped away, shaking his head, disgusted. Segrè reconsidered the scratch pad, and smiled, and then set furiously to work.

The pale man was very tall, and wore a long black coat, and wide-brimmed black hat, like a Quaker, and his skin was the color of cottage cheese. When he stepped away, with Segrè lost in his math, the pale man looked at me, and as he crossed into the darkness cast beneath the awning of the ranch, I saw his eyes catch the light in an odd way. The rings of them were a floating, ghosted green. He considered me like he knew me, and he nodded.

Then he was gone. For a while.

In 1969, I was working on NERVA—nuclear rockets for deep space exploration. We were up next. After Apollo, we were tasked with coming up with rockets that could burn for months, for years, to get our men to Mars and farther.

I was at Mission Control when Armstrong and Aldrin dropped the little lander towards the moon, though not in any official capacity. I stood off to the side in the "pit", a gaggle of NASA scientists present just to be present, but within earshot of the whole thing. Needless to say, it was very exciting.

What most don't know is that the computer onboard, tasked with side-scanning radar to find a suitable landing spot, threw an error in descent, and mission control went from calmly calling out rates, to frantic, mad questions.

I've watched four documentaries on it. I've even dug up archival footage from the Library of Congress. You can see me, once, watching with my mouth wide open. You see Gene Cernan a lot, along with a couple of other guys I knew, and still know.

You don't see the pale man.

When the lander threw the error and everything failed, he was there, leaning in next to Gene and saying something. Gene called it, and Armstrong put that fucker down like he was parking a damn car in a driveway. I was forty-eight and I had never, ever seen anything better than that moment. Not one single thing even came close.

Now. I saw the pale man, but I didn't see *him*, at least not then. Not yet. It wasn't time to see him yet.

They cancelled NERVA in 1972, and I went to work for the Air Force designing nuclear missiles. It paid to have TRINITY on your résumé, I suppose. I'm sure the pale man has seen it all.

I saw him again on September 18, 1980, at Little Rock, Arkansas. The day went normally for me. That evening, at about 6:45 I got the call, and the Air Force security showed up almost the moment I hung up. It was like being thrown into a blender. I was on a plane in thirty-five minutes, and in Arkansas by 8:50. When I hit the tarmac in Little Rock, I was still wearing my slippers.

Some idiot had pierced the skin of a Minuteman II by dropping a lug wrench on it, causing a leak. I had three levels of government staring at me, in the command room at the base. I had to ask the Secretary of Defense to repeat his question over the phone.

If there is an explosion, will the warhead detonate?

I was intimately familiar with the W53. After all, I had spent the last six years designing its replacement. Would the safety protocols engage in case the rocket exploded, preventing a nuclear detonation? It was hard to say, but the math of the initial design was sound.

Then, the pale man was there. He smelt of oranges. He wore a security badge. His teeth were thin and at their bases, nearly transparent, like some sort of animal. His eyes were yellow brown. When he spoke, his breath smelled of yeast.

"The math is sound. The warhead will not detonate."

I nodded, and repeated what the pale man said to the room, and to those present on the phone.

At 3 AM, the hypergolic fuel exploded and flung the warhead one hundred meters from the bunker, where it landed, but failed to detonate. A general clapped me on the back and laughed, but my mind was elsewhere.

In that time, my life quieted. I consulted. I read the journals. I talked to my friends—who grew fewer by the year—in the organizations which utilized the sciences I dedicated myself to.

On the evening of December 2, 1991, I received a phone call from that same general. He sounded drunk, and dangerous. We had exchanged Christmas cards since 1980, and I knew he sang my praises at the Pentagon. So much so, I had to turn down offers from Reagan and Bush, or their people.

Still, the phone call.

If we went toe-to-toe with the Soviets tonight, what kind of losses would we be looking at?

Now, to say this was a terrifying question was an understatement. Here was a man who could at least put in motion a nuclear exchange, even without the want of his superiors, if he felt like it. So, I exaggerated. Though I thought the Soviets were in much worse shape than anyone believed, I told him that an exchange, any exchange, would mean the end of the world. Who knows, maybe there could be a winning scenario.

He thanked me, and hung up. Sixteen days later the Soviet Union collapsed.

I talked to the pale man.

He didn't run when I saw him, and hailed him as a friend. Instead, his hand came up to match mine, in a mechanical nature, and he waited, towering over the others at the mall.

"Hello it is a fine day for the talk," he said, and his voice was like a South African pronouncing English phonetically off a teleprompter.

"We have met before," I said, and tried to smile.

"Yes. Many times," the man said, and his tongue, I saw, was such a deep red, as to almost be blue, like defrosted chopped meat.

"Why are you here?"

"You are my largest problem. Of all of them, you alone are the one I cannot solve," he said, and his voice rose and fell at odd points, as if he could not properly meter some script.

"I see," I said, though I didn't.

"You are required. The fallout table. The W54. The Damascus incident. The phone call. These stretch the entirety of your length, and you alone are required to maintain them."

"Are you from. . ." I saw then.

"Yes," he said. "Yes, yes."

I nodded. I suppose I knew that, somehow.

"Why are you here?"

"Man must survive."

"Why me?"

"An irrelevant question. There is only when."

"Are you here to kill me?"

"No. But you must come with me."

The light in the Cretaceous cast an orange glow through the vault, and onto a slab of stone the scale of some titanic archway, but which was nothing more than a table in the vast stone library. The book on it was two and a half feet across, and nearly three feet tall, and the thin metal skin on the outside was etched with a name, followed by titles. A doctor of nuclear science. A human of little consequence, who happened to be the junction point of some master plan he would never fully understand.

The scrawled, handwritten notes told the story of the sallow, pale man, and their chance meetings across time. The English characters were unsteady, but the handwriting was careful. To the human, who would never be human again, the story was important.

Outside, on the stone balcony the size of a football field, the huge conical creature considered the yellow white sky, and the moon, hung with the lights of the settlements there, winking in and out. The creature was not a native, but the time and place was full of wonders.

The creature had been born human, 66 million years in the future, and would play out its last days here, in an alien body. It was a problem never solved; simply removed from the equation. An impossible knot clipped neatly from some invisible skein of time.

SKOPTSY
By Jonathan Sharp

It's fucked. It's all gone to fuck. Mitch is dead and I'm running. Running for my life. Running away from, from total fucking madness...

It was supposed to be another easy job. Take Mitch, go up north, and kill some unwelcome squatters that had pissed off a small time Geordie gangster.

Walk in the park the Boss said.

Didn't play out that way though.

1:05 pm. The Lucky Egg Chinese Restaurant, Jesmond.

Fuck knows how much he'd paid the Boss to get us up here to sort out his shit, cause Richmond was slime. Fat, overweight, with a face the colour of recently boiled meat. He was chain smoking and alternating between stuffing his face with sweet and sour pork and pawing the girl beside him.

He looked less than happy at our arrival.

"Ah wazn't expect'n a lass, like."

The girl giggled. Despite the thick cake of makeup and the skimpy outfit, she looked about all of thirteen and drunk or stoned.

Mitch grunted and looked set to walk out.

I already didn't like Richmond, but the boss had warned us about him. In a world of nasty people, he had... a reputation. Smack, underage fuck movies, selling teenage girls...

I'd have happily pinned his grubby little hand to the table with a chopstick.

"Look, you called in the cavalry, we're here and we'll do the job. And we'll do it properly. I understand your own men got... messed up?"

"Aye, tha did like, reet fuck'n messed up an'all. But yr a lass."

He looked at Mitch, sizing him up.

"What ah need is hard fuck'n killas, like yah man there." He waved towards Mitch.

Mitch was ex army, ex private security and built like a tank. He looked the part.

"Listen Richmond," I leaned towards him and smiled. "I don't scare easily."

Mitch just grinned back at me and let me convince him.

3:30 pm. Khan's Halal Butchers, Blaydon.

I'd scared Richmond enough to know who he was dealing with. Fat fucks like that are nothing compared to a horde of pissed off Taliban.

It had started raining and we were at the arse end of Newcastle to pick up the tools for the job.

I didn't catch the kids name, it didn't matter.

"Richmond sez you'd come for these."

He unzipped a black hold all.

Mitch whistled appreciatively at the AK's.

"Are these clean?" I didn't want to be using anything traceable.

"Oh aye, Richmond got these babies for you from the paddies."

"What?"

"Y'kna, the paddies, they got no need fer s'many guns now."

This just got better, guns from Northern Ireland.

The kid gave us a mobile phone as well. "There's only my number on here. When yer done, ring me and toss the phone. Me an the lads'll come and clean up the mess."

6:24 pm. Somewhere off the A68.

Even with sat nav I could tell we were in the middle of nowhere, I wasn't entirely convinced we weren't actually in Scotland now. The farm was totally isolated and miles from the main roads. I let Mitch drive the Range Rover, good job we were in a four-wheel drive.

We pulled the car over in a wood about a mile from the farm. By now it was pissing it down with rain, I figured that ought to cover us on the way in. We changed into black gear in the car. After hearing what had happened to Richmond's crew, we'd brought stab vests as well.

I could see Mitch had one of his hand cannons with him. He's a big guy and he likes big handguns. Desert Eagle sized guns.

"Some extra insurance for us," he grinned and handed me a Sig that I slipped in the pocket of my jacket.

We took the AK's and set off through the trees for the farm.

6:47 pm. March Sike Farm.

The rain had eased off a bit; we'd got a vantage point in the trees about a hundred meters from the Farm Buildings. The place looked old and run down. Lights were visible in the farmhouse and in the larger of the two barns. No other sign of movement.

I could hardly believe this place was important enough to warrant us being here. But I know from experience, there are some kinds of business's that require privacy. Fuck alone knows though why Richmond had been stupid enough to rent the place out. Especially to them.

Time to wait and see what was going on.

8:31 pm. March Sike Farm.

After almost an hour and a half, finally some movement. In the twilight, a group of kids came out of the farmhouse and made their way across the farmyard towards the largest barn.

They were all naked. Most of them were stick thin.

They'd all been mutilated.

It was almost impossible to distinguish the boys from the girls.

"Fuck me Jess, just what the fuck are we looking at?" breathed Mitch.

"Shshhh... Stay down and let's just see what's going on."

We watched as this procession of butchered children, made their way across the farmyard.

Finally two adults appeared. Like the girls before, the woman had been mutilated, and she wore nothing except thick white stockings. Over her scarred chest had been daubed the outline of a white bird with its wings spread wide. She was carrying a huge kitchen knife in each hand.

The man, he was something else…he looked older, with snow-white hair and a long beard. He also was wearing the same thick, white stockings and a leather apron. I couldn't tell if he was cut like the boys had been. But the apron seemed to cover a huge bulge in his stomach area. It moved. I swear it moved.

This is who had fucked up Richmond's men? An old couple and a bunch of kids?

This is who we've come here to kill?

Mitch was looking uneasy. So was I.

"Jess, I don't like this."

"Mitch, we're here to do a job, just like we always do."

"Fuck it, I didn't take one in the leg from those Taliban fuckers to murder a bunch of kids."

"Mitch, you know the deal. We take the pay, we do the job, and we walk away."

"Fuccccckkkk."

The rain was starting to turn heavy – that and the noise that was coming from the barn now… it sounded like some kind of Slavic hymn singing. That was going to cover any noise we would make going in.

We split up. Mitch was going right in and while I circled around to come in from behind.

Staying under cover I worked my way around the back of the farm. Before I'd managed to cover the distance to the barn I heard the gunfire.

Something had gone wrong.

No point in being careful now. I sprinted the last twenty yards and burst through the back door of the barn. Everything seemed to go into slow motion

Mitch was framed in the doorway clutching the AK. One of the children was down, bleeding heavily from a chest wound.

The old man was facing Mitch, bellowing at him in what sounded like Russian.

So was the woman, she was waving around the kitchen knives and screaming at him.

She went for Mitch.

No hesitation, he pulled the trigger and her chest exploded, showering blood as she went down.

Almost immediately one of the children grabbed one of her huge knives and made to rush Mitch.

Again no hesitation, the assault rifle barked and the kid was literally lifted off his feet from the force of bullets as his face disappeared. The old man screamed a single word and the children stopped moving.

He motioned for them all to back off, and then he took a step towards Mitch.

"Don't make a fucking move old man, don't make a fucking move."

For a moment he seemed to stop, as if considering his next move. Then he began to laugh, a harsh rasping laugh that became a barking cough.

"You understand me old man? Don't move another fucking step."

The old man took a step towards Mitch, then another. He lifted his right hand to undo the clip of his apron.

We both fired at the same time.

Like a grisly marionette the old man danced as the bullets ripped into him from both of our weapons. Spinning around in a fountain of blood, his legs finally went from under him and he collapsed to the floor of the barn. As he hit the ground the children started screaming.

Mitch inched towards the body.

"No. Mitch stay back!"

Mitch ignored me.

The old man was lying on his back, amidst a rapidly spreading pool of blood.

Mitch moved towards the body, as soon as he was close enough he poked at the bulging apron with his assault rifle.

The bulge shuddered. Rippled. Pulsed.

Before either of us could react a tendril of mottled flesh extruded out from beneath the apron. Lightning fast, it poked out, forming a ropey snake like appendage. I swear it was intestine. It seemed to enlarge as it flowed towards the barrel of Mitch's AK. I saw him pull the trigger as the thing swelled over the end of the assault rifle.

The bullets ripped through it in a shower of blood and slime. Mitch didn't stop until he'd emptied the magazine.

"What the fuck, what the fuck..." Mitch was yelling.

Everything happened at once. Some of the kids rushed me from behind, trying to yank the assault rifle from my hands. Acting on reflex I heaved the gun backwards, it's heavy wooden stock crunching into one of the kids' faces.

At the same moment the old man's bleeding body heaved with a series of spasms and the apron fell away. No longer hidden, the ropey tendril reaching out to Mitch's gun had extended from what looked like a huge, pulsing, tumor, half buried in his abdomen.

Impossibly the old man's body lurched upright.

It couldn't. He was dead.

As the old man, or whatever was inside him, was trying to straighten up, I could see what was left of his abdomen was a huge gaping, bleeding mess.

With a final jolt the body straightened up.

The barn was momentarily silent.

The thing enveloping Mitch's assault rifle twisted hard and yanked the gun from his hands.

Mitch didn't hesitate. He turned and bolted for the barn doors.

He didn't make it.

With a sickening ripping noise, multiple tendrils burst out of the old man's chest. Like a dozen angry snakes they propelled themselves at Mitch. They punched through the stab vest like it wasn't even there.

He was lifted off the ground as three, four, maybe more of the tendrils pierced his large frame.

This was insanity.

Mitch started screaming. Screaming like one of those poor bastards that caught an I.E.D.

I could see the tendrils ripping through his body like hot pokers. He was a puppet being pulled apart by snakes of living, bubbling, twisting tissue. The tentacles seemed to act as one, folding back on themselves to burrow back through Mitch's body again. It was tearing him apart, killing him. Killing him in front of me.

I wasn't going to let it.

Wrestling free of the children, I dropped the AK, it was useless with an empty magazine. I pulled the SIG out of my jacket and aimed at Mitch.

Later—Time Unspecified. Location Unspecified.

It's fucked.

It's all gone to fuck.

Mitch is dead and I'm running.
Running for my life.
Running away from, from total fucking madness...

RED AMERICANS
By Cody Goodfellow

Out the window, Charlie Bledsoe watches the pregnant woman in the gray factory smock squatting over the trashcan by the bus stop. Gray plastic can, pocked with cigarette scars like cheetah spots. Her face wrung out like a rag, she screams and forces out something, slides off the can and lights a shaky cigarette. She drags on it long and hard, slams the lid on the can to cut through the umbilical cord, and limps away.

Brad Hurley is jubilant. "See, Charlie? They're tough stuff. Sturdy girls with guts like Dutch ovens. Fifty bucks says she doesn't even miss her next shift."

"You're sick," says Bledsoe, dropping three pale red Mao notes on the desk.

The newborn comes mewling out of the can, slapping the pavement and slithering after its mother, who spears it with her umbrella and atlatls it into the street. The bus stop security guard comes over and shoots it with his greasegun.

They're getting worse. Nobody wants to admit it because they've got so much tied up in the manufacturing contract. Almost a thousand girls and women locked up in dormitories the ten hours they're not on the clock. But every day, another girl on the factory floor turns up pregnant. Almost thirty percent of them are knocked up already. Even if the Party makes good on their promises to do the honorable thing, the hit to productivity is going to be staggering, if not fatal.

"We might as well go back to America."

"We might have to," Hurley says, "if you don't think of something fast, Charlene."

When Bledsoe found out how deep a shitpile the previous project manager left her to dig out of, Hurley, the factory's Chief Efficiency Officer, assured her that the asshole was taken out and shot and buried somewhere on the factory grounds. She promised herself that when she was done, she would dig him up and set him on fire.

Realive Baby was supposed to break Xmas. A masterpiece of misguided innovation at the company's blackout research lab two provinces over, Realive Baby radiated warmth, responded to touch, cried when it needed something and ate, pissed and shat, just like a real baby. The shit even smelled.

The gimmick was in a new proprietary material she's heard variously described as an organic polymer, a gene-spliced fungal colony, a stem cell breakthrough retro-engineered from vat-grown flesh for burn victims, to vague mumblings that it was actually a new form of artificial life. Whatever it is, the shit was woven into the silicone and rubber doll to form a durable but tender "skin" that got goose-pimples when it was cold, sweaty when it was hot, and required nutrients to stay "alive."

This last was the supposed master-stroke, for the dolls' organic matrix is dependent on another proprietary substance, a goo that they'll have to buy online and feed them daily, or the doll goes on maddening crying jags, as electrochemical hunger signals trigger the embedded voice chip. If neglected, the doll eventually "dies," producing a godawful stink every bit as bad as a real human corpse. Any other food gives it diarrhea and causes it to sweat out repellent odors.

The initial tests for the product the locals call Baby Consumer were disastrous, to put it mildly. Far from instilling any maternal instinct in the trial subjects, the shrieking, fluids and odors caused many of the girls to react like infanticidal baboons, dashing the squishy organic innards out of the plastic skulls and sometimes urinating on them in some kind of atavistic, primal rejection.

The company prudently shitcanned Baby Consumer 1.0 in June, but the project manager freaked out. Normally, they would've just demoted him, but he became some kind of crazy Right-To-Lifer over the fucking doll. Resisted burying them, tried to smuggle a truckload of them out in a trash truck. Claimed they were not just alive, but an incarnation of a god the factory workers told him was coming to REALLY break Xmas.

Thus, the bullet to the head and the unmarked grave. And with August around the corner, Bledsoe has to not only bring the hastily cobbled-together new version to market, she also has to get a handle on the plague of factory workers conceiving and birthing a hideous parody of Baby Consumer.

Nobody with her record would get buried out here on this goat-rope except as punishment, but they probably felt they were showing "sensitivity" by sending a woman.

The factory's satellite town consists of a row of worker dormitories, a recreation center, a miniature tract home development for corporate staff and an 18-hole golf course that is totally useless because it's overrun with a pernicious strain of four-leaf clover some assholes designed for holiday novelty landscaping.

The rec center has conference rooms, an indoor swimming pool, a theater, a roller disco and an eighteen-hole cathouse that is almost useless because the Ukrainian girls all have crabs and an unshakable biting fixation. Though built less than a decade ago, it still looks like an abandoned minimum security prison, and from the concrete dissolving like clumps of cat litter to the charming way water and sewage lines sometimes switch roles, it won't even be ruins in another ten years. Only all the aborted products in the surrounding landfills will remain to baffle alien archaeologists.

A dinner party for the regional manager, who flew in by helicopter from the provincial capital, umpteen hundred empty miles away. Bledsoe follows him and his escort out to a balcony overlooking the botched golf course to tell him what's really going on. Because Bledsoe's e-mails, formal progress reports, conference calls and spreadsheet projections apparently had too many syllables.

She kills her martini, regrets not bringing a spare. "Yes, we fumigated. Sterilized and repainted the whole factory, all the dorms. We tested the food, the water, the workers…"

"Did you check to see if they're not smuggling plums?"

"Yes, a doctor cleared all of them. They're females. Especially the pregnant ones..."

He picks his nose and studies his find, wipes it on the couch. "That's not true, is it?"

"Sir?"

"Don't call me 'sir', my name's Tim. I hear one of them was a...a shermaphro—"

"Hermaphrodite, yes, Tim... that's true. Statistically, they're rare, but they're out there. But incapable of getting anyone pregnant."

"Well, they're still freaks. Replace them."

"We did that once...again, it's all in my report...but the women came from the same place. Somewhere in Tibet or Mongolia, we can't get a straight answer. Some place with mountains, they all had trouble breathing when they got here, and hardly any of them speaks a word of Chinese...And you know how the Party is..."

"Fucking commies." The regional manager sets down his drink and picks up his cigar, absently tips a glowing ash into the lank dishwater hair of the girl blowing him. He does indeed know how the Party is, and the Party more than reciprocates his dislike. "But it's not slowing you down...?"

"No... but..."

"And nobody's died. Aside from the little bastards...which aren't, strictly speaking..."

"Oh no...Tim. Not even a layman would mistake them for human..."

"Then quit yanking our goddamn chain, Charlene. Jesus, Ops told me you had balls."

"Excuse me?"

"Darlin', if you're not gonna be another problem for us, you'd better get on the right side of this war..."

"What war is that? We're just making toys..."

The reeg grunts and pushes the whore away. "No, it's a quiet one, but it's total, existential warfare. They're running the same game on us we ran on the Russians. They're not even Communists anymore; they're just whatever they have to be to bury us. Drive us into bankruptcy, only with consumer goods, instead of missiles.

"You ever wonder what goes through their heads when they're injecting those molds and painting all that cheap, ridiculous plastic shit? They're making bombs and bullets, every one a thumb on the scale of debt. When we crashed the Iron Curtain and the Soviets fell, all we ended up with was a bunch of obsolete hardware and a vast, lawless market that counterfeited our goods instead of buying them. Between the Russians and the Chinks, just living their lives, they're driving us to insolvency and extinction."

"So...we're helping them, right? If this is a war, whose side are we on?" *Just tell me what to say, asshole...*

"We're still Americans, goddamit. I guess you could say we're all triple agents, now. Making them pay for every dollar they take in irreversible environmental devastation. They're trying to adapt to it, to eating shit and breathing smoke. We're adapting, too. We passed the point of engineering products years ago, now we're on to engineering the ideal consumer. The Chinese are trying to do the same thing. It's a race between walking fish over hot coals.

"Maybe now you'll think a little more before you shoot your fucking mouth off about what's going on here."

Charlie's nodding, trying to find her mouth to lick her lips and say, *Yes, sir*, when Hurley comes out onto the balcony and drives a steak knife into the vertebrae just above the regional manager's collar. Twisting the knife like a lousy *bunraku* puppeteer, Hurley maneuvers the portly Texan asshole over the railing and lets him fall, only just pulling the knife free before he drops out of sight.

"Were you as sick of that guy as I was?"

Replacing the regional manager proves a lot easier than replacing a factory floor. Hurley handles it, but she catches on quick. Let the Company think the Party clipped him, and vice versa. "It's not like there's an asshole shortage at the home office," he tells her.

Between the relabeled garbage bins in the restrooms and showers and the bonus for not missing shifts during pregnancies—which seldom run longer than nine weeks to full term—the Baby Consumer problem has faded to background noise.

And then Hurley disappears. A week goes by. She doesn't see him, but everyone else on site insists, *He was just here—*

A confidential memo drops claiming he's been relocated to another factory to troubleshoot a fucked-up production flow involving the Snoplow, essentially a miniature Roomba that chops and lays out digitally-scaled lines of snortable white powder. Demand has gone through the roof, but the robots are choking up on the gunk the coke's cut with, and a Russian ripoff is being produced in a neighboring province. Hurley has been promoted to industrial saboteur, with orders to reroute the cheap motors to the Russians and if possible, flood their factory with chlorine gas to make them miss the Christmas window.

A month goes by. Everything's been going smoothly since Hurley disappeared. She's more anxious about him coming back than meeting the new regional manager.

The head of security calls her in to look at something. "We've been *periodically* checking these security feeds…"

Bledsoe bites her lip. They're watching everything else. She's found six hidden cameras in her home and office. Why wouldn't they have cameras in the showers? She begins spewing the appropriate workplace-conduct boilerplate, but then sputters, "What're they wearing? They wear pants in the fucking shower…?"

"No, their legs…they just look like that…"

Nearly all the women and girls sport aprons of coarse black hair covering their genitalia, and many are covered from pubis to ankles in jodhpurs of matted or braided fur. They walk on the balls of their feet, as if their feet were bound in the hideous traditional Chinese style, their toes with outsized, curled nails almost like the split hooves of a goat. As one squats to scrub between her legs, Bledsoe notices a vestigial tail protruding several inches from the coccyx, almost covering the crack of the buttocks.

Jesus, the doctors somehow left all this out of the reports. But the doctors were locals, utterly terrified of the Party.

Pausing the feed on a bunch of them kneeling in a circle in the far corner of the cavernous shower, the security chief says, "This happened yesterday."

He lets it roll. The heaving knot of shaggy bodies trembles, linked arms keeping them together as they collectively expel their unwanted pregnancies on the tiled floor. A skinny, dwarfish figure with silver hair dances around them, shaking out a fine black powder that turns to mud on the unwilling mothers.

"They've been drinking this blue-black tea…we couldn't figure where they got it. We thought it was a narcotic, but it's just an analgesic mixed with something to make them miscarry."

Problem solved, then, she almost says. *Results!*

The women huddle together, exhausted, until the showers cut off. The silver-haired one, a prepubescent girl with an old woman's head, spills the last of her powder on the compost heap of aborted dolls and backs away bowing to it.

"That one," Bledsoe says, jabbing the screen, "what's her deal?"

"Shift super in injection molding. Freaky. Ngor Qo, or something... my guys call her Betty. The others are scared of her, like she's a witch or something, but she actually knows some Chinese, so we use her to handle the others..."

"Pull her out and send her to my office, won't you, Doug?"

"Sure... but that's not what I wanted you to see." He pauses it and turns to level his most paternalistic stare. "We put those burn barrels in the showers and everywhere else, but they've been coming up empty..."

"We don't have time to freak about problems that fix themselves..."

Doug lets the tape play. The pile of misshapen babies stirs and shifts.

Bledsoe groans. "Shit...what, are they in the air conditioning vents now?"

A limb stretches out, groping at air, tangled in umbilici and burst cellophane placentas. The rest of him spills out onto the floor and creeps out of frame, followed by two janitors with gas masks and snow shovels.

"Well," Bledsoe says, "at least we found Hurley." Staring even as she chokes back her lunch, she can't begin to imagine Doug has any explanation worth hearing. "Where is he now?"

Doug digs a ballpoint pen in his left nostril. "Nobody knows. None of the sanitation workers saw him. We made sure they weren't lying... Um... But I betcha dollars to donuts he's the one knows where all them babies are going..." He shivers, deleting the video. "Thank God we don't make dog food."

Dennis Fan has been Charlene Bledsoe's interpreter and the factory's Party liaison since she came to the factory, two months ago. Affable Hong Kong mannerisms, unaccented English, erudite sense of humor, and the first man she's ever worked with who could look at her and see a woman without making her into meat and mauling her in his head or with his hands.

Shitfaced at the welcome celebration, she made a pass at him and he dutifully took her home. She doesn't remember how it was, and she hasn't let herself slip again. Since then, she's also seen Dennis beat six recalcitrant workers bloody with his own hands, and order many more "education sessions." Three workers, at least, have been executed, by truncheons or forced ingestion of the useless weed killer they spray everywhere to keep the four-leaf clover at bay. Dead workers don't cause trouble, but the Party takes notice if someone starts wasting bullets.

Dennis smiles at her as Qo, the strange little witch, enters the office and bows to her desk, ignoring Bledsoe's invitation to be seated.

Bledsoe has done some Rosetta courses in Mandarin and Cantonese, but she doesn't make out a word of the gurgling purr Qo makes in answer to her questions. Dennis leans in politely, but fear and disgust oozes through his uncomfortable smile.

"She was not aware they were doing something wrong," he translates. "They were told to get rid of the things, and she helped them. Our medicine doesn't work...does not know them...but her herbs cure their ailments. That is why they are afraid...of her...no...afraid to kill her."

She girns toothlessly at Bledsoe. Apropos of nothing, one of Hurley's most colorful turns of phrase springs to mind—*ugly enough to stop a rape*. Qo turns away, looking out the window at the empty plains beyond the factory. Something comes out of her mouth, but Dennis just shakes his head minutely, sipping his tea.

"They're not words...not that I know. It's a very foreign dialect. These people have been in relocation camps for...some of them, for generations. They cannot even tell you where they come from. One says this plateau of Sung is in Mongolia...another, Tibet. Some look up at the clouds and smile and nod, others stamp their feet and bow to the earth beneath them. But this city, or monastery, that they call home...this Leng...we know that it does not really exist."

Bledsoe impatiently brushes her desk off. Dust everywhere... "That's fascinating, but where did the babies go, and what about Hurley? I know he was part of the ritual in the shower. I'm not going to do anything to her...and neither are you, okay?"

His smile goes away for just a moment. Then he turns and translates her question.

Whatever she is, Qo isn't afraid of anyone here. She chatters in a lilting singsong that leaves Dennis frowning as if personally offended to have to soil his tongue with it.

"They needed a man for the ceremony, because their god...no, their gods...they are two in one...one who is two. Male and female, yin and yang, but fluid, each partaking of and eating and killing and...loving, and becoming the other. That is why...they must keep her with them, because she is both man and women and neither. She cannot bear or sire a child, but has both sexes, both minds. What we call yin and yang, but their...true names... Zhar...and...Lloigor...through her, they seek to return from where their people have hidden them.

"The Chinese devils—you see, I try to translate honestly—invaded their plateau of Sung and they separated the One-in-Two and destroyed them... or drove them from the earth. The Chinese have one of their gods in bottles and they would make products of it...but...when they see...when we all see... then..." He shook his head, refusing to translate further. "It's perverse mountain people nonsense."

Finally, Qo sucks her mouth shut and grinds her black gums on a black leaf from the pockets of her smock. Dennis waves her out of the room and she starts to go, but Bledsoe stops her. "Ask her how her gods are coming back."

"It's not worth the trouble, Miss Bledsoe." He's always called her Charlene. He withers under her glare. "She says, 'They are already here.'"

Only Bledsoe catches the flicker of those smug eyes as she speaks, towards the display on Bledsoe's desk, of a finished, packaged Realive Doll, and then she's gone.

She's leaving the food court when a security guard accosts her. His helmet is on, his mask down. He murmurs in her ear, "Just keep walking, doll."

She climbs into a freight semi idling at the end of the line of golf carts. He goes around and gets behind the wheel.

Bledsoe looks out the window. Dennis and this week's dead fish-breathed visiting Party official come out the exit she just used, and walk right by the truck. She could scream and jump out, and the discreet security detail in gray sharkskin suits hanging ten paces behind them would shoot Hurley. She watches them walk by, shrinks down in her seat and watches them walk by. Maybe because she feels safer with him than with them. Maybe because, for all she knows, he's still a bigger asset to the company than she is.

Nobody is going to investigate this, because nobody wants to know. Nobody will write anything down, because nobody wants what we did here to be remembered. We made some shitty toys and killed a bunch of people. We didn't set the exchange rate. Merry Christmas!

And yet, when he throws the truck in gear and rolls out of the factory town, she starts in on him. "The Company and the Party are both looking for you."

"They better not find me, before I'm done."

"What'm I, a hostage? You know they don't bargain..."

"You're not a hostage. I need you." Taking off the helmet, he throws it out the window. His naked scalp is bloody and gouged like he shaved it with a sharp rock. "I've been thinking with my dick about this whole thing. Company wanted me to do it, but they didn't know what it was. The women, the dolls... can't you see what's trying to happen?"

"I don't see anything but people dying to make shit. The witch told me..."

"Qo? *She* should be doing this, not us. She wanted to. She probably would've, if somebody hadn't narced her out." She can't see his face in the dusty gloom, but his eyes catch the last pallid, setting sun.

"Fuck you for that," she says, "and fuck you for not doing your job, and fuck you for whatever the fuck you think you're doing now—"

She opens her mouth to say more, but the truck shudders and rocks arthritically as it veers off the road, and she looks out the window. "What the... fuck..."

The empty plains of dust now a broken chain of melted plastic mountains. The headlights swivel over walls of defective, discontinued, distressed and undecaying toys, kitchen gadgets, marital aids, athletic equipment, patio furniture, automotive accessories, and every conceivable form of forgotten, aborted, abominable promotional merchandise.

They just leave it out here like this? No... "You've been digging...?"

"As you can see, below the topsoil, there's not much dirt left. We only knew the general area where they buried it, so it's taken a while. Yeah, I imagine it would be pretty hard to find, if it wasn't calling to you..."

"What's calling to you?"

He throws open a door and, in the flat yellow dome light, looks at her like she's an idiot. "The babyfood, of course."

She starts to get out and then notices the pistol jammed under the driver's seat. Hurley's skipping over hummocks of deformed bobble-head dolls towards a massive hole with backhoes parked all around it. "Cloud cover's been on our side all week, but we gotta get this shit off tonight..."

Bledsoe grabs the pistol and slides out, tucking it in her waistband. She took a full self-defense retreat course a few years ago and has a gun in her nightstand at home. But she's never shot anyone. Not that she wouldn't, given the chance—

Hurley throws the truck keys to a worker in factory coveralls and orders two more to move the backhoes. He's not speaking Chinese. It takes her a moment to recognize the gurgling tongue Qo and the other workers speak. The goat-faced worker hobbles past her on crooked legs, leering at her as he passes and gets in the semi.

A chorus of voices scream, "FEED ME, MOMMY" from the ground beneath her feet. She jerks and goes for the gun. The sound is everywhere underfoot, croaking, screaming, discordant Baby Consumer voice modules embedded in charred doll torsos.

Hurley stands on the lip of the pit. About five feet down, a layer of fifty-gallon steel drums lines the bottom. Somebody took a pickaxe to them, ripping apart the lids so the contents bubble and foam like black yeast, out of the drums and up the sides of the hole.

"What are you doing?" Bledsoe demands, drawing the gun. "You're just going to get us all killed and fuck up the Christmas delivery. Is that what this is about, are you working for somebody else?"

He turns around and smiles at her, not even deigning to acknowledge the gun. "I'm trying to make amends for what we've done here. What we're all doing, here. Americans and Chinese, right and left, men and women...we shouldn't be fighting. We should be connected. Did you know there was a Gnostic sect that believed Adam was a hermaphrodite first? As punishment for eating the fruit of the tree, God split Adam into two bodies, two sexes."

"I don't care about any of that shit," Bledsoe says. "I just want the shipments to go out on time, and I want to go home." She points the gun at his knees. "Stop fucking up my program, Hurley."

The semi backs up its trailer to the edge of the pit, across from where they're standing. "When the Chinese crushed these people's home, they didn't just knock over all the idols. They killed their living, breathing gods, Charlene.

"This one god, it's really two gods—like the hemispheres of a brain, you know how one side's always dominant, but always trading places and faces until it's impossible to tell them apart, the difference is meaningless."

The semi's trailer begins to tilt on hydraulic struts. The doors swing open and a flood of flesh tumbles out.

"Divided, they were just so much ectoplasmic shit. The Chinese found this thing in the catacombs, this stuff, they didn't even know for sure it was alive, but they took it and tested it and filed it away and quickly forgot it."

All the half-plastic abortions from the factory fall like meaty sleet into the pool of strange babyfood. Immediately, clouds of steam roil out of the pit like the toxic vapors from lava meting seawater.

"Now Communism's dead, the kids who took over the Party are raiding the catacombs and they find this weird shit that acts like it's alive, and interacts with this other shit in an adjoining file, but nothing else, like they came from a meteor, or something. They couldn't figure out what else to do with it, so they sold it to us.

"But the other one is still around. It was hiding, waiting to be reunited with its mate. The people ate it so it couldn't get taken away. Hiding in those women..."

Ground quivers underfoot, cold plastic melting and clinging in toxic blobs to her flats as she stumbles backwards, away from the mouth of the pit bulging up and out like the mouth of a volcano.

She's shooting and he stops every bullet, they sink in like stones in a river of milk. His skin ripples and shimmers, and so does hers.

He takes the gun from her, takes her hand and they melt.

Together, trading memories and scars, hormones and genes, flesh and bone and she is shared more intimately than with any sexual partner, than anyone who ever loved her. And if being shared is a violation tantamount to rape, then no words exist for the outrage of sharing him—vile dreams of lust and rage and degradation, and at his core, a fear more primal and acidic than any terror of hers, of being unmanned, of becoming like *her*. And yet here he is, turned inside out and swirling over, around and inside her, until somehow, she feels the tide shift, feels him drawing back and taking from her all that she would have thrown away to get ahead in that shit job that was everything to her yesterday. What he's stealing is a deeper outrage than rape, he's stealing her gender—

She tries to withdraw, but they are conjoined by pulsating flesh. She can't get away and he's laughing at her and reeling her in, he's going to digest her like a benign tumor, going to consume and have all that she could have been and more, he's going to be its priest and the bearer of its mad, binary gospel. And she's just going to roll over and let him—

Fuck that, she thinks.

I'm stronger than you. My fear of you is stronger than you are. I don't have to be like you or play your games. I was made to make people, you just tear them down. You can't have this power. It's going to have you. I am not your bitch. I—

Am—

Your—

Mother—

She staggers back up a shaky slope disintegrating and sliding into the twin mouths of the ever-expanding pit. Swallowing backhoes and bow-legged workers and sports memorabilia and DVD clamshells and defective vibrators and she stumbles over the top of a ridge clumsily, she's gravid with the bloat of Craig Hurley's dead weight. She looks down into the writhing, Siamese abominations and calls out their names and their birthing orgy-battle shudders to an uneasy silence, and she tells it what she wants.

Party workers and soldiers swarm the factory. The Tcho Tcho workers file out one fire exit to line up in the dust, while workers in gas masks drag the wreckage of the assembly line out the other end.

Dennis Fan is waiting in her office with the new regional manager. Taking no official notice of her disheveled condition, he demands an explanation.

She briefly outlines the change of production policy and apologizes for any inconvenience it may cause to their fulfillment schedule. In the interest of efficiency, the workers are now the total means of production. The uninvited parthenogenesis is now their primary product.

"Actually, it comes at the best possible time," she says. "We're going to refit for a whole new product. Not so much a different product, as a modified version for a new demographic. If you'll excuse me now," she gets up from her desk, bows, and makes for the door, "I need to review our prototypes."

She takes a company Range Rover down the street to the recreation center and books a massage. The new girls promenade out, and she picks one that stirs the alien weight dangling from her groin to leaden tumescence.

She watches the way it walks as she follows it down the hall, the serpentine glide of girl-shaped plastic smoke. She circles an arm around its hips and gives it a squeeze as it unlocks the door.

"FEED ME MOMMY," the masseuse squeaks.

"We'll have to fix that before Xmas," Hurley gurgles, deep inside her.

We'll fix everything before Xmas, she thinks, and follows it inside.

SHADOW TRANSIT
By Ferrett Steinmetz

Last night's blizzard had choked the roads, leaving the cabinet factory short-handed for the Friday shift. So Michelle's boss had called to give her a choice: she could come in for an emergency shift today and keep her job, or she could take the day off she'd requested to visit her daughter at Shadow Transit, and get her ass fired.

"Thank you," Michelle whispered, glad beyond belief. "I'll come in. Just... call them for me? Please? I'll give you the number, they won't listen to me. Make sure they tell Elizabeth that Mommy's sorry."

Jackson made his apologies, saying how he was sure Lizzie was needed wherever she was, but he had quotas to meet. Michelle barely heard him. She felt the giddy relief of a kid hearing that school was cancelled. Her boss had made the choice for her: she didn't have to play with Lizzie this month, and pretend that everything was okay. No three-hour drives out to the Colander, no watching teenaged guards struggling to remember how to pronounce English words, no worrying about what Lizzie had meant for days afterwards. She was free for another month, and hated herself only a little for it.

It was going to be hell digging the Pontiac out—she'd be lucky if she could get that rattletrap to start up—but she'd have had to do that anyway to visit Lizzie. She'd been putting it off, not wanting to make the effort, but now she had to get to work.

As she pulled the shovel from the hall closet, she stepped on one of Lizzie's old Barbie dolls that still littered the floor. It snapped underfoot, a noise that sounded to Michelle like her daughter's spine snapping.

She knelt down, feeling stupid as the tears rolled down her cheeks, promising God she'd be good if the Barbie was whole. Then she balled her fists; *something* listened to prayers, but it was sunk deep in the ocean and refused to drown.

The Barbie's leg had popped free from the torso. Michelle snapped it back into place with quivering hands, then carefully refitted the Barbie back, face-down, into the groove in the dusty shag rug. It felt like lowering a body into a grave.

That groove was where Lizzie had dropped the Barbie a year ago, when the Shadow Transit agents had come for her.

Michelle looked over Lizzie's other toys, her breath squeezed tight in her throat—but no, they were all where Lizzie had left them. The Raggedy Ann still lay in the middle of the living room floor, the wooden blocks in their pseudo-Stonehenge configuration.

But she'd moved one. She'd broken the chain.

She'd doomed her daughter.

Michelle blushed with shame. That wasn't how magic worked; a twelve-year-old Shadow Transit agent, stammering glottally as she tried to remember how to form human words, had let that slip. Still, every time Michelle was tempted to tidy up, she couldn't bring herself to break that fragile web. She still believed that by keeping all the things Lizzie had loved perfectly in place, she kept some mystic gate open to guide her daughter back home.

She wanted her Lizzie back. Even if the way Lizzie played with Barbie dolls now scared her.

The Shadow Transit agent who'd told her about magic had disappeared soon afterwards. Michelle had wondered how that agent's mother felt when she got the letter explaining how her child had made the ultimate sacrifice for humanity's safety—the government never told you exactly what happened. *It's not safe to understand their exact missions*, they said, and Lizzie had bled enough of the alien waveform into Michelle's head to know that was true. But to not know how your daughter had died?

Michelle imagined two soldiers delivering that manila envelope, imagined wringing the paper in her hands as she wondered whether her daughter had been chewed up by some snarl of extradimensional math, or gotten an embolism from a mispronounced syllable, or whether she'd just gnawed her wrists open because the Dreamer never stopped broadcasting its cancerous thoughts from under the sea...

Michelle buried her head in her hands. She could keep her job. Or she could go to the Colander and exercise her monthly visitation rights. And if Lizzie died before she got out there again, wouldn't she spend the rest of her life wondering if today's visit could have made the difference?

She had to go.

She packed a lunch bag of peanut butter sandwiches, trying to figure out how she'd pay the rent—but just as she was figuring out how to tell Jackson she wouldn't be in today, he called back. Shadow Transit had informed him that firing Miss McGindy would be an extremely inadvisable action. His voice quavered as he offered her an extra vacation day.

Michelle headed out, afraid of seeing Elizabeth, afraid of not seeing Elizabeth.

The drive out of Denver wasn't as bad as she'd feared, even though Michelle's CD player was on the fritz again and she had to listen to Christian AM radio the entire time. As she'd expected, the road through the peaks to Shadow Transit wasn't plowed. She cursed, wondering how she'd make it through the drifts—but then an army supply truck roared up the road. She tailgated, half-blinded by the plumes of snow it kicked up, letting it break up the snowbanks for her.

Michelle suppressed a flush of irritation as she fishtailed up the peak. Shadow Transit wasn't even really in Colorado, so why'd they make the trip so inhospitable? It was as though they wanted to discourage all visitors, even though the psychologists assured Michelle she was critical to Elizabeth's developmental adaptation to externally-induced linguistic waveforms.

By the time she made it to the gates, her thighs ached from working the clutch. The Colander had no waiting room, just a small, heated shack for the guards—so Efro hiked through the snow to meet her at her car, wearing nothing but a dark trench coat over summer shorts. He was a lean black teenager, waiting with an anesthetized calm as the guards frisked her in the windy parking lot. The guards, hardened military vets, glanced down rather than make eye contact with him.

"Trip all right, Missus McGindy?" he asked, as though being up to his bare calves in snow didn't bother him at all.

She nodded absently. It should have reassured her, having the same escort four times in a row—they usually degenerated quickly, growing increasingly wild-eyed until one day, they weren't there and no one would answer questions about them—but it just made her want to ask him about puberty. You weren't supposed to discuss your Shadow Transit kids with the outside world, so the government gave the parents a forum you had to dial up to using a special modem, where everyone's real names were obscured.

Still, a man called DELTA OCHRE (Michelle's code name was ARROW PUCE, an ugly name she'd requested to change) had posted that once the kids made it through adolescence, they were safe. Well, comparatively safe; fireman or fisherman odds, anyway. The post had been scrubbed within fifteen minutes, and DELTA OCHRE's account purged—but Michelle had wondered if the post had been deleted for being true, or false.

It's not like Efro would tell. The parental gate-escorts were infamously closed-mouthed. Would Lizzie live long enough to get her turn activating the Colander? Or was the Colander what eventually drove them mad?

Efro led her into a titanium bowl of a room, laser-etched with distorted holes that seemed to twist in the corners of her eyes: the Colander. "You know the drill," he said, pricking her finger with a needle and smearing her blood onto an onyx plate screwed into the floor. "I'll chant. When I give the signal, close your eyes and think a human thought."

They wouldn't tell her what a human thought was. *Telling you would defeat the purpose, they'd said. You'll do fine unless you're not human, in which case we strongly suggest you tell us before the gate activates.*

She'd swallowed back fear and imagined the scent of Lizzie's hair, convinced she'd be transported deep undersea... But thoughts of Lizzie were, apparently, enough.

Efro chanted; Michelle clutched the bag of peanut butter sandwiches, crusts cut off, to her chest. Come the signal, Michelle thought of the way Lizzie had always begged for pea-butter sandwiches at dinner. She squeezed her eyes shut, felt squashed like a tube of toothpaste, and when she opened her eyes they stood in the Habitrail—Michelle knew the visitors' section by heart, though she had no clue where it was located. Some of the forum-parents theorized it was on the moon.

But now Michelle looked out of place in a curved children's playroom in her thick woolen coat, while Efro looked positively comfortable in his shorts.

"Sit down," Efro said. "Elizabeth's been waiting all day."

"A good kind of waiting or a bad kind?" Michelle asked, but Efro had already closed the rounded hobbit-hole door behind him.

Michelle squatted onto a bean-bag chair, sliding uncomfortably on the curved floor. The room was packed with toys, as befitted Shadow Transit's spectacular funding. As always, Michelle searched for a hard angle anywhere in the room, but found only oval cubbyholes, rounded crayons, circular television screens; even the PlayStation's case had been customized to a flattened sphere.

Its official name was the Shadow Transit Research Center, but its ovoid, windowless rooms made it look like a high-tech hamster cage.

It was cumbersome, but Michelle understood why the Shadow Transit kids were terrified of right angles. When Lizzie had bled signal into her, Michelle had glimpsed our world from the Dreamer's perspective. She'd realized hard angles were intersections of dimensions, and that there were things curled up in every hard edge like a spider that—if they noticed you, noticing them—could slither out to drag you back through the angles of time itself.

It sounded as crazy as saying two plus two equaled purple. And it *was* crazy—but also true. The rules the Dreamer bled into our universe were dead-real, as arbitrary and unarguable as quantum physics. Trying to pack its concepts into your head meant losing other human touchstones.

Michelle clutched the lunch bag to her chest, eyeing the door warily.

What human thoughts had Lizzie lost?

Michelle wasn't sure how to tell if her daughter was going insane, because kids weren't stable. She remembered how Lizzie would boldly greet her favorite aunt one day and then hide behind Michelle's legs the next. Lizzie slept through the night for years without a nightlight, and then suddenly developed a terror of the dark. That was just how kids were; their personalities fluid, like water, ever-changing.

Lizzie had become more serious and regimented since coming here—but wasn't that what happened when you put a kid in military camp? Lizzie used to love snuggling up with Mommy to watch The Little Mermaid—but now, Lizzie said she didn't like the way movies lied. Was that okay?

They let her visit only once a month. There would be changes even if this was just summer camp. But she couldn't tell what was normal, because none of this was normal...

Michelle winced as the door clacked open. In a way it'd be easier if Lizzie came in as eye-jittery as the older kids, creeping between spaces. But Lizzie was always so happy, so bright, so eager to play...

Oh, Lord, don't let her play.

"*Mommy!*" Lizzie cried happily, her eyes clear and shining, and hurled herself into Michelle's arms so hard they both tumbled off the beanbag. Michelle buried her face in Lizzie's brown hair as Lizzie squeezed her tight.

And for a time, everything was okay.

"You hungry?" Michelle asked, unfolding the crumpled lunch bag. Lizzie still hadn't let go; she made purring noises as she kept her face buried in Mommy's shoulder. "I brought peanut butter sandwiches, just the way you like 'em..."

"Yuck," Lizzie proclaimed, coming up for air long enough to stick her tongue out. "I hate peanut butter."

That was new. Michelle swallowed back an irrational sadness as she refolded the bag and put it aside; one less certainty in coming here, now.

She struggled with what to say next. Conversation was so difficult; therapists monitored their every word to ensure Michelle minimized her contamination. A simple "What'd you learn this week?" could lose you visiting rights for two months.

"So...what *do* you like?"

"*Mommy!*" She squeezed Michelle, adding a little butt-wiggle this time.

"So you just wanna snuggle Mommy? The whole time we're here?"

"Mrf." Lizzie burrowed into Michelle's coat, the same way she'd snuggled beneath the covers on sleepy church mornings. *Maybe she'll just stay this way the whole time*, Michelle thought guiltily. *That'd be nice.*

Except it wouldn't. Lizzie had fallen asleep in her arms during one visit, and Michelle had been a wreck all that month. She'd laid in bed, awake, wondering whether Lizzie's eagerness to drift off in her arms was evidence of a new form of trauma.

"So..." Michelle started, then paused. Lizzie could volunteer information—it was deemed traumatic to make children keep secrets from their parents, even if said secrets might chip away at the parents' sanity—but as the guardian, you could never ever ask questions.

The half-answers, though, were dreadful shadows.

She wished Lizzie still liked movies. Movies were safe talk. They wouldn't let Lizzie watch TV, and the cabinet factory was pretty boring, and what else did you *talk* about with a kid?

There was only playtime.

"...do you want to—to play, sweetie? Maybe some Uno, or dominoes, or, or..."

Michelle forced a grin. Her smile was a stiff mask, but Lizzie beamed back.

"Teacher says get ready for claa*aaa*-aasss!" Lizzie sing-songed.

Michelle did not wince.

Lizzie instructed Michelle to set all the dolls in the room up at little desks, being quite specific about where each doll sat. That was new—the full-room classroom of teddy bears and Weeble-wobbles, not the barking of orders. Lizzie was an obedient child, but in playtime, she became quite bossy.

It's the natural reaction to a strict teaching environment, ENTANGLE INDIGO had posted. *When they get their hands on some power, they want to play with it.*

"They never let us just play," Lizzie beamed, clapping her hands. "Even the videogames are just more tests. *No*, Mommy. No. Giorgio-doll sits by the rail. I *told* you."

Michelle put all the dolls in the right places, noting the space cleared for her at the center. Meanwhile, Lizzie had found a stick of red greasepaint. She drew three wavering lines over her left eye and into her forehead.

"I am Mrs.. SHATTERED TAUPE," Lizzie said, standing straight up. "Yes that is a funny name, but that is the name you will call me. Shattered. Taupe. And if you make fun of my name, you will get the bowl full of stars and you do not want the bowl full of stars... *Do you?*"

She glared at Michelle, the effect accentuated by her greasepaint scars. Michelle shook her head. She couldn't ask what the bowl was.

Lizzie nodded once, in satisfaction. "Now we grade you." She snatched a box of gold sticker-stars and walked around the room, placing the stars on the dolls' foreheads—sometimes just one star, sometimes four or five.

"Are—are those the bowl of stars?" Michelle asked, hoping the therapists would recognize she just going along with Lizzie's playtime. Lizzie whirled on her, mock-angry.

"Words are different *things* over there, Lizzie!" Elizabeth-teacher said. "Their words are us! They can manipulate us through words! We need to speak their language before it makes our whole world sick! This is why all the little boys and girls are dying to learn this language, and this is why you must not speak unless we tell you to! Say the wrong words and you twist yourself into the bowl of stars *forever!*"

The blood drained from Michelle's face. Lizzie's scowl loosened into sadness. "But we love little girls at Shadow Transit, and Elizabeth is new, so Elizabeth just gets a time-out. Is that okay? A time-out?"

Lizzie searched her mother's expression, fretting. Michelle remembered to nod. Lizzie smiled.

"Time-out for little girls," she repeated, and knelt down to sticker a baby doll's head—five stars, ten stars, a sheet full of gold stars until the head was wrapped in a glittering disco ball.

"These," Elizabeth-teacher said, flattening three stars against Michelle's forehead, "Are 'Ceptor-genes. You don't want too many. Three is baby-bear just right."

Lizzie picked up a single Barbie with no stars, tossed her off to one side, face-down.

"That one has no stars," Michelle said. "Is she safe?"

Lizzie gave her a mischievous look. "Noooooooo." She shook her head as she drew the word out like taffy, then tittered. "She's in terrible danger. But she doesn't *know*."

"We must protect her. Right?"

Lizzie nodded absently. "Okay! *Teacher-time!*"

"Is my time-out up?"

"*Stray words kill! Always raise your hand!*" Michelle obediently raised her hand. "Yes, Elizabeth, your time-out is over. And since you are a good girl with only three 'Ceptor-genes, you may try to draw a gliff."

Lizzie climbed on a stool to tug a Dora the Explorer backpack over Michelle's head, then thrust a Magic marker into her hand. "Now you can see Dreamer. Draw."

"Draw what?"

"*Don't look at Dreamer!*" Elizabeth-teacher yelled. "Just listen. But not too much! Just hear whispers, the whispers will make your brain twist a little, then outline the twist. It's like coloring-books in your mind."

Michelle scribbled on the paper, crying. She'd glimpsed the Dreamer just once, when Lizzie had woken shrieking, broadcasting signal and filling Michelle's head full of visions—so full she needed triple-doses of sleeping pills to get through the night—

Because when she slept without the drugs, Michelle remembered a thing the size of a continent with a face like a waterfall of slime, curled up in a space that shouldn't exist under an oceanic shelf, twitching as it slowly wakened—and underneath it churned millions of things, like bubbles in the bottom of a soda glass, each such a violation of three-dimensional space that it made Michelle want to slit her wrists rather than acknowledge them, each ready to rise hungrily when the Dreamer awoke...

The next day, Shadow Transit had arrived unbidden to take Elizabeth. That was their job, they explained. The Dreamer would wake soon, sure as Satan. They needed anyone who could understand its visions, to help fight it. And half-terrified of the Dreamer, half-terrified of Lizzie, Michelle had transferred her custodial rights to Shadow Transit.

Elizabeth-teacher whipped off the backpack. Michelle's purple-crayoned scribble lay lifelessly on the desk. But Lizzie brandished something *she'd* drawn on a sheet of butcher's paper, a twisted star that flickered between states like an optical illusion. The paper crumpled and flexed as the sharp-edged sigil in the center struggled to pull itself free...

"You made something new!" Elizabeth-teacher yelled. "*What does it do?!*"

"I—I don't know..."

"Nobody does!" Lizzie yelled, holding the paper high in exultation, running around the room. "*But it's new! A discovery!*" She grabbed the doll with the gold-starred head, popped the head off at the shoulders with a cry of "BOOM!" and flung it into the corner. She found the dolls with more than four stars, yanked their heads off, flung them all into the corner. Then she got a tablecloth, laid it solemnly over the heads.

"Nobody knows what it means," Elizabeth-teacher said, shoving the squirming insignia into Michelle's face. "Not even the smartest doctors. *Do not turn your head away!* No, you must look at it, and look at it, and look at it until either your dolly-head goes boom or you can tell us how to use it. Otherwise "

She stomped on the face-down Barbie. Pink plastic limbs flew like shrapnel.

Michelle sobbed. Lizzie slashed three lines through the sigil; it stopped twitching. Lizzie crumpled the paper, then crawled into Michelle's lap. "It's okay, Mommy," she pled. "It's just playtime."

Michelle wanted to ask how close this playtime was to reality, but she couldn't. Shadow Transit was watching.

Lizzie's concerned look deepened. "It's just *play*, Mommy," she said, wiping away her mother's tears. "We're learning to speak it. That's how you got here—the gate's made of un-words, my head's made of un-words..."

Michelle scratched at the tears on her cheeks, feeling the throbbing ache of *I'm a terrible mother, I'm a terrible mother.* Comfort shouldn't flow from child to parent. Maybe she could be a good mommy if she could just stay, just follow Elizabeth in class, but even then there was so much at stake...

Lizzie wrapped her arms around Michelle's neck. "No more playtime for Mommy," she whispered—and Michelle sensed a mournful loss in her daughter's voice, the same loss Michelle had felt when she'd realized there would be no more peanut butter sandwiches.

She was unable to cope, so her little girl was growing to fill the void. Maybe that was why all children grew up.

"We can watch a movie," Lizzie suggested.

They put on The Little Mermaid, which had too many tentacles now for Michelle's liking. And during the climactic scene, when Prince Eric drove his ship's prow into Ursula's belly and the music was at its loudest, Lizzie whispered a helpful secret in Mommy's ear.

It was exhausting, trying not to think about what Lizzie had told her, so Michelle stopped for coffee on the way home. The lights at the truck stop seemed too bright, the people moved too fast, but she couldn't bear to be alone.

She looked at the waitresses, and the truckers in the booth texting their loved ones, and the weary mothers towing squalling children through tire-tracked snow. So many people.

They kept a wary distance from Michelle, because Lizzie's gold stars were still on her forehead. She hadn't taken them off. Because she knew.

Michelle kept thinking of what Lizzie had whispered in her ear. Lizzie had sounded cheerful. But Michelle couldn't ask. So as always, she assembled the shadows of Lizzie's playtime into a shape as hard to look at as Lizzie's sigil.

It'll be over by summer, Mommy, Lizzie had whispered. *He wakes in March.*

Lizzie had sounded hopeful, even excited. The sound of a child who'd been told that it would be a thrilling fight they could win. And who knew?

Maybe they could.

But Michelle looked at all the people in the truck stop, their foreheads bare of gold stars, then thought of rising creatures, twisted angles, face-down Barbies snapping.

Baby Rhyme Time: Youngsters Enjoy Initiation at Innsmouth Public Library
By Deborah Walker

Thirty babies and toddlers, ranging from the age of two weeks (well done, Mrs. Beatrice Draggers) to two years, attended the first Baby Rhyme Time at the Innsmouth Public Library this week.

Miss Marberly Phillipson, Head of Juvenile Development Services, said, "I am delighted to see so many little ones here today. One simply cannot introduce a child early enough to the magic of the written word."

The youngsters enjoyed some traditional rhythms and were introduced to a few songs that are unique to our own Innsmouth region.

"It is amazing what children of this age can understand," continued Miss Phillipson. "Some of the youngsters have an almost instinctive grasp of our traditional songs."

The youngsters enjoyed several stories read by Miss Phillipson including *That's Not My Dhole* and the perennial picture-book favourite *The Very, Very, Sleepy Octopus*. As a special treat Miss Phillipson has adapted some of the Innsmouth's most treasured books to suit the tastes of the children.

"We have a wonderful heritage here in Innsmouth," explained Miss Phillipson. "It is our duty to pass it on to the little ones. I have adapted some of our special books to suit a child's understanding. But it is important to retain the integrity of the original. I believe it is a mistake, a serious mistake, to allow the message of our texts to be weakened. Children, especially the children of Innsmouth understand more than many outsiders might imagine. Children love books, and while I'm not advocating we allow youngsters direct access to our esoteric sections, I believe that the messages we instil at an early age will have a lasting effect on our future—on all our futures."

Mrs. Alison Transents, mother of Archibald (age 18 months) couldn't agree more, "When Miss Phillipson brought out her special story book, I had to hold little Archie back. It's as if he recognized some of the characters in the story. He particularly enjoyed the illustrations."

Miss Phillipson is a strong advocate of early learning. "It is my aim to get every child into the public library. I was amazed when I saw some of the children, who could barely speak, grasping the harmonics of some of our more complex chants. With simple repetition and constant reinforcement in the home, there is no doubt that these children will be adept in our traditions by school age."

Perhaps surprising, one of the most popular songs was spoken in a traditional language. Some parents may find some the following extract challenging!

"Ph'nglui mglw'nafh Cthulhu R'lyeh wgah'nagl fhtagn."

Miss Phillipson, who is something of an adept herself in these matters, will be glad to assist parents in mastering the correct pronunciation of this rhyme. Interested readers may like to attend Miss Phillipson's Manuscript Sessions—*An Easy and Fun Introduction to the Ancient*—held on alternate Thursday evenings at the library.

"Of course, parents might prefer my English translation," laughed Miss Phillipson. "It is not a literal translation, but I believe it captures the essence of the original."

Miss Phillipson has kindly allowed us to reproduce her translation for use in the home environment.

> Peek-a-boo, Ancient One
> Great Old One of the sea.
> In R'yleh
> Deep and silent.
> Awaken me. Awaken me. Awaken me.
> Hiding still.
> Peek-a-boo!
> You see me. You see me. You see me.

Mr Barnabas Wright, Director of Innsmouth's Leisure Services, attended the first Baby Rhyme Time. He fully supports the library's initiative, "I believe we are reviving some of Innsmouth's most ancient traditions. These fragments of text have been passed down to us through the ages. It is gratifying to think of countless generations of mothers singing these same words to their children. These chants have a timeless appeal. That is why they have survived—and will always live on."

Mrs. Vernonic Nahastra, mother of Mirabelle (8 months) certainly agrees, "I would never have thought to bring Mirabelle to the library at such an early age. But you should have seen her little face light up when she heard the rhymes. It was almost as if she understood every word. I shall be definitely including Miss Phillipson's chants in our bedtime routine."

"We have some very exceptional history here at Innsmouth," commented Miss Phillipson. "Knowledge can be instilled in even the youngest child. It is my duty and my privilege to pass on our special legacy to these innocents."

And to judge by the cries of delight when Miss Phillipson led the special chanting, I think the youngsters of Innsmouth are very pleased about that!

NYARLATHOTEP'S WAY
By Tom Pinchuk

Sensible folk wouldn't seriously expect the faceless god Nyarlathotep's temple to be tucked away in some neglected corner of the Hollywood Hills. Desperation has an awful way of making some notions sound more believable, though...

A cool wind picked up, whistling through this little canyon just as the sunlight turned a smoggier amber. He hugged his arms tighter and sniffed. Then, he traced a thumb down his nose, across his chin and round his throat—anxiously scrubbing moisture out of all the grayed bristles. As the temperature dropped, it brought on the unpleasantness of hot and cold weather, alike. Moist and chilly, at once.

Serge was homeless. In his internal dialogs, he preferred the term "transient," as it framed his circumstances into some grander historical tradition, but he accepted "homeless" as being straighter to the point. More direct— precisely because it was more dismissive. Few would ever look at him long enough to see past the frayed hoodie, holey sweatpants and chewed-up high-tops. The only possession which might get them to look twice was the scratched-up violin that always stuck out of his backpack. Such second glances never lasted long, but he recognized the attention while it lasted. And since he'd never debase his instrument, and his art, by busking on some corner, these fleeting moments were savored. His audience focusing on what mattered most, if only for a blink.

He slowed, nearing a bend, and checked the torn, yellowed paper sloppily taped to the underside of his sleeve. It was a page he'd ripped out of an almanac in the Long Beach Branch City Library's occult section, however long ago. The relevant text only took up a quarter of one side—a paragraph no thicker than five sentences. And by now, he could recite it with eyes closed. Of course, memorizing sheet music and actually playing a piece are hardly the same thing.   That went for his art, and for everything.

His eyes roamed, searching for the stairway described with such specificity—finding only a couple brown, water-starved shrubs. An anxious reflex made his neck twitch, right around the crook of his jawbone. He was wound so tight, it took only a second of uncertainty to get that acting up. Serge looked at the paper again, but didn't linger on it long enough to honestly check for some detail he may have missed, somehow. He was already stepping up, already pulling a branch aside, already finding what he'd come for in the narrow just ahead...

A flight of cracked, stone steps, leading up to a crooked, stone door frame. Dead weeds poking out of all the jagged fissures like so much unkempt pubic hair. A still, deflating sight that'd inspire neither awe nor dread in any beholder.

Frost breath seethed from Serge's brown teeth as the crook of his jaw pulsed. This stair was in such disrepair as to seem abandoned—*had he found it too late?* The path he'd walked was the steepest tributary of a public hiking trail snaking through the mountain ridge's posh mansions and grandfathered shacks. Its incline was sharp, and far from leisurely, but it was open. It was accessible. Any joggers could climb up, if they felt so determined. And yet...no spray-paint marked the stone. No dried dog shit littered the yellowed grass.

Still, how foolish would he be to think he was one of only a few to come here?

The cloud of shapeless anxiety swirled. What if the secrets promised inside were long gone? What if they'd been claimed already? What if somebody else had learned of the temple long before he had? Or, worse yet, had just stumbled upon it? How old was this almanac he been relying on? Could it be out of date?

Serge squirmed along, despite the doubts, awkwardly angling so his violin's scroll didn't scrap on the rock. He pivoted once he'd passed the shrub, and lost his footing as its branch sprung back in place—"sealing" him into the narrow. As last steps in long journeys went, it was fittingly clumsy, and undignified.

The temple's inside was as disappointing as the exterior. All Serge found was a stained, felt poker table with a service bell lying on it—sideways. It sat between two bar stools with faded, checkered cushions, and underneath a naked tungsten bulb hanging above. The air was stale. Something about that smell, with the rocky floor, made him think of the supply closet by the boiler room he'd worked around when he was a janitor in the 90s. He'd just spent all day—traveling thirty-five miles between Hollywood and Long Beach on a public bus, plodding up this trail for over three hours—to reach a cramped nook just like the one he'd used to sneak smoke breaks into. What farce.

He drew his hood back, and idly twisted a gray ponytail out while he contemplated the table. The contemplation went on several minutes. Then, he started to blush. It was the rush of blood to the cheeks that comes when one slowly recognizes the trappings of a prank around him. This felt like a con. And he, the patsy.

Anger simmered, but was doused quickly when he remembered one particular detail from the almanac. "Nyarlathotep" was only one of this god's many mercurial guises, it said. To worship him, it stressed, was to accept transience as inherent, and fundamental. What was true yesterday might not be so today, but could perhaps be true again tomorrow, and so on, even shifting from moment to moment. Serge had been attracted to this Great Old One, over the others described in the book, precisely because of that turn of phrase. "Transience." How neatly it aligned with the label he preferred.

But he'd yet to make any direct contact since then. His untested philosophical interest would have to turn into active worship, now. Here. Finally. And if it were to do so—if he were to prove his devotion, and earn the boon promised—he should be prepared to tilt his thinking even further. Learn to embrace transience in more aspects than he had already.

The angles of the concept sharpened as his eyes adjusted to the dimness. There, beyond the table...a rag-worn curtain materialized. Seemingly. As if the dust before it had thinned. Serge squinted, making out the expansive, black symbol woven into the surface. A bust dominated by a set of snarling fangs. Eye-less. And crowned with an ancient pharaoh's headdress. That was Nyarlathotep's most infamous face, unmistakably. An awesome and dreadful sight, at last. And just as the book described.

He flinched. Was its appearance delayed by the slow reflex of his dilating pupils? Or was there some theatrical timing at play? The surprise confirmed that he'd found what he'd sought—and asserted that it was more than it seemed. He felt a gaze upon him, now. Not from the face on the curtain. There were no eyes there. No, it was observing him from some vague, surrounding somewhere...and it was watching to see what he'd do next.

If Nyarlathotep took on different guises when he appeared to mortals, should not his temple be just as protean? The realization stiffened the hairs on Serge's neck. Had he stepped into a glamor of the god's conjuring? Would it shift further?

The poker table before him no longer seemed like mere discarded junk. It had been set according to a design. He saw that, now. And he would surely be judged by his reaction to it. Such was Nyarlathotep's way, as the almanac had described. Self-conscious, Serge pinched his nose and messily wiped out the dusty globs of snot that had balled inside it. Then he took the service bell, turned it upright and tapped quickly, for fear he shouldn't hesitate a second longer.

The bell chimed. And the chime echoed. But no answer came.

Anxious he may have done it wrong somehow, Serge tapped again, and again—doing the same as he'd do when the green man at a crosswalk wasn't popping up.

"Yes! I heard you! Shit..."

The voice was irritated. Groggy. And young.

"Have a seat. And...uh..." the voice trailed off. "And sit tight. Yeah. *Be over in a sec.*"

Serge obeyed—on reflex almost—dragging the nearest bar stool over and twisting his backpack off. None of the oddness of that response really registered until after he'd sat down. Be over in a sec. A sec? Who had just spoken to him?

He frowned, but still carried on, setting his pack down gingerly and taking care to part the zippers so no teeth scraped his violin as he slid it out. By the time he'd sat back, with the instrument laid across his lap, any perceived affront had slipped his mind. Instead, he thought of the petition he'd rehearsed, countless times on the way—rolling through it, just one last time. Then, he looked back at the curtain, focusing on the dark god's visage, searching for any rippling in its fabric which might hint at what was happening on the other side.

And he waited.

He didn't have a watch, or a phone, so he couldn't track the time, but the first ten minutes or so were a stretch of coiling anticipation. His hearing heightened, picking up the slightest rustle or groan over there—every little noise, a clue. The mental image he started piecing together dimmed once the smell of smoke crept into the stale air. Serge recognized the flavor of weed.

He tried to figure out what to make of that for the next ten minutes, or so. And even when he realized he hadn't heard anything further in all that time, he still hadn't decided. There was no stirring. No puffing. Nothing. After a while, the stink thinned, and he was back to where he was before he'd touched the bell. He thought to tap again, but then thought against it, for fear of irritating the one he'd come to petition. That circle of second-guessing carried on until there was no denying that the voice who'd answered earlier had either forgotten him, or left.

Enough. He tapped the bell. Its chime echoed. Then, there was a groan beyond the curtain.

"Ah...right."

More rustling. The curtain was pinched from behind its right edge, then yanked back. The cleric stepped out. He grabbed the other bar stool and took a seat before Serge's stare had even finished going cock-eyed.

"What do you want?" he said while raking his eyelids. So rushed and unceremonious was the entrance.

This was not the cleric Serge had a pictured. Not at all. A barefoot teenager with smooth, golden skin, and the most uneven, tousled bedhead. Half of his white hair was flattened to his scalp, while the other half poked straight out. He wore a gray robe, but had pulled the top half back such that it hung off the belt, leaving him topless. Indeed, it seemed more like a blanket he'd hurriedly wrapped himself in after stepping out of bed.

"What do you want...?" he repeated, spinning his fingers around insistently.

Serge stood slowly—balking, but only for a moment. He'd rehearsed this scene so many times before, it didn't take long for the practice to guide him. He bent the knee and breathed deep.

"I...petition Lord Nyarlathotep, seed of Azathoth. He that mankind knows, and fears, as Lrogg, Ahtu and Shugoran also. The Dark One. The

Black Pharaoh. The Crawling Mist and the Floating Horror…"

The "cleric" smirked crookedly. Serge was enunciating this litany with such care, but still managing to roll all the R's with a consistency that betrayed his Baltic accent.

"Howler in the Dark, and Messenger of the Old Ones. To him, I pledge loyal worship, knowing I am unworthy of his attention, recognizing I do not deserve charity, for I am insect crawling beside his boot, and…"

The novelty wore off fast, though. Serge kept going on. Bored already, the cleric puffed a cheek, and clicked his tongue.

"You really did some homework, huh?"

"I… I…" Serge stammered, unprepared for any breaks from script.

"We're good. I got it. So…" The cleric started mouthing slowly. "What… do… you…want?"

"My…my music. I work so many years—whole life. Learn history. Theory. All of it. All genre. All tradition. No one respect art more than me, and yet… and yet…"

"It's a simple question."

Serge gulped dryly. Even if he'd rehearsed, so many times before, it still took a lot to admit this aloud.

"Success elude me. Somehow. I should play concert hall! I deserve! My violin should earn me million dollar…!" He held his instrument up to demonstrate.

"Maybe you just aren't any good?"

"I know. I know…" Serge trailed off, lowering the violin and hanging his head. "I know the way. In head, I see it."

"You see music…?"

"See. Hear. The same. I see music on sheet, but do not hear when hands play. No matter how I practice."

His eyes were slick—blinking tears away for dignity's sake. Not that the boy noticed. Attention drifting, once more, he'd plucked a cigarette from a carton lying beside his chair leg and was feeling his robe up for something.

"I have… how you say? Taste. But not…"

"Talent?"

"Talent, yes. The talent, I deserve. And I…request Lord Nyarlathotep grant to me."

By now, the boy had found a lighter. Somewhere.

"So, what do you want from him? Music lessons…?" he asked, having only half-listened.

"No. I take enough. I give enough. Today, I think it just circumstance of birth."

"...the shit does that mean?"

"That...that I just not born with talent. Even though I deserve. So many people—they have it, somehow. The world give to them? They have success. Get to play music, for money. And they do not even appreciate."

Taking a drag, the cleric leaned back and looked off—puffing out the corner of his mouth for a good, slow moment. Serge leaned forward, waiting for some response, until the boy just snorted.

"What is funny?" Serge asked.

"Why come here for this?" He waved his cigarette back at the curtain. "Why him?"

"I think long time. If this is what world say is 'natural' for me...Nyarlathotep, he is to turn what is natural upside-down, no?"

"Ahhh..."

"I look up his other...how you say? 'Guises?' And I find he make arrangement with others before."

"Right. Sure." The cleric took another drag, but a snicker cut the puff off. He recomposed himself after a couple coughs. "Okay. Okay. Do you... have any friends?"

"Sorry?" Serge asked.

"You know...'friends?' " the boy mimed quotation marks.

"What that have do...?"

"Who are you comparing yourself to?! Like, who're you living with? Damn it..."

"Ah. None at shelter like music. No artists there. No culture. All idiots there."

"Who doesn't deserve this money then?"

"Oh. I do not meet them. I see ads for concerts in paper. Hear them on the talk radio, sometimes. But it has been all life, yes? I take music lessons as boy—watch brats in class go on and success. So many."

Serge bit his lip. Raw, old nerves were being irritated. He faced the boy with renewed conviction.

"Lord Nyarlathotep help me? I pay any price."

"What? All the gum wrappers in your pocket?"

"Excuse...?"

The boy combed his fingers through his hair, twirled a fistful of it, and smiled again.

"Let me talk with him for a sec." He stood and rushed to the curtain, like the notion had suddenly occurred to him. "Don't think we'll even need your soul, or anything."

He came back with a burlap sack he'd fished off the ground back there. Serge raised an eyebrow—it looked like something he'd have carried potatoes with in the old country. The boy was barely choking back another snicker as he pulled it open around his waist.

"We're going to...commune. Yeah. We'll commune, right now. Hang on..."
He dunked his head down...
"Hey! Can you grant a wish tonight?!"
...then popped back out.
"Hm. I think he's sleeping. Give me a sec."
Down again. The cleric yelled into the sack. Then he gasped, and yelled again. Each muffled tone started as a low hum, then grew into a guttural howl—the last one trailing off into warbled gibberish because he was rolling his tongue.

As these obnoxious sounds echoed in this close space, Serge thought first of the last time he'd gotten to gargle mouthwash. However long ago that was. As they carried on, another memory surfaced. An earlier one—the opera singers back at the old conservatory. And the vocal exercises he'd hear them run through in the studio down the hall. Both thoughts made his cheeks redden.

He smelled a prank's stink again—but another glance at the aspect on the tarp quelled his umbrage. Transience. Mustn't forget it. For clearly this was another test, and if he lacked the patience for it, how suited would he be for an audience with Nyarlathotep?

The boy reemerged finally, licking his lips after all the shouting. Having his head down there had tousled his hair another way, too.

"He's up, now. And kinda crabby. But...uh...let me see."
He ducked in, but then turned back just as fast. "Wait... what'd you call him before? The Crawling Fog?"
"Ah...ah..." Serge stuttered, unready for this to become a dialog again. "Mist. The Crawling Mist. Do you not know this...?"
"Right. Nice."
The boy smirked before disappearing again. Serge tried not to notice, but couldn't pretend he hadn't.
"Oh, Crawling Mist! So...this old, Russian dude wants to play the violin better. I think...? Can you, like, make him good at it?"

The bag bobbed, like he was nodding at some silent answer. When he turned to Serge this time, he didn't bother taking his face out. "He's thinking about it. Don't worry."

Then he nodded some more. "Uh-huh. Uh-huh. Uh-huh..."

"Should I...?" Serge started.

The cleric hissed at him sharply. "Hey—shut up."

He twitched, reacting to something he heard. Serge leaned in and turned his ear, trying to catch any snippet from the other half of this "conversation." Might the dark god actually be speaking from another realm?

"Look, this guy—he came all the way out from Long Beach," the boy said. "Yeah, Long Beach! I know. I thought it was hilarious, too. But, listen... he knows a shitload of stuff about you. Like, everything. Ha ha. Aren't you impressed?"

Being represented like this was wholly unbearable. Serge knew he shouldn't interrupt—understood why he shouldn't—but still could not help himself. The crook of his jaw pulsed, like a gag reflex was coming on. He stepped up, and raised the violin with bow drawn, offering it as if Nyarlathotep might actually hear.

"I play for him? Perhaps?"

"Didn't you say you sucked?"

"No..."

"Why would he want to hear crappy playing?"

Serge's nostrils flared. "My music is not crappy."

"Wasn't that the whole reason you came? What're you making me ask him for then?"

"Success! I want success! I say this already! Success! Please!"

Now, it was Serge's shrieks that were echoing. His composure, and his patience for this little shit, crumbled by now. Trembling, he bit his lip. And when the cleric said nothing in return, he added, "What must I do, ah? I tear heart out of chest and give to him. Tell me!"

"Did you get all that?" the boy spoke into the bag. "Dude wants this, real bad..."

One more pause. A few more nods. "Uh-huh. Uh-huh. Gotcha."

Then the cleric pulled the bag off, at last.

"Okay, the big guy needs a couple things. And lucky you—the sacrifice isn't too bad."

"Sacrifice...?" Serge gulped hard.

"Yep!" The boy clapped his hands, and rubbed them together eagerly.

It took just a few, fumbling paces for him to understand what an absence of footwear truly meant out here. The harmless pebbles that stuck to his soles quickly stung when pressed against cold dirt. He tried to adjust his gait, so at least the arches weren't touching ground, but the shuffling only made him step on this one little rock at an even more awkward angle. And there had to be dozens more—just as little, and hard, and sharp—lying all throughout the narrow. They would have been tough to spot even if he wasn't walking in darkness.

Serge winced, opting to just hold still, and not step further until his eyes had readjusted.

He pulled out the quarter he'd been given, and turned it around in his palm. Its dull copper edge glinted more brightly when the moon struck it at different angles. And in each flash, he looked for significance. When he was walking barefoot down those stone steps, just now, he'd rubbed the bulge this quarter made in his pocket for the same reason—feeling for something, anything, which might differentiate it from some regular coin.

The absurdity of that became clearer at about the same rate his eyes were adjusting. What had just happened inside—how his audience with the cleric had concluded—all of it was rolled through his head like the details of a dream. Not that he was forgetting portions, or was even fuzzy about them. Rather, he was having trouble understanding why those developments had seemed at all sensible to him then. They did not connect in any rational way, now.

"There we go," the cleric said, flapping his outstretched palms as Serge handed his chewed-up high-tops over. "Oop. Socks, too."

Serge groaned slightly. He might've been able to remove his shoes while standing, but he had to get down on his ass to slide the socks off. And when he sat, his backpack—and the violin inside it—dropped on the ground harder than he would've liked.

He was also ashamed to unclothe his gnarled feet and blackened toenails, but it wasn't like anybody saw. Preoccupied again, the cleric was pinching the shoes' collars together between his thumb and index finger, freeing a hand so he could fish into his robe again.

"Got it. Now...here." He pulled a quarter out of the same spot where he'd found the lighter earlier. Flipped it. Palmed it. Then held it out just as the transient finished removing his socks.

"When you get home, or wherever, buy something for your viola with this," the boy said.

"Violin, you mean?"

"Huh?"

Serge examined the coin. "What...can quarter buy?" He asked slowly, careful not to offend.

"Well, it doesn't have to cost twenty-five cents exactly. It can be, uh, six bucks. Three-fifty. Doesn't matter, 'kay? Just, whatever it is, you've got to pay in cash, and this has to be part of what you pay. Got it?"

Serge squinted cautiously. "I...think so? But, why?"

"Whatever you buy is gonna make you the, uh...success you're asking for. In two months. Yeah. You'll be on the radio. That's what the big guy's offering."

The squint turned moony-eyed. Even at the merest suggestion.

"But... what of sacrifice?" Serge asked.

The cleric held the shoes up and jingled them around. "Told you. Got it."

Serge touched his hand to his lip, almost kissing the quarter because it was pinched between his fingers. For the first time in so long, he laughed. Joyously.

"Thank you. Thank you..."

By now, the boy had lit another cigarette up. "Hey...you earned it." He smirked, and puffed.

When his frost breath started twinkling in the moonlight, Serge finally turned back to the staircase.

It had vanished. No shadows hid it—he could see everything in the narrow, now. It was just simply gone. No theatrics as it vanished. No clap of thunder. No whooshing wind. It was simply there one moment, and not there the next. Like an eyelash, blinked away.

He checked the underside of his sleeve. The yellowed paper was still there, but it offered no further insight.

Back there, somewhere. Nyarlathotep had torn his ratty tarp down, and was now sprawled out across it. He sat up long enough to tie the high-tops' laces tighter, then lay back and wiggled his toes around, giggling at the scratchy sensation of smooth, golden skin against mildewed fabric. He hadn't bothered putting the socks on, though. Maybe later. He was pleased enough with himself at the moment.

The boy grabbed a clump of white hair with his right hand, then idly slid his left down until it found his crotch—just busying his hands as he mused on all this.

Taking that wretch's soul would have just been too easy. He offered it freely, without even stopping to consider its actual value. And the boy could have simply taken it, as he had with so many other mortals before. The getting was routine, though, and such possessions no longer amused him. Their taste was trite. For he'd plumbed the pleasures of flesh so thoroughly, he'd come to prefer what men called "fetish" when assuming mortal guise.

Simple gratification no longer compared to gratification that asserted an abstract. As such, the business with the transient was all the sweeter for how inconsequential it'd been rendered by the end. With minimal effort, he'd brought that man to such a point of desperation as to seriously, and sincerely, seek a lifetime's desire behind some bushes on a hiking trail. There'd be cruel irony in that wish being granted at an awful price, certainly. But that trick was played—ho-hum beside the more awkward irony of a wish being dangled close, and then just casually shrugged away. This could have been the most important night in Serge's life. Now, it was just a question mark, and would always remain so.

The transient would take that coin and use it to buy varnish, or something; fully aware of how silly the superstition was, even as he still went through with it. Sooner or later, he'd get past the debasement of his art and busk on some corner—on Hollywood and Highland perhaps—telling himself he could win tourists' attention away from the actors dressed as Chaplin and Marilyn. He'd mistake coincidences surrounding his playing as signs of improvement. And for a while, he'd believe things might actually be on the upswing. Then, two months would pass without incident, and it'd be undeniable that nothing was actually changing. The crowds would ignore him again, and he'd be back at the shelter, playing in public no longer.

The cruelty wouldn't show in some sudden bout of hysteria. No, it'd lie in quiet desperation, drawn out tepidly over the days, weeks, months and years that'd follow. Ever after, Serge would think of this meeting and wonder if he'd done something wrong—failed a test of "transience" – or if he'd actually been part of some smartass' practical joke. Or if it'd been both. Or neither. No answers were ever coming...

For such was Nyarlathotep's way.

STRIDENT CALLER
By Laird Barron

Languid days of fucking for rent didn't faze rambling man Craven. One summer, he witnessed a woman and a horse die on tidal flats in Alaska. A blonde woman and a sorrel horse doing that romantic canter near the surf as seen on the cover of many a bodice-ripper. Mud caught them fast. They'd screamed as the sea rolled in. Nobody could do a damned thing. Later in his youth he'd blown a state trooper to avoid a possession rap. After a few homeless months in winter, he'd gratefully eaten a roadkill coyote that a big Aleut chopped in half with an ax. He'd done worse.

Now, a hell of a long way from the Last Frontier, his dark curls specked gray, and granite abs gone a tad soft, he'd done it *all*. Unlike many of his friends and fellow travelers, he hadn't gotten hooked on liquor or addicted to dope or caught an embarrassing, career-ending disease. Jack of a dozen trades and possessed of not half-bad looks, his mutably convivial personality proved sufficient to succeed at the job of survival. His sole motivation at this stage of the game? Three square meals a day, a roof overhead, and minor pleasures where he found them.

Craven discovered the secret to longevity. He tended to roll with life's punches, such as his mistress Deborah's unpredictable moods and strange demands. *People like you disappear every day, Princess,* she'd murmured when they first met after a literary reading at the Kremlin Lounge in New York City. Craven might've been a rootless drifter, yet he'd read his share by campfire light and the electric shine of dirty bulbs in flophouses from Seattle to Poughkeepsie. He knew his way around the Beats and better still the women who frequented the cafes and bars made famous by reprobate poets and other lettered scoundrels.

They'd slipped upstairs to the jazz club and got loaded. Deborah licked his earlobe while they shared a dance. *Pretty lost boys disappear and nobody cares. Better come home with me to be on the safe side.* He'd accepted both the widow's pet name and her offer of protection. Like a grateful dog, he made peace with the monthly dinner parties that saw him banished to his chamber at the end of the hall where he flopped on a poster bed and listened to muffled conversation and raucous laughter until dawn. No problem. Eccentric socialites weren't his crowd. He didn't dig séances or any of that weird shit either. The routine had begun to chafe mainly because it defied his nature to put down roots. Eight months so far. How much longer could he play Midnight Cowboy?

A familiar wanderlust whispered his name. Craven fantasized about the open road as he rinsed away Deborah's cloying musk. The water hit in cold pellets. No electricity since the storm first broadsided that morning. He dried himself with a fluffy towel on the landing before the half stained glass window. Late, late sun emerged in a brief glory of lambent redness. The squall had ended. Another approaching storm mantled the Catskills in the west; a front the color and texture of smoke from a great fire. Pieces of the neighbor's sycamore were scattered in the yard. A branch speared the camper shell on Craven's '83 Datsun. The marble fountain frothed—twin columns of nymphs supported a basin carved into the improbable likeness of a bloodthirsty ape. Twigs bobbed like skeletal fingers clawing from the turgid depths.

The driveway went for fifty yards through sycamore and pine. The dairy farmer across the rural blacktop road had wisely called in his cows. Odors of tramped soil and cowshit persisted in the empty pasture, green and powerful after the downpour. A tiny mother-in-law cottage nestled on the far edge of the property—this was the abode of groundskeeper Andy. Gardener, handyman, and sentry, Andy was a late-career Boris Karloff-looking sonofabitch who stalked the grounds while wearing the scowl of an ax-murderer on vacation. Craven hadn't exchanged two words with him. Gardener Andy kept a low profile, appearing and disappearing in a swirl of dead leaves.

"Dude, you are morbid as hell today." Craven spoke to hear his own voice echo in the foyer. Were he to leap into the Datsun and drive, the bright lights of Kingston awaited him twenty minutes east. He wouldn't leave quite yet. First, because he enjoyed the kinky pleasure of balling Deborah, and second, there wasn't enough gas in the truck to reach town.

Artemis crouched at the end of the hall by the bedroom door. Craven rescued the brindle pit bull during his hippie-at-large days in the Pacific Northwest. Time and cynicism had rendered the wriggling puppy an inscrutable grand dame. Sunlight came through a rain-dappled pane and fitted a glowing band across her eyes. The rest of her bulk sank into shadow. Eyes without a face, man. Something Saul Bass would film, or a still from a Fulci giallo flick.

Craven went into the amphitheater-style living room where Deborah napped on the couch with a travel magazine spread open on her breasts. Her belly and thighs were caressed by the wavering lines of a prism as it revolved in the skylight from a string. Seventy-fifth birthday coming next month, she possessed the florid sumptuousness of an aging yet ageless Italian scream queen.

"Vic, Vic," Deborah said, stroking herself. She talked in her sleep. Crazy shit, too. Claimed to not remember her dreams. Probably a lie. She was cagey like that. Free with her body, yet coolly impersonal. "Don't bother. Don't. Come here, baby. Don't open the hatch. It's too late. Oh, well."

He touched her foot. Canary yellow toenails, canary yellow fingernails. Bobbed gray hair, a trimmed bush with a brunette dye-job. Heavy on the eye shadow and mascara. Violent violet lipstick. Her habit was to remain stock still for a few seconds upon waking in order to gain her bearings. He knew she'd revived because he could see her eyelids flutter behind the smoky lenses.

"Jesse. Where am I?" She had a hell of a voice, its richness cultivated by dint of studio lessons and a few thousand "little-pick-me-up" snorts of coke from her snuff box.

"Home," he said. "Snug as a bug in a rug."

Deborah propped herself against a cushion. Her gaze shifted to his legs and tracked upward. "Put some clothes on. No son of mine walks around in the altogether." Usually it took a few seconds for her to recall her son was a rock journalist named Erik who lived in Chicago. She never registered embarrassment at her lapses. At least she hadn't yelled Erik while they were getting it on.

He grasped his cock and gave it a twirl. "Perhaps it has eluded your notice that you too are decadently naked."

"No power?" she said.

He shrugged. "Life in the country."

"Be dark soon."

"Hint taken." He slipped into a silk robe that had belonged to Deborah's husband. Crimson with a cowl bunched around the shoulders and embroidered by gold stars. Craven strolled around the house and lighted candles and oil lamps and wall lamps in cloudy antique glass bowls. There were a lot of lamps and bowls. Deborah suffered from mild nyctophobia. This marked the third major power outage since Craven moved in, thus he knew the routine.

Artemis stoically shadowed him. He paused to let her do her business in the backyard, then resumed his circuit, eager to complete the task before sundown. While night and darkness held no special dread for him, neither did he relish the idea of traipsing the house during a blackout. The place was creepy enough during broad daylight.

The pad almost qualified as a mansion, a Hammer Film hybrid of American Gothic and Mission Revival that rich kooks once built atop cliffs with primo views of the ocean. Three stories with a maze of narrow passages and thick carpet and a plethora of mismatched rooms. The décor skewed toward the macabre. Rooms were straight out of salacious occult flicks of the North American hippie era—garish yellow curtains, fisheye mirrors, heavy wooden furniture, liquor cabinets, lava lamps, gargoyle light fixtures, and oval doorways hidden behind psychedelic velvet hangings. The perfect place to host a dinner party and then watch the guests vanish one by one.

Dearly departed husband Victor earned his bones as an entertainment lawyer before he and Deborah retired to the mid-Hudson Valley. A connoisseur of Roman/Greco and Medieval European art, he'd possessed the means to acquire plenty of it. His library shelves creaked with leather-bound tomes of esoteric lore. In the den, an oil painting of seven hooded magician apprentices supplicating Satan hung above an abandoned mahogany rolltop desk. Someone had carved a Latin phrase into the hutch.

Craven didn't read Latin. Victor had mastered it, Craven knew because he'd spent a long evening on the internet, panning for gold. Victor passed away at home seven years ago. Obituaries always say "passed away" if the details are prurient or scandalous. A brief mention in *Variety* also played the death coyly. Craven figured it *had* to be an OD or suicide.

Framed photographs of young, lush Deborah in the buff were salted here and there throughout the house. A smaller photo was tucked into an alcove—Deborah, perhaps thirty-five, in a string bikini on the deck of a boat. White ruins dotted a distant, hazy shoreline. Victor clutched her waist. He wore a Hawaiian flower print shirt and grimaced at the camera, tongue protruding; a comedian strangling on an invisible noose. Someone knelt on Deborah's other side. A man with large hands (his head was cut off by the frame) and wide shoulders under a linen tunic. The man pinned the shiny corpse of a squid to the deck with a spear from a spear gun. The squid's tentacle lifted slightly, forty years frozen in mid-convulsion.

Craven once jokingly asked her if Victor practiced black magic. She took it seriously, or pretended to. *He tried. He committed fully. We had a third child, you know. Victor was a disappointment to our father.* Whatever she meant by that—Deborah had a mind full of cats. Her games and her delusions were often inseparable.

Dusk claimed the land as Craven finished. The wind picked up and a hard rain started in. Thunder boomed, closer and closer. Artemis slunk away to hide under the bed. The dog feared few things except storms. She developed that dread back when Craven hiked the Olympics during late summer and high winds lashed the trees. Man and dog cowered inside a flimsy tent. Men rationalize forces beyond their control. Dogs do not.

Craven experienced a pang of nostalgia as he fetched a camp stove from the garage. He boiled tea for Deborah and they sat at the island in the kitchen. A large black skull candle flickered between them. Tall shadows climbed the walls.

She poured cream from the mouth of a pewter faun. "I dreamed I went to a café in a small town. A girl in an apron came around and poured complimentary tea for the morning customers. Everybody drank tea and either died or fell into a coma. I did not drink the tea. On the next table lay an old book with gilt lettering. Part of the title read—*Conversing with a Barbed Tongue*. Someone behind me said, *Yes, that one. Pick it up*. The horrible whisper frightened me. I leaned over and picked up the book. It smelled like a piece of soft wood that had lain in the muck of a swamp. The pages were gummy with mold. My hand went numb. I woke to you standing there like a slowly spreading Adonis." She waited for him to respond. Finally, she said. "What would you say it means?"

"Dreams never mean jack shit." He gulped hot tea. She had revealed a dream, which represented a first in their relationship. He should feel some sense of closeness, of bonding. He felt uneasy instead. A taboo had been broken, a line crossed.

Lightning hissed near the yard and its blue stroke cast Deborah's face into a death mask. He jumped. She smiled patronizingly. "Conversing with a Barbed Tongue. That's suggestive, don't you think? Like a rare tract an exorcist would stash in his files with a bottle of good wine for a paperweight. Or a tract the Witchfinder General keeps in his traveling satchel of horrors."

"It also sounds like a chapter some fallen angel would dictate to some Franciscan monk," he said, smiling to let her in on the joke. "The Apostles got theirs. I'm sure a demon would jump at the chance to say its piece for the record."

"The weather channel forecasted this storm on Tuesday." She apparently disliked it when he spoke more than one sentence at a go.

"I suppose that means your dinner party is canceled." He tried not to sound smug.

"Yes and no. There might be a gathering." She took his hand and kissed his fingers. Her eyes gleamed with tears, although her unkind smile remained. "I hope not. But if they decide to visit, I am sorry."

"Hey, your place, your rules. Kind of weird to come over in this weather, though." He laughed and squeezed her hand in a gesture of cheap graciousness.

She pulled away and stared into the skull flame. "I minored in music."

"Oh? Makes sense. Useful skill for an actress." Craven lifted the cup to his lips. Empty.

"Aspiring actress then. I dabbled in so many things during college. The world didn't truly open for me until I met Victor." Deborah reached into a drawer and brought forth a flute and delicately held it to the light. The instrument glinted, dull, loveless, and the color of dried blood. "This is ."

"Your flute has a name. I knew a coal miner who played a harmonica. Every single night after supper. He didn't name it or anything."

"His wasn't an object of power."

"No. It was a plain old cheap harmonica."

"Objects of power are always named. is a recorder, not a flute. My family has passed her down through generations. Hollowed from a child's radius in the days of antiquity, she belongs to a set of nine. A recorder, lyre, didgeridoo, hichiriki, drum, whistle, sitar, violin, and a horn." Deborah went to the center of the kitchen. She breathed notes through the recorder. Her black silk robe clung to her breasts and hips as she swayed to a harsh, discordant melody. Thunder served as her metronome. Her playing was terrible and compelling.

Craven's stomach felt odd. "Uh, wow. Does your family own the other instruments?"

She stopped playing, although she didn't lower the recorder. "That would be utterly mad. Nobody owns such instruments. We are stewards."

"Sorry. I didn't realize."

"I am not terribly accomplished. Victor trained as a pianist in childhood. Law school stripped that joy from him. He became cruel after our honeymoon. He showed me the world, for a price. I was his slave. Our son too, until he fled home and lived with my sister in Alaska. To think a cold, hostile land would prove more nurturing than his own home." She rotated, bent at the waist and shook her buttocks with the aplomb of a burlesque dancer. The recorder notes climbed a notch.

"A slave?"

Three long notes that bled dry. She looked over her shoulder at him. "You think I'm melodramatic."

"Deb, your ass is dramatic. That's all I know."

"Men enslave women in a thousand small ways. Victor's possession of me was simply more overt. Early on I defied him. I only complied half the time. He decided fifty percent wasn't adequate."

Down the hall and slightly muffled, Artemis howled. She snarled and then fell silent. Craven didn't enjoy the shrill fluting either. Or the rolling thunder. The cacophony set his teeth on edge.

Deborah ceased playing mid-note. "Not all music soothes the savage breast." She straightened and remained motionless for several seconds. "The great dark is gathering around us.   is like a needle that pierces the black membrane and sucks ichor of the devil gods. It will begin in a moment."

The flame of the skull candle bent to the left and licked the wax rim.

"Deborah!" Someone shouted from downstairs. Deep and authoritative and angry. "Bring him to me!"

"Who's that?" Craven stage-whispered. He'd almost fallen off his stool.

She finally turned around and sighed theatrically. "Take a guess."

"I don't have a clue. Although, I am sure I just pissed your old man's favorite robe."

"You sorry sonofabitch!" a different angry voice cried from the same direction as the previous.

Craven pinpointed the roaring to the billiards room. He'd locked the exterior doors and seen no one during his sweep of the premises. An intruder could've hidden in a closet or under a table. Unpleasant explanation. Although, every explanation was unpleasant.

The stranger said, "Deborah! Deborah! Deborah! Deborah! Deborah! If

I have to come get him…"

"You'd better go," she said. Her tone was mild. "He'll come up here. He'll come, and then…"

Craven snatched the biggest butcher knife from the block. "The fuck I will. Is this a joke? Where's your cell? Get Five-Oh on the horn." He whistled for Artemis. Normally a dependable watch dog, the sound of a stranger's voice should have brought her running.

"Jesse, calm yourself." Deborah smiled. Unctuous and facile. Flies and honey and so forth.

"The fuck I will. Artemis!"

"Jesse—"

"The phone. Give me the goddamned phone." He realized he'd pointed the knife at her and tried to rein himself in. "The phone, Deb." He followed her chin gesture and took the pearl-case cell from where it lay upon a knick-knack shelf. He hit 911 and as the circuits did their thing, he watched the stairs that spiraled downward into gloom.

The angry voice boomed through the speaker, "YOU SMARMY BASTARD! NOW YOU'VE DONE IT! PUT DEBORAH ON!"

Mushrooms, peyote, acid, nitrous, glue, melted Styrofoam…at one time or another Craven tripped balls on pretty much every substance that could take a man for a ride. Looking into Deborah's luminous gaze, a madman on the cell in his left hand, cleaver clutched in his right while thunder crashed and lightning blazed, he entertained the notion she'd slipped something into his tea, because the moment stretched and his emotions felt too unstable. "Deb, are you screwing with my mind? Why?"

She played a treble note. Yellow eyes flickered in the shadows. Artemis padded into the kitchen and sat next to Deborah, head pressed against the woman's leg. They stared at Craven. He stepped forward, not entirely clear in his head what he meant to do, and the dog bared her fangs. Artemis didn't growl and that was far worse.

"Shit." He remembered nursing her with an eyedropper and how she'd looked at him as if he were everything in the universe. The sting of tears surprised him almost as much as Artemis offering to take his hand off at the wrist. He backed to the top of the stairs and listened. Ceiling timbers creaked and wind chimes sang. "Whoever's down there, better run. I'm gonna put the hurt on you, pal." He sounded convincingly rough and ready—the command voice he'd learned from listening to cops. He'd summoned this voice in the past when confronted by fellow vagrants vying for a patch of ground, or intimidating teenagers who thought a seedy dude hitching along the highway would make excellent sport.

He went to his room and dressed with the haphazard efficacy of a man in a hurry to escape before an angry cuckolded husband arrived on the scene. Pants and shoes make a world of difference when it comes to prowling through a dark house. No use wasting precious mental energy in a vain attempt to sort the situation beyond his grasp of the apparent facts—Deborah was a kook (old news) and she'd put one of her whack-job socialite buddies (or her weird gardener) up to shenanigans. He didn't give a flying fuck at a rolling doughnut as to who, what, or why. The cleaver went tucked into his belt and he selected a nine iron from Victor's golf bag in the closet. It swished reassuringly as he executed a few practice swipes in the air.

A flash of orange light caught his attention. He peered outside. Fire engulfed the Datsun. Andy stood nearby, naked but for Wellingtons, and inked with kraken tentacles. The gardener smoked a cigarette, his head tilted to regard Craven's window. The sycamores and the grass of the lawn reflected the blaze. Hooded figures lurked amid the undergrowth, obscured by darkness and whipping smoke.

Deborah's recorder bleated from the kitchen. Its melody rapidly descended through a complex sequence of stops and blats, then ceased. The storm died at that moment as well, and the house fell silent. Craven hustled back, yet she and Artemis were already gone. Two choices presented themselves to his tunnel vision—bolt through the front door and make a break for the road, or venture into the basement and attempt to collect his turncoat dog as that's where the crazy widow must have taken her. Probably only had a few seconds to decide before the cultists, or whomever skulked in the woods, busted through the door to drag him away for ritual sacrifice or gods knew what.

Really, no decision at all. He followed pale, shifty lamplight down into a passage. He glanced into a succession of rooms—billiards, guestrooms, bath, storage--each empty. At the end of the hall double doors painted white and black let into a home theater. The doors parted. Reddish light dripped.

Deborah knelt at the threshold. Her hair lifted, as if pulled by a strong wind. "You wouldn't come. You wouldn't submit. The membrane is tender, but resilient. It always seals. He takes blood with him. Always blood."

Past her, within the room itself, a disk of watery red light shimmered on its edge like a freestanding mirror. An entire vista of hellish landscape suggested itself—a lunar maw and jagged, mountainous fangs; a sea of crimson, rolling vertically. A man's silhouette receded toward the heart of the disk, slightly hunched and dragging an inert object. The front door crashed in above. Deborah covered her eyes and bowed her head. Craven simply reacted. He ducked into the spare bedroom, wriggled through the window, and ran until he reached the highway. A guy in a BMW eventually gave him a lift to Kingston.

The police took his report with straight faces. Two cops visited Deborah. A young cop and a much older cop. All the old cop said upon their return was that she'd decided not to press charges. Craven was not welcome at the house and his meager belongings were in a box in the trunk of the patrol car. The young cop handed over the box with a bland expression of professional disdain.

The box contained spare pants and shirts, socks, and Artemis's vaccination tags. Craven had no idea what to do next. The old cop told him there was nothing to do except get gone while the getting was good. He did.

A couple of years later, Craven hopped a train chugging through California. He shared a cold boxcar with a hobo who did a tour in the Persian Gulf. The men drank a bottle of Knob Creek and talked about their lives as the engine traveled through haunted industrial star fields.

He told the hobo about the time he'd escaped a bunch of Satanists. After a long silence, the hobo asked him, *why are you crying, man?* and he rolled over and dreamed of being hunted through the primeval forests of the Olympic Peninsula, Artemis a fleeting shadow—sometimes ahead, sometimes behind, always near.

Craven lurched to his feet. Still drunk and half in the dream, he went to the gate and screamed her name, "Artemis! Here, girl!" He clutched the gate and leaned precariously into the wind. The train rushed onward and carried him farther and farther away.

Dawn splintered far off at the rim of galactic nothingness. He left the train and ambled to a park near a withered forest. The dead forest decayed beside a river that had slowed and stopped. He slept with his face pressed against a picnic table. The rough wood smelled of acid rain and whiskey and his own bile. The edge of the sun broke through the crust and burned white as the eye of an acetylene flame. He raised his head and watched a mutt wandering listlessly among busted glass and scraps of paper. Pigeons scattered from its ragged path. Craven whistled. The black dog swung around unsteadily. Collarless and skinny as a stick. Its matted sides heaved. One eye drooped shut. Dry foam caked its muzzle.

Craven had a hank of beef jerky in his pocket. He shook the jerky and whistled again. His lips were cracked and it sounded feeble. The dog limped toward him, whining deep in its chest and panting. He dropped the jerky. He held his hand the way a man does over the heat of barrel fire, shifting it this way and that. The dog whined again, yawned frightfully, and bit him with seeming diffidence. One chomp of green fangs, sunk in good and deep. The dog thrashed as instinct commanded, and finally released. It wheeled stiffly, like an automaton, and moved away and eventually disappeared into some underbrush.

Dark blood oozed and filled the punctures in Craven's hand. Blood dribbled down the back of his arm; its tributaries dripped onto the table and spread. He wrapped his hand in a bandanna. The bandanna had been with him for a while, but he couldn't recall where he'd picked it up. Wearied beyond repair, he rested his forehead against the wood. The sun kept coming, kept drilling through the icy shell of night and burned the top of his skull like it might actually thaw him out.

Nobody ever came to the abandoned park except for hobos, scavengers, and birds. In a while, sparrows began to flit down from the dry branches and peck around the bench and atop the table. Much later, a bird alighted upon Craven's shoulder. It plucked at his hair. He let it.

LUCKY CHUCK TAKES THE SUNSHINE EXPRESS
By John Palisano

It started like so many of these things start: with a girl and a promise. Sunny was very persuasive, and extremely attractive. She was one of those girls that was a modern hippy, so I didn't think should be hung up about hooking up with a slightly older guy. Hell, I could dream, couldn't I? Like the old cliché goes: life's short. Carpe Diem. All that self-help pseudo spiritual mumbo jumbo. Don't judge me.

Sunny invited me to go on an all-expense paid trip to Las Vegas. How could I resist? At 52 years old, I thought I might feel strange hanging out with a bunch of people in their 20s, but I got over myself. Heck: the worst thing that could happen is my spending a lot of time by myself while everyone else clumped together. So what? I needed to get out of San Diego for a little while. Wake up again. I wasn't born to sell overpriced solar panels. That was for other people...people who'd given up and couldn't do any better. I was just there temporarily. Going on four years temporarily.

That's the same pitch I gave Sunny when she parked her sundress and Birkenstock-wearing butt on the bench next to me. "You look sad," she said.

"You'd be sad, too, if all you had to eat was a peanut butter and jelly."

She sang, "It's peanut butter jelly time" and I thought I might strangle her right there in front of anyone who could see, no matter how cute she was. I was sure the judge would give me a pass.

"Seriously," she said. "There's something about you missing. I can tell. That's why I wanted to come say hi. There's something you could use."

Here it comes, I thought. *The fucking hard sell.*

"I hang with a group of people called the Travelers. We go places on spiritual retreats."

"Damn it," I said. "I knew there had to be a reason you came and sat next to an old man like me."

"You don't look old. What? Are you thirty or something?"

"Cute. But I'm not swinging, no matter how cute you are. Don't have the coin to get involved in any of that."

"You don't have to pay for anything. It's taken care of. We just like to spread the love."

"You're the bait and then the boyfriend knocks me out, I'm not stupid."

She laughed. "I don't have a boyfriend. I'm a free spirit." She handed me a circular business card. A really pro looking job with a fancy sun design. The flames looked kind of like orange octopus arms, all squiggly, with dots that could've been seen as suckers.

The Travelers

Ride the Sunshine Express to Bliss

The Cool You Spa and Resort

There was a website at the bottom.

"Look it up. No strings attached. We take people on spiritual journeys so they can find themselves. That's all. Our way of giving back. Kind of like tithing. Check around. It's no joke. My email is on there. Let me know. We're leaving Friday for Vegas. We stop in the Mojave on the way in. Do our thing. Then it's Saturday and Sunday to ourselves. You should come."

"I'll get back to you," I said. "You bet."

I felt like a desperate, lustful, chauvinistic jerk checking out her knock-out figure as she walked away. I felt even worse that night when I went online and searched the blue sites until I found a girl that kind of looked like her, and then fantasized the guy in the clip could've been me. Then I looked up their site. Looked legit. I went to Yelp. Lots of great reviews. Probably plants. No complaints on the Better Business site. A straight Google search didn't bring up anything of concern. They seemed like just what Sunny had pitched. I emailed her:

> Hey, Sunshine. Nice meeting you. Checked everything out. I'm in. If I get to sit next to you.
> Love, Chuck

I added a dumb little smiley face. What did I have to lose? Nothing. Flirting on the net was easy. Who cares? Who could blame me for having a little goof?

She wrote back within the hour.

> *Yay, sweetie! You're so funny! We can sit together. I can introduce you to everyone. So happy we met!*

She copied the details of the where, when, and how underneath. Friday morning I found myself standing on the curb at Downtown Station waiting for a bus to pull up. A guy in a dark blue jumpsuit asked if I was going to Denver. "Not until tomorrow," I said. He shut up after that, which was perfect. He took his Coffee Bean sippy cup, and his slurping lips, down the sidewalk away from me. I overheard him asking other people about Denver.

To my right a group of skinny kids unloaded out from a skinnier car. Two of the guys sported spotty auburn beards with beads worked in randomly. Had to be Sunny's friends. I sized my competition up. Damn it. I looked more Jimmy Hoffa than Jimi Hendrix, though it was through no fault of my own. I'd been selected by Age to be the example for twenty something's of where hard living might lead you.

As soon as I approached them they freakin' recognized me.

"Chuck," said the taller of the two beards. "Glad you came. Sunny mentioned you."

"She tried to steal my peanut butter and jelly time," I said.

He looked me up and down. "Don't worry. There's food on the bus."

"I wasn't being serious," I said. He looked back blank. "Forget it. If you have to explain a joke..."

There were others nearby that'd gathered. I noticed a woman holding a backpack as if it were a life preserver. She was heavier than she wanted to be. The oversized black pajama outfit gave it away. It made me kind of upset. I thought that maybe these kids preyed on people who were sad and a little broken. I fantasized about choking the beards for about six seconds before one spoke. "Lost you there for a moment, didn't we?" He had a sweet smile.

"The kids these days are calling it 'ADD' but I'm just constantly thinking about multiplying. Can't help it."

Someone laughed in back of me. When I turned I saw a striking brunette about my age. "We all have multiple levels within us," she said. I didn't believe she believed what she'd just said because her smile seemed to contradict her. Was she kidding?

"Mine usually come out by the third beer," I said. "Are we going on a trip, or what?"

"You have perfect timing," she said, pointing over my shoulder. I turned to see a pretty generic looking black bus turning into the lot. Its marquee read: The Cool You!

"That's us," I said. "Cool You people."

I felt two hands clamp on both shoulders and squeeze a little. "Now that's the kind of spirit I love." It was the brunette again. She was way stronger than I'd expected. She smelled expensive.

"Either you're a masseuse. Or a plumber. One or the other, with a grip like that," I said.

She let go and laughed. "I guess I'm a little of each being a spirit guide."

"I thought only wolves and dolphins were spirit guides?"

"You're very funny," she said. "I love your spirit."

The bus pulled up. A small crowd had assembled around me and I was kind of dumbstruck at how many there were seemingly out of nowhere. I counted about thirty. Most were young. Sunny was not amongst them, to my dismay. Damn it, I thought. She was definitely just a recruiter.

The woman behind me hurried past and made it to the foot of the bus. Her high cheekbones were rosy red, and her raven hair looked like it'd been cut and styled the day before. She was very well put together, which made me suspicious.

"Good morning, everyone," she said. "My name's Aria and I'll be the connection for everyone today."

Some asshole said, "Namaste", which Aria thankfully ignored.

"I see some familiar faces, and a lot of new ones. Thank you. You're probably wondering if we're going to try and sell you a timeshare, or get you involved in a pyramid sales-thing. I can assure you we are not. This trip is our way of reaching out to people. We strive to awaken the Spirit inside each and every one of you. That's it. No catch. We're just asking that you spend one night with us under the desert sky. We sing. We dance. We're merry. You'll love it. And then you can enjoy Vegas. On us."

"Cool," a guy next to me said. "Sounds like a rave."

"Or Burning Man," said another. "Hells to the yeah."

My skin had peeled off and was doing its best to hide behind me. Those were the last two kinds of places I'd want to go. I cursed myself for being a desperate, old-fashioned, dirty old man. I was getting exactly what I deserved for listening to my...

The door opened behind Aria. "Pile in," she said, turned, and went inside. The group followed her. Scanning the crowd, I saw a few people close to me in age: two ladies, including the one with the backpack life preserver, and an older one that looked like a blonde owl.

As soon as I made my way onto the bus I spotted Sunny sitting more or less up near the front. She spotted me, said hey, and patted the seat next to her. "Saved your spot!" My heart didn't skip a beat or anything, but I was definitely psyched.

I sat.

Sunny looked me up and down. "You didn't bring any bags?"

"Nah. It's only a few days."

"What are you going to change into?"

"Figured I'd spend most my time at the pool. Got my trunks underneath. What else do I need? I hate to be weighed down."

"I can totally relate to not wanting material things." Sunny draped her arms around me. "You're going to fit right in with us."

Sunny didn't smell expensive, like Aria did, but she smelled clean, kind of like baking soda and incense. I sure hope she liked the smell of Irish Spring and Arm and Hammer because that's what I was wearing.

A bunch of her hairs stuck to my five o'clock shadow like Velcro. I didn't push it away; I dug the connection. She didn't either. Sunny leaned her head on my shoulder and snuggled in. "There are just some people you meet and you instantly feel comfortable with them. Like you: you're a lot like my Dad. You should be my Dad on this trip."

Shit.

Aria was in front of us, holding on to the tops of the two front adjacent seats. "Everyone buckled in and ready to go?"

The bus left Downtown Station just as Sunny started to snore. Aria shot me a brief smile before she sat down in one of the seats in front. Across from me the two fellows were busying themselves each reading the same thing: it looked like a photocopied booklet—a regular page folded in half and read sideways. The logo on the front was the same one from the business card: the sun with the fire that still looked an awful lot like octopus arms. Or squid arms. I could never figure what the heck was different between those anyway. Something about it just bugged me.

The scenery changed. Downtown San Diego turned into the less occupied, greener suburbs. A short while after that we were back on a highway, only there wasn't so much around us. We hit the desert in what felt like record time. Sunny twisted away from me and curled up next to the window. I thought about her saying I should be her Dad and it made me angry. I'd have to have had her really young to be her father. Shoot. I wasn't that old. Right?

The entire situation felt kind of silly and off up until then, but I swear things took a detour. I can't put my finger on it, but there was a point a few minutes after we crossed into the desert where the lightheartedness was cast into shadow. The sand around us took up more and more real estate until that was all there was, other than road.

There were huge boulders and I couldn't help but think what might happen if one were shaken loose from an earthquake. We'd be crushed. That'd be that. The melancholy part of me took over and shrugged the thought away. At least it'd be quick and the endless struggle would be done.

The air they pumped in wasn't quite cutting it. I bet it was low in oxygen or something, and it smelled like vinyl. I tried fighting it off, but I fell asleep, my chin on my chest.

And I just couldn't get that damn picture of the sun out of my head. It was like it was burned inside, stuck spinning, and I couldn't get it to stop like when I pull the chain on my ceiling fan and it just gets faster instead of shutting off. The flames around the edges uncoiled and wiggled. The sun lost color and inside became an oily texture with metallic green and blue rings that went out into infinity. Reptilian webbed wings unfolded. A low rumbling drone sounded, starting, and played, subtle intricate overtones fading in.

My stomach twisted and I felt like my lungs didn't fit, that they'd smother my heart. I wanted to go back home to my place, to my simple routines, but knew that there was nowhere to go where I wouldn't be seen or found. The beast saw me and homed in on me and memorized me and would follow me wherever I hid. I belonged to it.

The arms uncoiled, rolling toward me inside the dream ethosphere, where you can't do anything but watch, but you keep willing your body to do something or your mouth to open, but neither will because you're too passive in that in-between state. You're just along for the ride, the hell with it all. Go with it. You're dreaming, after all, right? It can't hurt you. What it can do is color your day after you wake up, your psyche thrown off the rails. When I came to, I was certainly feeling pretty bleak.

Sunny was next to me, headphones plugged in, looking out at the red desert. Red? As I looked closer I realized the color came from the setting sun, which cast its long, thin shadows across the plains. The palm trees had given way to succulents and rocks. Dry washes stretched under low bridges. The air inside the bus was too cold and I wrapped my arms around myself. I still felt disconnected and off from my dream.

"We're only about twenty minutes away," Aria said. I turned to see her looking at me, a slight smile sneaking through. I nodded. She was a beautiful woman, but the radiance I saw seemed to be coming from a place other than peace—I felt a lot like a wounded gazelle in a cheetah's gaze.

I yawned and rubbed my fingers through my hair. I wanted to go back to sleep, but I didn't want to dream about monsters or angry, murderous dark stars. Just a plain old rest would be good. Maybe I'd get that later, after whatever it was they wanted to show us was over.

A short while later the bus slowed. We pulled off the highway and went on another, smaller road. I didn't catch the name. The desert looked gorgeous at that moment—all strips of orange and red light painted across the plains. Even better? The punishing heat had given way to a comforting cool. My stomach made an embarrassing noise, and I hoped there was food straight away.

Sunny came to. Her eyelids were puffy, her expression reminding me that of a sleeping cat's. "I had the craziest dream," she said. "I fell in a well that went on forever, and there were these fish people there trying to grab me and pull me down, and I couldn't breathe."

"I think it's the desert," I said. "Bakes your brains. Makes you see things that aren't there."

"Mmm," she said. "Right. Good thing we're close. I need to forget about that."

"Good idea. Let's keep things happy, right?"

She shut her eyes and put up a grin. "Right."

The place we stopped at didn't look like much: a simple southwestern building, with faux adobe trim and matching red mud colored paint job. Aria stood up just as the bus stopped. "Alright, Travelers. Wake up. We're home for the night. The Cool You is about to come out." Her voice was strong and clear, but had just a little rasp to remain endearing. No wonder she was a leader.

There actually were a few people sleeping, I noticed. Pretty funny. Glad it hadn't been just me. That ominous feeling still stuck in my gut, though. I'd hoped it was just my being hungry.

Aria stayed up front as people shuffled off. When I passed her, she said hi and I felt really special. Sunny was right behind me, and seemed a little bit in a trance. When we were off the bus and on the pavement I mentioned it to her. "Oh, I always get like this when I come out here. It's just the way I channel things, I guess."

Folks milled around us. No one knew each other so well, so they were all asking each other questions about where the were supposed to go and do. "I'm starving," I said. "Is there food anywhere?"

She lit up. "Oh, yeah."

I followed her inside. The room looked anonymous. Folding tables and chairs. Catering trays filled a table up front. Normal stuff. Pasta. Some kind of chicken dish. Sides. All pretty boring.

Sunny's plate was stacked higher than mine. She proceeded to barely pick at it while I inhaled mine. Pretty unspectacular, but decent.

"I'm never hungry like this." I put a hand on my belly.

"Coming out here changes your appetite," Sunny said.

I went back for seconds. So did most the crowd. Everyone seemed about as hungry as me. There was murmuring.

Even though I was full, I made my way back up to the catering, but when I saw Aria heading for the same area, obviously bent on a speech, I doubled back. Back at the table, some jackass with an e-cigarette had taken my place. "Those things cause brain damage, buddy," I said, pointing at his affectation.

"Did I take your place?" He made no motion to move.

"I didn't want to sit there anyway," I said. "I've got better seats down front." I didn't, but I was trying to save face without making a scene. The inner part of me wanted to crush his larynx with my forearm and throw him out the window. But I was trying real hard inside not to be such a predictably angry, chauvinistic, territorial, overcompensating man. Not easy.

I did find a seat right up front. I didn't mind. It was better I not focus on Sunny. She would obviously drive me crazy real fast, even if we did hook up, and even if we became friends. I thought through the whole relationship in a blink. Again with the wandering mind and overthinking.

Aria had started in. Most of what she said at first were the typical platitudes. Thanks for coming. Hope you enjoy…yadda yadda yadda. I perked up when she started going over details. "We have private rooms for everyone here tonight, if you're wondering. The Travelers is a full resort. Again, I want you to know that no one is trying to sell you anything, or get you to sign up for anything, or even get your email address or phone number. In fact, all we ask is that you come to our big shindig in a few hours. There's going to be lots more food, drinks, and singing. We know that lots of people aren't into singing and dancing, and that's totally fine. Just by hanging out and watching, we hope you'll have a good time. Then we'll be off to Vegas tomorrow at ten. Are there any questions?"

I raised my hand. She nodded. "What's the catch? How do you all make money and stay in business?"

Her smile never faded. "We have many private benefactors who make this possible. This is strictly a human outreach organization. Our goal is for people to expand their spirituality for a night, and we feel the best way is by having others celebrate with us. That's it. There's really no other catch."

Someone else raised a hand. She said, "Are we allowed to talk about this?"

Aria laughed in a very practiced way. "Of course. There's really no secrets. This isn't an exclusive club. If you think someone might benefit from coming, let them and us know. But you certainly don't need to."

Another person asked, "Can we come back again if we like it?"

"Sure," Aria said. "We have many regulars."

Someone said, "Where are we staying in Vegas?"

"We've got rooms booked for everyone at the New Life hotel."

Of course it'd be the New Life—the damn hippy, New Age hotel where everything was green and vegan. Well, hell. We wouldn't have to stay there the whole weekend, just sleep and shower there. Fine with me.

"Is there a religion attached to all this?" another guy asked. "Like, is this Christian? Or Buddhist? Something like that?"

"None of those," Aria said. "We like to refer to ourselves as Travelers. Souls on a journey toward a deeper, more meaningful spirituality."

There was something in her face that went a little dark, I thought. There just had to be something about all of this—some ulterior motive. My stomach was tight from it, to be honest. Were they taping us? Were they using us for something? Harvesting information? Market Research? A reality show? I was feeling a lot like an animal being herded into a slaughterhouse. Again, there was nothing on the outside giving off warning signs, but my instinct was going apeshit.

Our rooms were small but clean. There was nothing about them I could sense that was off. I'd grabbed my keycard from a sign- in desk and found myself down and away from most the others. I moved fast on purpose. I needed a break, which I hadn't felt I'd gotten. I just wanted to be alone for a while. No one else. I was grateful for the brief moments. Shutting my eyes, it'd only be about an hour and a half until the nighttime event went down. I wasn't down for singing and dancing, but I sure would be up for a drink or seven, and maybe a little more to peck at. Heck, it'd be a good experience, if nothing else.

I set the alarm on my phone and shut my eyes again. Dreams didn't come. I hovered in my thoughts, and heard steps and voices passing my room and outside. I didn't care. I just liked being still for the first time in a long time. I thought about Sunny, and how I'd gotten there, and then thought even further back––to the many other choices I'd made in life that had delivered me right into the belly of the beast. Maybe if I'd worked a little harder in school, had gotten better grades, made it into good college, I might have found myself, and found a special someone to share my life with. Then I thought fuck that noise. I saw full well how happy all my old friends who'd gone that route had become. Most were on kid number four and marriage number two, but still at job number one.

Boom. Boom. Boom.

The whole place shook. Yeah. You bet I was startled. I sat up and looked around

Boom. Boom. Boom.

A moment.

Boom. Boom. Boom.

It sounded like an earthquake. That's exactly what I thought it was until I heard other percussive, musical sounds joining in with the loud booms.

I got up off the bed, grabbed my keycard, and made it out to the hallway where I almost slammed into a really young girl with long black hair and an even longer face. "They sure as hell are making sure everyone's getting involved, whether they like it or not."

She heard what I said, but didn't answer back. I didn't think her mind could comprehend everything all at once, judging from her expression. I shoved past her just as another set of the booms shook us.

I looked around me and saw lots of folks streaming out of their rooms and heading outside.

There was a lot more happening than I thought.

Funny thing? Time felt stretched out and sticky right then, like when you first get up in the morning and can't get your head together, or when you've drunk just enough for things to get hazy.

Most everyone had gathered by the infinity pool. One of the bearded guys sat on the lip of a stage playing a large drum that appeared made from curvy bones and a tanned skin. There were others doing the same.

People crowded around some kind of action I couldn't get a good look at. I had to push my way through to see what was going on.

Sunny danced. Her movements were trancelike. She reminded me of an eel, her limbs swaying in curved gestures. She was a natural, and stood out. Others danced, too, but they had that off-rhythm jerkiness that seemed built into the DNA of Deadheads and hipsters.

A woman's voice sang from the opposite side of the crowd. Aria stretched her arms up and tilted her head back.

"Cool you. Cool you."

It seemed like such a nerdy thing to sing. I felt like I was knee deep in cult shit quicksand. Every instinct fired and radioed for me to get the hell out of there.

"Cool you. Cool you." Other sheeple joined in.

There was nothing cool about it, but I had to watch. At least it was fun watching the girls dance. Thought it would've been funner with a drink. But I'd not really taken one in a long time. A few weddings and countless funerals before, drinking washed away what I thought I was supposed to be. I flashed back to thirteen. My folks watching me audition for that sitcom. I got on. Lasted throughout the rest of the run. I was on my way. Found booze. A little wasn't enough real fast. Then I was out. Get him some help, they told my folks. Bring him back when he's okay. They did both. The doors were closed. No one remembered. No one cared. I was on the outside looking in. That was that. Must be some secret blacklist. My folks never judged. Loved me the same. Were proud of me. I never forgave myself. Somehow I always go back to that audition. Maybe I could get a do over? Make better choices.

Too difficult having my nose rubbed in it. Headed south to San Diego. Just needed to get out from under all that.

Same thing I was doing out in the desert. Shed that skin. Burn it. Open up that spirit. Inside I was looking for some kind of comfort. Some kind of ...something.

Dance.

No.

Forget your comfort zone. Go.

No regrets.

Forget the drinking.

It'll keep your mind off it.

Others my age were flailing about. Fuck it. Get undignified. What's dignity ever gotten you?

It caught on, the dancing, the chanting, the music. Some people drummed on their thighs or chests. Lots were singing.

Cool you. Cool you.

Cath you. Cath who?

What the hell were they saying? Damn hippies were messing it up.

I danced, too. I didn't have to try too hard because it'd crowded in.

F'gathon.

F'gathon.

Great One.

Great One.

That was one special person next to me. I regarded him for a moment. What was he doing? It had to be a cult. That was some weird stuff he was saying and singing.

Cat. Who. Loo.

Cat. Who. lol.

F'gathon.

F'gathon.

"Hey buddy?" I said. "It's cool you. Not that other stuff."

He ignored me and went on with his gibberish. He pointed up at the massive rock above us, like he was willing it to roll off its perch and crush us all.

I looked around to see if there were any chicks nearby. There were, but none of the good ones, so I kept to myself. Always a lech, aren't I?

Then I lost myself for a few moments. I got into it. The music. The drums. The dancing. Let it all fall away. Forget all the noise, man. Come on.

For a blessed few minutes I did.

Right before the screams and gasps.

Here was the catch.

People broke away. The music stopped. People made sounds like trapped animals.

As they hurried backward, away from the open desert, I saw a massively long translucent, blue-tinged area stretched as far as I could see. It didn't look like glass; it seemed to be some kind of membrane. Nothing I've ever seen compares.

Below, it was like looking at the Grand Canyon, only the rock were shades of gray and black. A large formation of rock moved. Snake-like things coiled around it, each the girth of a Jeep. Whatever it was had to be about the size of a cruise ship. Only thing I could compare it to. There was nothing alive to compare the thing to: it was too immense. An eye opened, its glossy black surface saw us...saw me. I wanted to run far away. I wanted to dive in and be a part of it. Can't explain that bipolar desire. It drew me in like it had mental magnets that aligned my thoughts toward it like a million iron filings.

I realized it was hovering in water, as though it were deep in the ocean. But we were in the middle of the Mojave. There's no way there's that much water underneath.

There were huge connecting tunnels. I instinctively had a feeling they connected elsewhere. Tunnels that must have stretched all the way to the great seas, deep, deep under the bedrock. I couldn't quite comprehend what I was looking at.

Then the membrane crept up and I felt like I was going to fall right in. How the hell was this even possible in the middle of the desert? There weren't any loud noises. The earth hadn't shook. It had simply just opened up.

I stumbled back and fell on my butt. Others fell the other way. The woman who'd held her backpack as a security blanket went over and vanished. I couldn't see down, and she didn't seem to have made any sounds. Others went overboard, too. I crept back away from it as fast as I could.

A tendril oozed its way up and out of the membrane and onto the desert floor. It was only the size of a garden snake, but as it slithered forward, I saw...we all saw...that it was only the tip of one of the thing's larger arms.

The tentacle was up and on the sand, followed by two others several yards apart. They swung back and forth, sweeping members of the Travelers down into the abyss.

Lots of screams.

I'd made it up and turned tail.

It wasn't until I'd made it back to the building that I turned.

The beast, for lack of a better word, had lifted its head up and out of the chasm. It looked around, sweeping people and party gear off the desert floor and into its impossible home.

I didn't see anyone I recognized.

Sunny.

Aria.

The beards.

No one I knew.

Those fucks. They knew this was coming, didn't they? It'd been a trap. No wonder they didn't care about our contact information, or anything long term. We were just meat for the beast...sacrifices...so they could get some extra spirit points with this thing.

The beast rose into the desert sky. Holy Hell it was massive. It's skin was dark and I saw what had to have been dark bat-like wings sprout from its back. The enormity of the beast blocked out most of the moonlight, as though a huge black curtain had been pulled up and over. That made seeing details pretty damn hard. The smell was more immediate: like bad breath and spoiled fish. I had to cover my face.

The darkness was absolute.

Screams seemed muffled.

Something grabbed me. I jumped a mile high.

"Come on."

Sunny.

Her hand grabbed the crux of my arm.

Pulled me back.

Away.

My feet felt familiar purchase. Concrete. Cement. Something. There were large cracks, but she pulled us around them. I was completely blind. How had that thing taken all the light?

Then there was not concrete under my feet, but sand again. Inklings of moonlight. We escaped the shroud, somehow. I felt lucky and grateful. At least I'd had a friend in her.

Her hand grew tighter around the crux of my arm...impossibly tighter.

My eyes adjusted.

Sunny's face looked like she'd been injured. Damn it.

Not injured.

Changed.

Worm or snake-like things wiggled from where her mouth was supposed to be. Her eyes were black obsidian like the Beast's.

She pulled me close.

A dark kiss.

One last...

I almost went for it.

I ducked.

She was strong, and instead of getting away, I slipped to the ground. I used my free hand, very quickly slipped it under her fingers. They felt like a rat's tail instead of human skin. The move worked and her grip freed.

I bolted.

And ran smack right into a car.

No. I didn't get inside and drive away. I crawled underneath. Figured if I went inside I'd be a sitting duck. I didn't have the keys. Hotwiring only worked on old cars, and in the movies and TV. Not in real life. Even if I did, the beast would see the headlights…would see me driving away. That'd be that.

So I hid like an insect, burrowed under like a rodent.

So what?

I made it.

I kept still the rest of the night.

I heard them pass me several times. They were looking for every last one of us. They couldn't find me.

The sun inched up and the pitch black gave way to the punishing desert. I could see nothing around me.

The building was still there, but there were no signs of life. The bus had gone. I slowly crept out from under the car. I could see the road we came in on and made a run for it. I ran as fast as I could, early in the desert morning.

What if they come back? What if they're still here, somewhere?

The membrane, the chasm, the abyss…all had closed.

Maybe they'd just drugged me. Maybe the whole damn thing was one insane trippy hallucination.

Fuck it.

If it were, I still wanted out of there.

I made it to the main highway. Cars sped by, oblivious to what lay in wait only a few hundred yards into the desert.

It all falls off into oblivion. Into nothing. You're on the edge of nowhere.

I stuck out my thumb. Most people sped by. Who wouldn't? I wasn't a hot blonde in Daisy Dukes, after all.

But, eventually, someone stopped. Another blonde, only she was older than me. Small miracles. "Need a ride into town?" she asked.

I was a little lost for words.

"Hop in," she said. "I don't bite."

And like so many other things in my life, the next part of my story had

once again started with a girl and a promise.
 Wanna hear what happened after that first drink in Vegas? So...

The End.

NOTEBOOK CONCERNING THE CLASS STRUGGLE IN DUNWICH, FOUND IN THE RUINS OF A CONSTRUCTION SITE
By Kevin Wetmore

From the Journal of Neil van Skloot, late of Miskatonic University
State's Evidence #A1207639-J
Currently in the Open Cases file of the Arkham Police Department
Monday, January 30, 1989 - First Day of Classes, Spring Semester

This is going to be the semester when things change. Miskatonic students cannot continue to be the same stupid sheep they have been. These scions of New England who, because their ancestor left Europe three centuries ago and came here and, after perpetuating genocide on the indigenous peoples, immediately set up an oppressive capitalist system to benefit themselves, think that they have the right to do whatever they want sickens me. Their money, their unquestioned privilege, their privileging of their own socio-ethnic heritage are all abominations.

This school is not much better. It perpetuates class difference, educating the sons of the oppressors so that they, too, might one day take up the lash (metaphorically speaking). If Miskatonic would sell just one book from the "rare and forbidden" room in the library, the funds raised would pay for every program at every public school in the whole Miskatonic River Valley (not that the public schools are any good—indoctrination, not education, is their goal—and they use their monopoly on the teaching of literature, science and the arts to perpetuate the status quo!) M.U. does the same thing—keep the scions of New England as scions! I must work harder this term to wake my fellow students up from their nightmare of conspicuous consumption and indirect oppression of the working class.

I know I can succeed. I convinced the trustees of Miskatonic to divest in South Africa so that we might end apartheid. I was the only male on the "Take Back the Night March" organizational committee—working with my sisters to fight male oppression and sexual violence. Nicole and I have worked hard to change this campus. I use every opportunity to open the eyes of my fellow students to the oppression and repression perpetuated around the world, often in their name. But they, for the most part, ignore or mock me. I founded the Student Socialist Circle in my freshmen year so that like-minded individuals can organize and change this campus and this world for the better. Most of the students began to call me "Commie" and "Red Neil" as joke nicknames, but the joke is on them, as I wear them with pride. I need to remind myself that they cannot help their short-sighted stupidity as they have been indoctrinated into the system since birth. This year, things are going to change, I can feel it.

Tuesday, February 7, 1989

ENOUGH! *The Beacon*, the Miskatonic student paper, after a public debate on the "crimes" of the university administration, called me a "privately funded revolutionary" and said if I was so committed to the redistribution of wealth I should start with my own family's fortune. The author stated that I was obsessed with shaming students into social action without realizing my own privileged position. "Neil van Skloot fails to recognize he can work with the poor and underprivileged in Africa and Latin America because he does not need to work full time during summers and breaks from school. He can afford the cost of travel to do such volunteer work, while others who must pay their own tuition labor in the dining halls and laundry rooms he seems to think are beneath him." As if! They also accused me of going to "sexy" (their word, not mine) places to do charity work instead of the soup kitchens and homeless shelters near M.U. As if these were not symptoms of the greater problems of American society. I'm looking to cure the disease and they want me to buy a box of tissues with which to blow their ignorant noses!

I'm tempted to demand the university give me the funds to start an alternate student newspaper, one that will tell the truth and not just offer sophomoric writing (pun intended!), reviews about things nobody cares about, and ill-informed opinion pieces. An alternate paper might wake some in the student body up to the truth about their university, their nation and the world!

But I will not treat *The Beacon* with the contempt it is beneath. Instead, I shall take the high road by proving them wrong. This year, the Student Socialist Circle is partnering with the Greater Boston Habitat for Humanity to build houses for the poor and underprivileged in the Miskatonic Valley. Nicole, who is local, told me of an area to the northwest of here, an unincorporated area just to the north of a village called Dunwich in the upper Miskatonic Valley. During spring break, while the selfish philistines go to "party" in Tampa or Daytona or some other community that panders to the lowest human urges, we will build low cost housing both for the local residents and for Latin American refugees, fleeing the right wing death squads (funded by the American government, I note), thinking they will find a better home here, despite the institutionalized racism, the right wing culture and the fascist local, state and federal governments.

I will show these philistines at Miskatonic how to change the world, how to help the masses here and abroad, how with my own two hands, some tools and some lumber, we can make the poor and impoverished less so. They'll see, the bastards.

Thursday, February 9, 1989

I don't blame *The Beacon*. I am not making a difference. I am a hypocrite. My passing will mean nothing and no amount of fighting the power structures will make any difference. You can't fight the powers that be, they are too entrenched. The see themselves as gods and for all practical purpose they are right. Days like this I think it were better I were dead.

I don't deserve Nicole. She is an amazing woman and should not be with someone like me.

LATER:

I must remember not to give in to despair and self-loathing. I must not listen to those who despise me for trying to make the world a better place. They are the ones who are pathetic non-entities.

Tuesday, February 14, 1989

While the sheep at Miskatonic celebrate the corporate-created holiday of "Valentine's Day" in which they practice the outmoded and oppressive courtship rituals designed to keep our sisters subservient to men, I blew off classes to drive out to an area to the north of Dunwich which is one of the poorest parts of the state. Nicole and I do not observe this "holiday" and she had her Womyn's Literature seminar anyway.

I persuaded my father to give me the money to buy a parcel of land on which to build the houses and went looking for an appropriate place. (Even though he will get a substantial tax deduction for donating the land to Habitat for Humanity, I want to think some of the things I have said during our many arguments have finally opened his eyes, mind and heart, and not just his wallet). I thought I had found the perfect site just off the highway, where we could also be respectful of the environment and reclaim some old property falling into abandon. It was next to some marshlands, at the base of a hill. There was nothing there—just some overgrown ruins of a house, which we could easily demo and build on.

I found out in the town records that the land has not been occupied since the late twenties, when it belonged to a local family called the Whateleys. But they vanished with the death of their last member, and the land has sat unclaimed since. I might even be able to get it through squatter's rights if we just start to build there. We can then use my father's money to buy building supplies.

The strangest things happened towards dusk, however. After I learned the property was unowned I went back to the land to measure it out and take some photos. I parked my car at the side of the highway and walked onto the land. There was still some snow on the ground, but I anticipate it to be gone by spring break and hope to convince someone who does such things to donate and pour the concrete for foundations for some houses. I figure we could get about a half dozen two or three bedroom houses on the land. That's six poor families that will own their own homes free and clear!

As I was taking notes, a local came out of the woods. He was dressed in an old oilskin coat, wearing a hat and ancient boots. He carried a shotgun (at least I think it was a shotgun—I find firearms unnecessary and dangerous and so do not know them). He just walked right up to me and said, "Whatchyu doing here, son?" I could see as he spoke that he was missing some teeth. He could have been anywhere between fifty and eighty. He had clearly lived a life of poverty, and his diet and lifestyle reflected that. He spat some tobacco on the snow and looked back to me for an answer.

"I don't know what concern of yours that is, sir," I told him, letting him know I would not be intimidated just because he had a gun, but being polite to show I was in solidarity with him as a believer in the working class.

"Folks 'round here mostly stay off Whateley land," he said. "You ain't from around here." He said it as a statement of fact, but there was also a grin playing about his lips.

"I thought it wasn't Whateley land anymore," I told him. "I heard the Whateleys died out. This land should be used to help people."

He made the strangest noise I had ever heard. At first I thought he was in pain, but then I realized he was laughing.

"Always Whateley land," he said when he was done laughing. "And this land ain't never gone help people. You should go back to Boston."

"I am not from Boston, sir," I informed him. "And the Whateleys are gone. This land will help the living, the poor, and the people who need it." It frustrates me when I hear working class people like this still devoted to this New England notion of land belonging to colonizers who took it from the Native Americans still belongs to the descendants of the colonizers, long after they are dead. The classicism perpetuated by even the poor in New England is the greatest enemy to progress in this nation.

"Where you from?" He narrowed his eyes.

"If you must know, I am from Miskatonic University. The Student Socialist Circle will be building houses for low-income and immigrant families in this area and I think this land might be perfect," I informed him.

Again he made the strange croaking noise that was his laugher. "Ain't nobody building on this land, boy. Go back to Miskatonic. Hell, if you go to school there you should know better than to come here and try and set yourself up. The land won't have it."

"I'm sorry you feel that way, sir," I said to him, "But these dwellings will be built." His reaction to the news was most likely a combination of xenophobia, racism and that curious New England quality of not wanting anything to change, even if it will benefit the masses. Most likely he wanted to keep hunting and poaching on these lands and was trying to scare me off.

"Good luck to you, then, son," he cackled and started to walk on through the land towards the marsh. "Strange things happen out here. City folk should know better, but gotta learn the hard way. Whateleys won't want you here."

I watched him trudge off into the marsh. I returned to my car and drove the forty-five minutes back to the university. I told Nicole the story of my meeting with the man while we made dinner together. She's the one who suggested I journal about it, as I was clearly disturbed by it still. I just don't understand why the rural poor, such as this man obviously was, would side with the elites against their own interests and against their fellow disenfranchised.

Thursday, February 16, 1989

Heard back from the Dunwich assessor's office. No one owns the land technically. I informed them of my plan to build low-income housing on the land. The woman on the phone politely but coldly suggested that was a bad idea, but admitted when pressed that she could not stop me, nor would any town officials do anything to stop us, nor were there any Whateleys or their heirs to claim the land. This is happening! Tomorrow I will drive to the Dunwich town hall and purchase the property.

Monday, February 20, 1989

We are now one month away from the start of spring break. Victories and setbacks abound. I was able to convince a cement company to pour six concrete foundations on the land. They will be uniform, flat slabs. That way each house will be built identically (so no one will envy their neighbor for having it "better") and there will be no basements, which is probably a good idea given the proximity of the marshes. Basements would probably flood from time to time. We want these to be easy and inexpensive to maintain. They will be there on the 15th, so the cement has time to set by the time we show up on the 20th to build.

The bad news is that while I was able to get *The Beacon* to do a story about the project, so far only Nicole and I have committed to giving our spring break to the building of houses. I was really hoping more members of the Student Socialist Circle would volunteer, but they all gave the excuse that they have no actual experience in building things. I don't have the experience either, but I am giving of my time and effort. Besides, how hard can it be? We're all highly educated young people. We're the ones who are supposed to change the world!

Still, even if it is just Nicole and I, we can oversee the pouring of the foundations and begin the project. Perhaps once our fellow students or the locals in Dunwich see what a great idea this is and how it is actually happening they will volunteer to help finish.

Wednesday, March 1, 1989

Building permits arrived today. I was fortunate enough to find an architecture student at Miskatonic who was able to create blueprints for simple wood-frame houses that we can build. A local lumberyard that does a lot of business with the university was willing to give me a discount. I figure we can go up on the 15th and oversee them as they pour the foundations. Then on Monday the 20th we will frame the first house. We can set up a tent on the foundation then and sleep on-site, saving us transportation time.

Friday, March 3, 1989

Again went to the site. The man was there again. Another man was with him. This new one looked older and even more bent and broken than the first, but there was a fierceness to his eyes that made me walk onto the land more slowly than I might have. It was almost as if they were waiting for me. I was determined not to let them intimidate me. Instead, the conversation took a most strange turn.

"You fixin' to build a house here?" the new one asked.

"No," I responded and he looked suddenly relieved. "I'm 'fixin' to build six houses here. For low income families. Surely you must see the value. . ." I was not able to finish the thought.

"Listen, city idiot. Asher here tells me you're a college boy. Wise up. Tain't a good place to build. Nobody wants you to build here. Strange things happen here. If you're a crusader, like Asher here says you are, do yourself and those folks you're gonna put in these houses a favor and find another place to do it."

"NIMBY, huh?" I said with as much distain as I could muster.

"What the hell you talkin' about, boy?" said the man whose name I now knew was Asher.

"It stands for 'not in my backyard'. You guys don't want poor people or Latin Americans living on the land that you hunt on. I get it. But time has moved on, this land is available and you need to start living in the eighties." I knew they didn't know any better—they had been brainwashed by generations of capitalism and class oppression.

"Pipe down, ya damned fool!" the fierce man roared at me. "You don't get it. I'm trying to warn you; no good will come of you building houses here. There are things in these woods. Things that have been here long before there was a Dunwich. Whateleys weren't right. Land ain't right. Find somewhere else, or them folks you're trying to help will end up dead."

I was shocked. You've heard of things like this, but this was the first time I had experienced such blatant discrimination. "Are you threatening me? Are you threatening the residents who will live here? Get out of here before I call the police." While law enforcement is yet another tool of oppression to maintain the status quo they can be useful in situations like this.

"Trying to help you here, son. Don't get so all in a pucker. C'mon, Asher. We've said our piece and college boy here doesn't know beans when the bag's untied!" He started to walk back towards the woods.

Asher continued to stare and me then asked, "When you gonna start building?"

I rolled my eyes and said, "If you must know, we break ground on the twentieth."

The man walking away stopped in his tracks and whipped around. He and Asher looked at each other. He then said, "Yer building during the full moon? You are a damned fool. Good luck, son. Say farewell to them what you love before you come back here, 'cause you ain't gonna see them again." And with that they both walked away. So curious and so frustrating. Still, folks like that explain how Reagan got elected. Twice.

Friday, March 10, 1989

Tools, check. Nails, screws and other hardware, check. Everything, including the lumber, will be delivered to the site on Monday the 20th. This is happening!

It looks like it will be Nicole and I and two others on the first house in ten days! Steve R. and Dennis K. said they would join us. I suspect they are both nominal socialists — it's more of an intellectual pose on their parts, but I guilted them into working with us, since they are not going anywhere for break. If you're in Arkham, I told them, you can be in Dunwich and make a difference. Do you think sleeping in every day will make the world a better place?

What's more, Dennis has done work study in the theatre department so he has built sets. He will be our foreperson, showing us how to build a house. (I figure the two processes are similar, right?)

Nicole and I have purchased the food for the week. We'll be "roughing it" and cooking on a camp stove. The plan is to set up two tents on the property while we build. Nicole and I in one and Dennis and Steve in the other. I even got a Beacon reporter to agree to come out at the end of the week to take photos and write a story that will appear in the first issue after spring break. All the philistines with their tans and their hangovers will see who used their break to make a real difference in the world, instead of giving in to hedonistic, selfish pleasures.

Wednesday, March 15, 1989

I again skipped classes to drive to the land in Dunwich to oversee the pouring of the foundations. The gentlemen from the concrete company showed up at 8:00 am and poured the cement for the slabs. Each slab was a 20 x 35 rectangle, arranged so that each home could follow the model laid out by the architecture student: kitchen, bathroom, living room and two bedrooms. Nicole pointed out that we had not thought about the plumbing or how to connect the houses to a water supply. BUT, I knew a house had been here earlier and the marshland was right there, so a well must be possible. I will arrange as soon as possible for a plumber to come out and advise us on how to set that up. How hard can it be?

Everything else is all set. We will drive up to Dunwich on Monday morning in two cars, mine and Dennis's. I also hung fliers around campus, letting folks know what we're doing in case anyone staying in the area for break decides they want to stop living selfish lives and join the folks who make a difference for others.

Friday, March 17, 1989

I am giddy with excitement. Classes are over. Admittedly, I have missed a great deal of them setting up this project, but let's be honest: Miskatonic perpetuates an inherently unfair and oppressive system. When I tell this to my fellow students, they ask if I am not a hypocrite for going to school here.

I digress. Everything is good to go. Nicole and I have a quiet evening at her place, making dinner together, reading poetry aloud to one another and making last minute preparations.

Sunday, March 19, 1989

Tomorrow's the day!

Monday, March 20, 1989

I write this by the light of a lantern in my tent. The day went well. We woke up at six, before first light and drove to Dunwich. Dennis showed us the correct way to hammer and screw, and by mid-afternoon we had two frames for walls up on the first house, mounted on the foundation and put together.

The snow began to fall lightly in the afternoon, so we set up the tents quickly to ensure they would be on dry ground. We decided to put the tent on the slab we were building and hang some of the sheetrock before Steve and Dennis left. They planned to drive back to campus tonight, but said they would stay in the tent starting tomorrow night. Nicole and I figured if the sheetrock were up, and the tent was next to it, we'd be out of the wind, which tends to whip up at night around here.

Nicole and I lit the stove and made dinner after they left. It gets very dark here very early. Away from the city, there are no lights other than what nature provides. Since it had been overcast all day, the second the sun went down, this area was pitch black. We had our flashlights and the lantern for the tent, but I did not realize how dark it gets, even with those light sources.

LATER:

Nicole and I went to bed early. Partly because it was so dark and there was nothing to do and partly because we wanted to get up early and get going on the building. I have no idea what time it was (oddly, my watch stopped working sometime around sunset!), but I was awoken in the tent by strange noises coming from the woods and the marsh. It sounded like a booming. Like something was stomping on the earth, or a small earthquake that we could not feel was happening nearby. I also heard what sounded like a distant scream. Something was moving out in the woods. It woke Nicole, too, who swore she heard whippoorwills, although they must have flown south for winter. We listened for a while and then the sounds stopped. A little while later we drifted off into an uneasy sleep. I know I had horrible dreams, but I don't remember any of them. I'm writing this by flashlight, hoping that by journaling about it I will fall back asleep.

Tuesday, March 21, 1989

We were awoken by Dennis and Steve, who drove up after dawn. We did not mean to sleep in, but my portable travel alarm clock (which I had set for six) did not go off. It had stopped working during the night. Nicole and I both woke up exhausted from the night before. We were also stiff with the cold, and we were damp, as our breath during the night must have condensed on the inside of the tent. After a warm breakfast courtesy of the camp stove we began the great work again.

Two more sides finished and the four of us have put up four wall frames in two days. There were some setbacks. We've broken some boards and I thought this would go much faster than it has been. At this rate we won't even finish the first house. But it doesn't matter. What matters is that we are using our spring break to make a difference.

LATER:

As soon as the sun set, the noises began again. Dennis was really creeped out. He swore he saw fireflies out in the marsh! Fireflies in March! Not likely. I think his imagination was running away with him.

We told them about the noises from the night before so if they recurred Dennis and Steve would not be surprised and panic. We ate dinner and huddled around the camp stove for warmth. The three of them argued that we should drive back to Arkham tonight and then return in the morning. I argued they were letting irrational fears and their selfish desire for comfort dictate their actions, when by staying at the site overnight we could maximize our time there for building the houses. Though unhappy, they reluctantly agreed to stay. We went to our separate tents. Nicole and I argued. She accused me of being the selfish one. She called me a megalomaniac and even threw that "privately funded revolutionary" line in my face. We went to bed without speaking. As I write this by flashlight, I can hear from her breathing that she is not asleep, but simply being petulant. She will feel differently by the end of the week.

STILL LATER:

I am alone. They have left. Even Nicole. Something was moving in the marsh. Something big. We could hear it. It woke up all of us. Dennis and Steve were so frightened they did not initially leave their tent, but "whisper yelled" to us through the fabric. When the booming began, Nicole leapt from her sleeping bag and clung to me.

"I bet it's the locals," I told them. I explained about Asher and his intense friend. I said it was probably them out there, hitting a garbage can against a tree or rock or something. They were trying to frighten us away from their hunting grounds.

"These are hunting grounds, but not for people," joked Steve. At least I think he was joking.

After half an hour of the racket, Steve and Dennis announced they were running to the car and going back to Arkham. Nicole begged for us to go with them. "It's cold, it's dark - I mean real dark, and there is something out there. I don't want to stay here. Why can't you understand that?"

I explained that we were not staying for ourselves, and therefore we could not leave for our sake. "There are poor people here in Dunwich depending on us to build these houses," I explained.

"No," she countered. "Nobody is depending on us to build these houses.

The locals laughed at you and told you not to build here. This is stupid. And dangerous."

"I'm glad you finally had the courage to tell me what you really think. So helping the poor is stupid, huh? And you want to run because you're scared of the dark? Because it's a little cold? Because you hear 'monsters'? You're such a child. You have no dedication to the cause."

"I'm not afraid of monsters," she said, calling me several childish names. "That could be a bobcat or a panther or a mountain lion. And even if it is the locals, if they want to drive you off, what do you think they are capable of?"

"If you were a true socialist, you would not be afraid," I told her calmly.

"Screw you," she responded, unzipped the tent and ran out, calling for Steve and Dennis. It turned out they already left, so she took my car. I had forgotten I had given her the keys to run errands in town earlier in the day. So I was left alone at the site, with no car and no one.

Screw them all. I can do this on my own.

Wednesday, March 22, 1989

I thought Steve, Dennis and especially Nicole would come back today and apologize for their foolish behavior. I was wrong, and they are the ones who are pathetic.

Today was beautiful. When I awoke it was warmer than usual and the sun was shining. It was the first clear day, the first day not overcast since last week. No snow on the slab, but there was a curious smear of something that looked greenish purple. I assumed one of them stepped in the marsh and wiped their feet on the slab yesterday and I hadn't noticed.

A quick breakfast and I got to work. I was determined that by the time they showed up they would see what even one determined person can do. I began hanging up plywood and drywall. I started working on framing the roof. I built up as much as I could during the day, and then the sun began to set.

Tonight is the night of the full moon, according to Asher. I figured I'd see him or his buddy today, but I saw no one. Now that I think of it, I heard nothing either. Usually there are some noises in the woods, even in early spring. There should have been wind blowing, branches snapping, melting snow dripping, the birds that stay for winter—I heard none of this.

I ate a lonely dinner by the light of the camp stove. It is not easy being a warrior for progress, but this is the sacrifice I make for others.

LATER:
The noises are back and closer still. I swear there is something right outside the tent. I heard it coming through the woods, circling into the marsh, and then finally approaching the site. I have a hammer and a crowbar next to me, in case it is a bobcat or panther, like Nicole suggested.

It sounds like something is hitting the walls I have built. The full moon is shining down and I can see the shadows of the roof beams through the fabric of the tent roof, shaking as if they are being struck. Time to show these locals that a committed socialist doesn't get afraid, they take action! I write this so that if these philistines are out there with a shotgun determined to stop me one way or another, someone will know what happened here.

The news article below, from the Miskatonic Beacon, was taped into the journal by Neil's roommate.

MISKATONIC STUDENT DIES IN ACCIDENT DURING SPRING BREAK
Monday, March 27, 1989
Anthony Dalton, Beacon Staff Reporter

Sometime in the late night hours of Wednesday, March 22, Neil van Skloot was killed when the house he had been building as part of a spring break project to help the poor of Dunwich collapsed on him as he slept in a tent. Van Skloot, well known on campus as an activist and ardent socialist, had been building the house, part of a group of four, with three other students. Those students, whose names are being withheld, stated that they had returned to campus the night before, as staying at the site had proved cold and "unsettling" in the words of one.

According to local police, who discovered the body the following morning, van Skloot, who had no experience in construction, had built a wall and roof that were not stable. "At some point in the night, maybe a wind put a little extra pressure on the structure and it collapsed on a tent that had been placed right next to it," said Dunwich police spokesperson Deputy Chris Aiken. "Poor construction, poor judgment in the location of his tent, this was an accident waiting to happen."

Van Skloot was killed instantly by the falling structure, according to Deputy Aiken. The deputy denied rumors being reported by students that enormous footprints had been found at the site, or that van Skloot had a look of horror on his face when he died. "Urban legends, all," said Deputy Aiken. "They always start up in response to a tragedy like this. Unfortunately, a young man made some bad choices and lost his life as a result."

A memorial service open to all members of the Miskatonic community will be held in Armitage Chapel at 7:00 on Wednesday.

FIVE MINUTES OR LESS
By Michael Hudson

Ray Morland sat reading in his armchair, surrounded by the modest spoils of his suburban life. A television set costing a week's pay hung on the wall, smeared with fingerprints and unused in some time. The DVD player and speakers attached to it were gathering dust, slowly becoming just another collection of useless crap in the Morland household. Ray and his wife had bought a lot of useless crap over the years. Decorative curtains and ornate furniture. Fancy appliances and engraved bathroom linens. They even had special dinnerware for the guests they never brought home. Ray hated all of it. The regularity of things, the inescapable normalness of his life was what bothered him. It wasn't what he had wanted, but Ray was too afraid to try and change it. Something drastic would have to happen, an opportunity would literally need to fall out of the sky before anything would change.

The smell of dinner crept in from the kitchen, but Ray wasn't hungry. Meals were just another ritual in their household, an item to check off the daily list of "normal people" things to do that alternated back and forth between being Ray's problem or his wife's. Tonight it was her turn and Ray could guess what they were having based on the day of the week. For his wife, equally disenchanted with their white picket fence lifestyle, the routine was easy and quick, but like so much else in their lives, it was boring.

On the second floor, Ray's two sons argued back and forth over a video game, not the same video game they had argued over last month, probably not the same one they would be arguing over next month. They had the volume turned up and music playing besides that in order to drown out the inevitable shouting that would accompany the game. In a house full of routine, that was theirs. Go to school, think about video games. Come home, play video games. Eat dinner, play more video games. Sleep and repeat. On some days, the Morland parents hardly saw their own children and while that had bothered them for a while, they now accepted it as part of the overall way of things.

A steady increase in volume from upstairs followed by a sudden outburst of profanity and yelling jarred Ray from his reading. He sighed and slapped his book shut as he stood to play the role of stern disciplinarian.

"I know I didn't hear what I think I just heard," he shouted toward the ceiling. "Maybe you two ought to shut it off and give it rest before dinner starts."

The shouting stopped and the music was turned down which Ray took as compliance. He ran a thumb along the side of his book to catch his bookmark, but felt only the smooth edge of the pages. He swore quietly to himself as he noticed his bookmark still sitting on the end table next to his chair. Deep down, as stupid and nonsensical as he knew it was, he blamed the kids for losing his place.

His wife had come out of the kitchen and was standing at the base of the stairs, arms folded, glaring at Ray. She was still in her work clothes, too tired to even bother getting out of her uniform before starting on dinner.

"You shouldn't swear like that," she said, "not if you're going to yell at them to stop doing it."

"They can't hear me when I do it," said Ray.

It wasn't the first time he'd had this conversation with her and he was certain it wouldn't end any better than it usually did. Their mutual frustration with life usually involved Ray bottling his resentment up inside while his wife vented at him every chance she got. Each argument, Ray thought, brought him one step closer to losing it. One more shouting match, he would tell himself, and that's it. He was going to go out into the shed and get a shovel—

"Are you listening to me Raymond?"

He wasn't. She had kept on talking about the kids, their discipline issues, and how it was their monthly visits to Ray's mother that was making them act the way they did. Ray had ignored it all and even managed to smile while he did, lost in thoughts of more pleasant things, which his wife took as him making fun of her.

"Useless," she said, shaking her head, "Can't even hold a conversation, much less a job can you, Ray?"

Ray looked across the living room in disbelief. "That escalated fast," he said mockingly, "normally you get your voice warmed up with some shit talk about my mother before you move on to me."

"I was talking about your mother, you idiot," she said in the same mocking tone. "Keep up."

The microwave beeped from the kitchen and signaled the end of the conversation. Ray's wife stared at him, considered saying more, but eventually turned back to the kitchen with a sigh.

"Dinner's almost ready, I just need to stir it," she said.

"Alright," said Ray, "I'll get the kids and we'll be there in a bit."

Ray hauled himself out of his chair and dropped his book on the cushion. He took a deep breath, looked at the bookmark still on the end table, and mumbled again about losing his place. He went to the base of the stairs to call his sons down for dinner, but a knock at the door stopped him as he was about to speak.

"Right at dinner," he said to himself.

Ray went to the door and checked through the peephole, expecting to see a salesman or a pair of Jehovah's witnesses wanting to sell him on something he knew wouldn't be worth the time it took to listen to their spiel. The eyepiece was dark, but Ray could still make out the shape of a tall man standing alone on his porch. Ray didn't know why, but he felt his chest tighten as he stared at the blurry, dark form on the other side of the door. A second knock startled him and with a shake of his head, he opened the door and stepped out onto the porch.

The man outside looked nice enough, tall and olive skinned, with a wide smile spreading across his gaunt face. Looking at the man, Ray felt the sudden urge to bow, but caught himself and offered a handshake instead. The man was unsettling and though he showed no outward signs of hostility, Ray found it hard to speak while looking directly at his visitor.

"Can I—help you?" said Ray, straightening himself with feigned confidence.

"Actually sir, it is *I* who will be helping *you*," said the man. "I bring a message of hope to you today along with the possibility for salvation."

The deep, booming voice caught Ray by surprise. The sounds of the kitchen faded behind him as the man spoke; and the neighborhood beyond Ray's wraparound porch seemed to disappear ever so slightly. As oddly enthralling as this man was, Ray was not in the mood for a religious lecture, not there in his doorway and especially not right before dinner.

"Look, I don't mean to be rude," said Ray, "but the wife and I just started a pretty interesting fight that I'm sure is going to pick back up over the dinner table. So if you don't mind, I'm going to head back in and get that over with instead of stand here and listen to your speech about whatever god it is you're peddling."

"Gods," the man corrected.

Ray was nonplussed. He thought for a moment, staring intently at the stranger then pulled his necklace out for the man to see. The gold religious icon dangled from the chain in the evening sunlight, sparkling as Ray twisted it in his fingers.

"See? We're all full up on faith here, so thanks but no thanks. Have a good one."

Ray let his necklace drop and turned back to the door, but the smiling man spoke up again.

"You're correct in thinking that I'm here to convert you, but you won't have to wait long for the end." The man's calm, baritone voice grew quiet, beckoning Ray away from the door. "There are horrors not of this world that will soon be revealed to us all."

Ray rolled his eyes. "Uh-huh. What did you say your name was?"

"I have many names," said the man. "Thousands of names in fact. But that is all irrelevant. Only my message and those I serve are of any concern."

"Okay pal, get off my porch or I'll call the police," said Ray, figuring that would bring a swift end to the conversation.

"The police aren't going to be able to help you Raymond," said the man, "not in the end."

Ray cast a nervous look over his shoulder as he stepped back out onto his porch, letting the door close behind him.

"How do you know my name?" asked Ray in a timid whisper.

No response. The gaunt man only smiled.

"How do you know my name?" Ray repeated a bit louder. "Are you going through my mail? That's a federal crime, you know. I really will call the police if you don't get out of here now."

The man nodded and spoke politely, disregarding the threat altogether.

"As I was saying," the stranger continued, "the police won't be able to help you in the end Raymond. Not when the Great Old Ones are among us again."

The air outside was suddenly heavy as Ray's chest tightened again. Something was wrong about the man's eyes, something not quite human.

Ray thought for a moment that there was someone else inside the man, just behind his dark eyes and olive skin, someone just beyond Ray's understanding. The tall man was a missionary, a joyful messenger gathering souls in the name of his Father. This simple, yet regal man on Ray's porch was waiting, lurking in the unnatural stillness that had followed him up the steps, whispering into Ray's ear a means of escape from a mundane life.

"Only I can help you now," said the man, "and I'm afraid our time grows short. The end is nearly upon us."

Ray made one last effort to tell the man off and return to the familiar, mind numbing safety of his suburban life. He did his best to stand upright, to give one last trembling protest, but the man, dark and smiling, towered over Ray as he spoke.

"Yeah?" asked Ray in the most defiant tone he could muster, "A lot of folks say that, you know, the whole end times thing. A lot of them say it and a lot of them are wrong. All of them in fact. What makes you and your Great Old Whatevers any different from all the others?"

The stranger leaned forward until his face was only a few inches from Ray's and responded slowly.

"My father, The Daemon Sultan, lies amid infinite Chaos, sleeping as the Lurker sits patiently at the threshold of this realm."

The scent of warmed over microwave dinner faded away and the sounds of bickering children ceased.

"Shub gathers her thousand, starving young and the Dreamer no longer sleeps beneath the frigid sea."

Ray had never heard the names before, but it made his ears ring to hear them. There was no logical reason for him to fear a few oddly named gods and yet Ray's heart thundered in his chest as the world slipped away around him.

"Rituals have been completed, sacrifices made, and I have shown many faithful followers the truth. We await Their return; all is ready for the end."

Ray began to rock from side to side, swaying gently on the porch in front of the stranger. The rest of the world had vanished, buried around him in silent, formless darkness, leaving Ray standing there alone with only a single, joyous voice echoing in his head. The stranger, ever smiling, continued with his message of conversion.

"I wish only for you to join us, Raymond. A short ritual of penance and the offering of a truly worthy sacrifice will bring you wholly into the fold as Darkness descends on your existence. We would welcome you as one of our own."

The stranger wrapped his bony fingers around Ray's necklace, studying the delicate religious trinket in the light before snapping the chain in one quick motion. He moved slowly past Ray, still swaying on the porch, and pushed the door open.

"You will of course need to shed the trappings of your old ways," he said as he tossed the broken chain into the bushes, "and your sacrifice must be of a great personal nature to be accepted."

Ray turned and glanced up at the stairwell as the sounds from within the house grew louder.

"It should only take five minutes, Raymond," said the stranger, guiding Ray into the house.

I could call them all into the foyer together, Ray thought, Could bring all three of them here in front of him. Truly worthy.

The ground shook and a deep rumble echoed through the house, snapping Ray out of his stupor. He looked in confusion at the tall man standing in his doorway, but the stranger was staring at something in the sky above them. A small, black dot appeared overhead in the red evening sky, growing rapidly, opening onto the darkness of space high above Ray's cul-de-sac. Stars gleamed in the background as the void grew larger and larger, until it opened over the entire city. At its center, floating listlessly in the darkness, a grotesque mass of innumerable mouths lay dormant, surrounded by long, slowly swaying tentacles. Beautiful music emanated from the void, carrying across the neighborhood in all directions, calming and peaceful to any that heard it, reassuring the frightened, and giving hope to those who needed it.

"Father returns," said the stranger and the music stopped.

The tentacles began to move. And the mouths began to speak.

Something inside Ray snapped to life. Ray grabbed the gaunt stranger by the arm and began to lead him through the door into the house

"I know you said five minutes," said Ray, trying not to think about the thing in the sky outside, "but do you think we can cut it to two?"

The gaunt man smiled and pulled a curved blade from his coat. "That all depends on your—" he paused, thinking of the right words, "—personal commitment to the task."

Ray nodded as he took the knife and slipped it behind his back. "Honey! Kids! We're having company for dinner! Come say hi."

Ray's wife, visibly annoyed by the surprise dinner guest, forced a smile as she entered the foyer. She cast an irritated look at the still open front door and then to Ray. The children were at the top of the stairs, not wanting to come all the way down to meet someone they felt didn't warrant their full attention. Ray smiled at his family. They were his ticket to freedom; his means of escape from a life he so desperately hated. Silence crept into the house as the stranger gave Ray a reassuring pat on the back.

"You have a wonderful family Raymond," he said. "They are truly worthy for our purpose."

Yes, Ray thought, *truly worthy*.

The stranger gave Ray a gentle push toward his family and, still smiling, closed the door on the Morland household.

THE BABY DOWNSTAIRS
By Chad Fifer

There is a baby living in the apartment downstairs. It's living by itself.

Two days ago, I saw it crawling around by the mailbox, nobody watching it. I was on my balcony and I saw it in the night. I heard it gurgling. I called the police. My heart wouldn't stop racing.

The baby was gone before the policeman showed up. He arrived, knocked, and I heard the apartment door open. The door closed. That policeman never came out again. I'm telling you, he never came out again.

Yesterday, the same thing happened, like a rerun. I saw the baby crawl out, grab some mail, crawl back in. I called the police; the officer came, nodded to me on the balcony, and disappeared into the apartment forever. Hours later, I walked the street, looking for deserted cop cars. There was nothing but the night and people in their TV rooms.

The baby downstairs knows how to cover its tracks.

A neighbor saw me peering into the baby's windows today and I jumped, caught. I blurted that a baby was living in there alone, in an apartment I could never afford, could he believe it? The neighbor walked away, suspicious. In thrall to the baby, no doubt.

Earlier tonight, I heard scratching at my front door, down at the bottom, where a cat might scratch. When I opened the door, there was only a filthy rattle on the ground, with the scrawled note underneath that caused me to run off into the night, incoherent, a shattered parody of a man.

Don't make me come up here again.
Sincerely,
The Baby Downstairs

GIFTS
By Robert Stahl

When Jakob Zann couldn't stand the buzzing in his head any longer, he swallowed the pill, a side effect of which made him nervous, so he was walking if off in the park when he heard the tinkling of a piano being played; *Für Elise*, one of his favorites. Curious, he followed the sound into a clearing. There she sat at a public piano in a tight t-shirt, sunlight glinting against her short blond hair, and she didn't say no when he scooted in beside her. They made music together, his nimble fingers darting around her clumsy ones. Soon the rhythm took over, like it always did, and his hands began to move faster as he improvised, lost in the mechanics of sound, of creation. It was a feeling close to godliness, he imagined, the unfolding notes and harmonies cascading off his fingers like sparkling flecks of water. When he looked down again, his fingers alone danced on the keyboard and she was turned towards him on the bench, staring. A crowd had gathered there in the dappled light and when he stopped at last, his chest heaving with exertion, they cheered and tossed dollars, begging for him to take a bow. He did, and she took him by the hands. Her skin was soft like cream and she smelled lovely, like lilacs in the summer. She kissed him on the fingers gently and strongly on the lips, and a fire raged inside of him for the first time, hotter than the glare of any concert spotlight. Shy though he was, he asked for her number. She scratched it out on a piece of paper and gave it to him. *Mary*, the name read.

That evening the buzzing returned, so he took another pill and ran scales on his piano until his thoughts calmed. He barely slept, worrying whether or not to call her. He called her the next day, even though his voice was shaking from nerves, and asked her to meet him downtown for a soda. Surprisingly, she said yes. At a café on 59th street, they talked until the sun went down and he begged her to join him for a walk in the park. She straddled him on a bench, not far from the piano where they'd met, and she kissed his fingertips over and over again. "What else can you do with these?" she teased. Eagerly, he demonstrated, and her body responded by wrapping tightly around his. "More," she moaned. The fire inside him burned for her, but when he pulled out his member it was soft, another side effect of the pill. Working his fingers back into her shorts, he was surprised to find she'd gone cold. "Not tonight," she said, and left him listening to her staccato footsteps as they faded down the sidewalk. That night in his apartment on Bleecker Street, he didn't sleep again, plagued with thoughts about her. When the buzzing returned in the morning he decided enough was enough. He wouldn't be enslaved to the pills forever. No, it was time for him to stop.

Today.
For Mary.
The pill bottle on the nightstand was moved to a drawer, and while bugs buzzed in his brain he forgot about going to class, forgot about eating. His only thoughts were of her. But when he called his sweet Mary on the phone, she didn't answer. So he called her again.
And again.
And again.

Her last boyfriend gave it to her hard and rough, just how she liked it; sometimes he called her names and struck her until she cried. But it was love, she knew. It was physical; she could feel it. Most guys didn't know how to give themselves that way. Except: last week he had dumped her because of her flirtatious manner. Upset and in need of attention, she put on her tightest clothes and went to the park. On a public piano, she played *Für Elise*, the only piece she remembered from her years of piano class. When she saw the young man coming her way, she thought she recognized him from campus. She didn't mind when he sat beside her and started playing, even though he was kind of awkward. By the time he'd finished, she knew she was in the presence of an artist. He was slight of build, hardly a man at all, but she kissed him anyway, giggling inside when he asked for her number; and she gave it to him, flirt that she was. He sounded so nervous when he called the next day she almost hung up the phone. But she didn't; he might be an interesting toy for the evening. He had a childish kind of charm, she thought while he sipped on his soda. But there was something about the way he looked at her, about his eyes, something wild, maybe even dangerous. It didn't matter in the end, because on the park bench, when he couldn't get it up, she decided to call the whole thing off. He couldn't give her the hard love she needed. A guy like him couldn't give her anything at all.

And when the phone calls started the next day! She knew she had made the right decision. Though he was talented, something about him wasn't right. "Better watch that flirting," she scolded her reflection in the mirror, but the girl in the reflection was grinning.

Without his pills, the buzzing in Jakob's head grew until it was like a jet engine in his brain, chewing up his thoughts and spitting out fragments. Why wouldn't she answer the goddamn phone? On the third day, when he learned she had changed her number, he smashed his own phone to pieces with his fists. He forgot about the outside world, watching with reddened eyes as the sun came up, went down, and came up again. He turned to the piano for solace, but his fingers only betrayed him, slapping impotently against the keys like lead weights. In his mind, his father's voice reminded him: *It is the duty, and the curse, of the descendants of Erich Zann to play the music that keeps at bay the black forces of the abyss*. Fiction or fact? Young Jakob never decided. In his misery he slammed the piano lid down and returned to thoughts of his love. His sweet Mary, who smelled like lilacs in the summer, who had kissed his fingers over and over.

With a few clicks, it was easy to find out where she lived.

Now gaunt and haggard, he stood in his garage with his hand immersed in a bucket of ice, staring at his ghostly white fingers. Once, those appendages had been so full of promise, dazzling his instructors with their exquisite dexterity, bringing audiences to their feet in applause. Now they were useless; he'd never be able to play passionately with them again. She had taken everything: his love of music, his ability to sleep, and his desire to take his meds. He turned on the saw and the spinning blade roared to life. For a moment, the tone of the machine's whirring pitch matched up with the buzzing in his head, and in that moment of clarity he wondered what she would do when the gift arrived.

And in the darkest corner of the garage, watched only by the eight eyes of a common house spider, miniscule tendrils of blackness emerged from the shadows. One of the tendrils drifted across the spider's leg, imparting a crushing feeling of coldness, causing the spider to flinch. The tendrils started to spin around one another, forming into a tiny sphere of darkness, gaining momentum and mass, forming into a cold-thing. The terrified arachnid scurried away in search of safer grounds.

By the time the package came, Mary had forgotten about Jakob completely. Winking at the mailman, she carried the small parcel to the kitchen. She sliced the tape with scissors and wondered why the paper was covered with tiny flecks of red paint. Lifting the lid of the shoebox, the fetid stench of spoiling flesh assaulted her and a scream tore from her throat as she saw them lying there like five fallen soldiers on a bloody battlefield, grayish-yellow against the delicate cellophane.

And in the apartment on Bleecker Street, Jakob Zann's graying corpse lay perched against the wall, one bloody hand clutched to its chest. Around the young artist's body, rising into the air like an ever-expanding swarm of hornets, the nebulous cloud of darkness expanded and whorled, at first rustling loose papers and finally growing into a howling wind that shook the blinds and splintered the windows. A hideous laugher queased into the room as the cold-thing was born into this helpless world at last.

NOW WE ARE NINE
By Joel Enos

When it came out of the dark spot in the wall, it was smaller than it is now. But it was no less demanding. It is quieter now and we are thankful for that. But it really only stopped its constant screaming because we finally figured out what it wanted. We slept little those first few nights. The sounds it made went from coo to caterwaul quite quickly, causing much frustration. After the first confusing few hours that initial night, my wife eventually put earplugs in and went to bed. I, who have never been able to sleep with something shoved in my aural canal, did not. I just lay awake listening to the truly deafening din.

I drifted off that first night after more than four hours of listening. Deliriously, I opened my eyes to find that it had moved across the floor, bravely leaving its dark spot, which it seemed reluctant to stray very far from, and entered our room. It sat on the floor on my wife's side of the bed. Her sleep was fitful, but the creature was silent, watching. It only began its unearthly howls when my wife once again awoke.

It needed sleep, we discovered. Our sleep. It was a sacrifice but we learned kept it quiet with a system of short naps, one at a time, out of view of it. Once it had its fill, it would move back to the other room, near the dark spot. And it would wait, quietly, till it was hungry again.

We couldn't just *not* sleep. That was not enough. We had to sleep and then become fitful and then be awakened, jarringly. It was the *lack* of rest you only feel when you are sleeping and awakened prematurely. It wanted that anger, that exasperation, that complete sense of not being able to control your own necessary cycle. It ingested that sort of sleep and it was hungry often. The eventual result, of course was that we barely slept at all.

So when we were three, we were hardly humans any longer due to exhaustion. But it was quiet.

Until the next one came.

This one wanted something else. And it made sounds that made our ears ring until we figured out what that was.

Understand that we did try real food on both of them but they did not respond to it. The meals sat on the floorboards untouched till they started to smell. And, of course, we are too sad about what happened to the cat to try and explain it to you but you can imagine it was unpleasant and something we wish we could forget.

We tried crying but the new one did not eat tears.

In the end, it was a type of hysteria that satisfied the new one's hunger.

My wife, from lack of sleep, had become dangerously clumsy, falling and twisting her knee quite terribly. The same affliction had brought out a cruel streak in me that I do not usually have. I was perhaps woozy with schadenfreude. The act of it all was akin to something like Chaplin or Keaton, a backward, slow motion, grappling of the air sort of tumble. The hilarity of it struck my addled brain hard and I laughed till it hurt, despite her pathetic state.

And the new one was silent. It devoured our laughter and it was satisfied, at least at the moment of ingestion.

The laughter was not something we could falsify. Whatever prompted it had to be truly humorous and the reaction real. So when we were four, we were indeed, not much more than our lack of sleep and lack of laughter, because once the laughter erupted from our exhausted selves, it was quickly ingested, never to occur again. Any event that had made us feel that whimsy would never have that effect twice. So we had to keep coming up with new reasons to laugh, no matter how diabolical, unreasonable...or cruel. We did manage. For a time.

And then we were five. We are now ashamed at what we tried to calm the third one with at first. And of course, initially, there was the complication involving the hole itself. Part of the third one, for a while, was stuck in the dark spot.

We had not witnessed the first two emerging from the spot. They were just suddenly there, with us, already out of the hole. The third confirmed our suspicion that the spot was the entry point as one tendril was deeply embedded in the spot. The poor thing pulled and pulled, working up a true scream that one could equate to the soul of a rabbit dying and going to hell. The tendril oozed a thick oily substance that stained the carpet and left a foul smell. The wife, who had taken to having long discussions with herself about her situation, leaving me out of it mostly, is the one who discovered the solution to both the stuck situation and the sound it caused.

Her discovery is why I feel that these words I manage less and less to document well, will soon be gone from me. Because when my wife stopped telling her tale to herself, as she sat, wan, with all three of them, near the dark spot, the third one was silent, and visibly pulled more of its confined tendril from the dark spot into the room. Oh, that tendril was a long one. It took days to come through completely. And it was always after my wife told her stories and explained her predicament.

The more she told, the more the third one pulled into the room and the quieter it was. But she could not tell the same story twice. It was not that she was not allowed to repeat herself for fear or boring the three. It was that once the tale was told, it was devoured, never to be uttered again.

I know that eventually she will run out of her story. She's dangerously close to that now. And once her story is gone and her tongue silent, I will have to start on my story. I've asked her not to tell my story for fear of duplication and thus, my days of sanity being even less than hers, once I begin.

Once I start my story, we will both be forgotten. But for now, we are five and we will try to stay this way forever. Because if we don't, I fear, there won't be anything left of us to feed them.

I wrote those words many nights ago. Things have changed, as you can imagine. I am having trouble finding my words to describe the life we now live. It is not what we had before. It is not who we were before. It is something else and there is not a word or words for it.

The fourth one emerged from the dark spot only two days after the third one pulled out its overly long tendril and took up residence on my wife's torso. As sounds no longer bothered us, the foul smell this one had was an effective prompt to action much more than another scream or wail would have been.

I wrote that last observation quickly and when I read it back to myself now, I do not understand it completely. My comprehension is decreasing. When I think about things, the smell diminishes. But only if I think of my situation. If I stop thinking of our slithering problems, I smell it again and I am ill.

I can no longer describe my wife as anything but yet another new addition to the strange denizens of the room. She no longer speaks to me. Or at all, much. Her stories are slow and hoarsely narrated. And though we seem to have satiated the smell of the fourth, it is the fifth that I fear will be the most damaging.

We cannot touch the fifth without pain. And that seems to make sense, as what it leaves after contact is not so much a wound or a scar, but a hole. It is less a new dark spot, but more a true emptiness, an erasure. It simply takes away a bit of us. My wife is barely there. The majority of her now exists as a roost for the third, which has its formerly trapped tendril wrapped firmly around her midsection tight enough to leave marks when it relaxes during sleep and gives her a moment of respite.

The fifth has been taking much of me the past day or so because the third seems to attack and injure it if it attempts to take more of my wife. Our balance is treacherously wobbling on a precipice at the moment. And I fear this is the end of our story.

Because the sixth and seventh crawled slowly from the dark spot at the same time.

Now we are nine.

THE THING IN THE FRIDGE
By Samuel Poots

"Hey Frank, we got some wee lad wants to see a policeman."

Constable Frank Harris didn't bother to look up from his copy of *The Sun*. "So?"

"So you can deal with him, I'm off to the Lion for lunch."

Frank sighed and carefully folded away his newspaper. "It might save a lot of time," he muttered to himself as Sergeant Walker stepped out the door, "if you just moved this bloody station to the Red Lion all together".

With a grunt of effort he lifted his weight out from behind his desk and wandered out to the station's entrance. Hockwold was a quiet town, for the most part. It was the sort of place which always seems to turn up in your memory in the grips of a permanent summer. In a country that was rapidly changing, it had managed to hold on to the image of a small south England country village. Such places don't tend to attract the criminal element, so no one really noticed if Frank and the Sarge left the front desk for an hour or three.

At first it seemed to Frank that the foyer was its usual empty and slightly dusty self. Then a movement caught his eye. A child's face bobbed momentarily into view before disappearing once more below the desk's surface. Frank leaned over and was greeted by a small, determined expression.

The kid stopped jumping up and down when he saw the constable watching him over the edge of the counter-top high above. He crossed a pair of pudgy arms and fixed Frank with the serious look of someone carrying out a sacred duty, and who, incidentally, has yet to have the horror of policemen ingrained into them by years of cynicism and guilt.

"There's a thing in my fridge." He pronounced in a solemn voice.

Frank blinked. He wasn't good with kids and avoided them wherever possible. Damn the sergeant. "Er, what?"

"You are a policeman." The kid said matter-of-factly. "Mummy said to tell a policeman. There is a thing in the fridge."

Frank nodded slowly. "And where is your mummy?"

"She is back home. With the fridge."

"Hmm, well you see," Frank began, speaking in the slow, measured tones he used when on holiday in France, "the police aren't for when an animal gets stuck in the fridge."

"No!" The little kid stamped his foot. "Not an animal! A thing!"

"And, er, what sort of thing?"

"Mummy said it is a great old thing."

"What, like really old cheese?"

The kid let his hands hang limply in front of him in childish exasperation. "Noo." He whined. "It's like an octopus thing. That talks!"

There was silence, of the sort kids often seem to engender in adults. Chances are if there had been another grown-up present it would have been broken by a snort of laughter, with everyone admiring how children are and don't they have such wonderful imaginations? Since there was only Frank, it didn't.

Both of the large man's hands slapped down on the desk top with a noise like the slam of thunder. "Do you think this is funny lad?" Frank roared. "You know I could arrest you for wasting police time!"

"Daddy always says you are wasting time anyway."

"Oh does he now?" Frank was beginning to enjoy himself. It had been awhile since he had shouted down some young prankster and put the fear of Frank into them. "And just who is your Daddy?"

"The mayor." The boy sounded as proud as if he held the position himself.

"Oh." Frank slowly settled back down into his chair, the pink colour draining from his face as though someone had pulled a plug. "And, er, how do you think your dad would react to hearing you've been telling lies?"

"I'm not lying!" The boy shouted indignantly, as loud as the constable had just been. "There is a tentacle thing in my fridge who talks to us and keeps stealing my yoghurts!"

"It's just that the police don't really deal with monsters under the bed.

Or even in the fridge." The berated constable brightened as a thought struck him. "Have you tried the fire brigade? They deal with cats up trees, maybe they can get this... thing out of the fridge."

"No. Mummy said to get a policeman."

Frank sighed. He was a beaten man and he knew it. It didn't help that he had been beaten by someone who had to be lifted up to use a urinal.

"All right," he said, throwing his head back in defeat, "I'll come and take a look. I take it you'll be wanting a ride in the police car?"

The boy sprung to life, hopping from one foot to the other in excitement. "Yeah, yes please! With the siren going nee naw nee naw nee naw nee..."

"Well tough." Frank started rummaging around in his pockets for the keys. "We're taking my car."

The boy's whining gave Frank the satisfaction of a small victory as he drove the car across town.

The child was still griping away when Frank drew his car up into the small gravel driveway of the mayor's flint and chalk house. The kid ignored the rose enshrouded front door entirely, running out of the car and clambering over a garden gate before the engine had stopped rumbling. Frank considered following before dismissing the notion. Like undertakers and postmen, policemen used front doors.

A few minutes after he had knocked the door juddered open. It revealed a short, round woman to whom the word "harassed" could accurately be applied. Bouncing by her side was the little prophet of things in fridges.

Frank knew the woman of old, though generally just as a smiling, supportive face behind the mayor. She had changed. Gone was her friendly, slightly vacant smile, an expression of genuine worry in its usual place of residence. Her hair was lose and uncurled itself wildly around her head, as if Medusa had suddenly decided to go for an afro.

"Mummy, Mummy," the small boy tugged excitedly on the lady's arm. "It's the policeman mummy. And he wouldn't let me in the police car."

"Get inside David." She said, pushing the child away before turning her attention back to the constable. "It's good to see you Mr Harris."

"Afternoon Mrs. Freeman." Frank said, politely doffing his cap, revealing a scalp shiny and free of hair. "I understand you sent your lad there to fetch me?"

"Yes, yes." She leaned out and looked up and down the street. "Please, can we talk about this inside?" She beckoned for him to come in and then scuttled back into the confines of the house.

Frank stooped to follow her and found himself blinded by the sudden gloom. A number of candles cast haphazardly around the room provided the only light, casting the expensive furniture in shades of twilight.

"Sorry about this." Mrs. Freeman's tremulous voice came from a shadowed corner. "I'm afraid the power is out."

Frank nodded, deciding not to ask why the curtains were closed, blocking out the mid-day sun. He felt his way across the room until he found a chair and sunk down into it, grateful to take his admittedly prodigious weight off his feet.

"Now, Mrs. Freeman," he began in a serious tone, "you know that pulling practical jokes on the police is a very serious business?" He could make out the shape of the woman, perched on a sofa across from him.

"Practical jokes?"

"Yes, all this malarkey your son has been spouting about a monster in the fridge."

"Not a monster." Mrs. Freeman snapped out. "A Great Old One."

Frank blinked. "Er, your son just called it an older thing."

Frank shrugged. "Well monster, Great Old Thing, what's the difference?"

There was a sudden flare of light in the darkness ahead of him. Mrs. Freeman raised the wavering match to the cigarette clenched tight in her lips. The low light did strange things to her features and Frank was reminded of how they used to hold torches below their faces when telling ghost stories, in the mistaken belief this would make things scarier rather than just blinding

"A monster, Frank," said Mrs. Freeman, her voice steady even as the embers of her fag shook. "A monster is the stuff of nightmares. A Great Old One is where those nightmares come from. They come from the darkness between stars, from the cold depths of the ocean. Most of all they reside in the dark corners of humanity."

"And now in your fridge." There was silence for a moment. "Well I guess it makes sense," Frank continued jovially. "I mean, a fridge is a cold and dark place too. And mysterious things do seem to grow in them, least they do in mine. Heh, I'm surprised that something hasn't started talking to me."

More silence greeted this remark.

"...Mrs. Freeman, you can't seriously believe that there is something evil in your fridge?"

"Yes, that's what I said!" Mrs. Freeman waved her cigarette at Frank wildly. "Don't be stupid, I said to them. Don't tell tales, I said. Then things got...weird." She inhaled deeply on the cigarette, blowing the smoke back out in a steady stream.

"It all started with my husband." She began again, her tone once again steady and controlled. "A few weeks after we got the Fridge, my husband... he started acting...strange. Staring at it. The worst part was when it started to stare back."

"Wait, the fridge was staring back?" Frank cut in. "I thought the problem was the thing in the fridge."

Mrs. Freeman shot him an annoyed look. "Yes, it is." She snapped back, her tone so sharp she must have been chewing on razor blades. "It twists the world around us all."

Frank nodded. By this stage his keen policeman senses, built up after twenty years in the most unexciting constabulary in the UK, had led him to a conclusion. This lady was barking. Absolutely, completely barking. She was so far gone from reason that she couldn't reach it with a big stick. And he was stuck in a room with her.

Admittedly, it was more interesting than sitting around in the office, and it would certainly provide him with a great story for the lads down the pub, but it was still a pretty awkward situation for a bobby to find himself in. Still, he was here now and it seemed pretty clear to him that the only way out was forward.

With only a slight groan of effort he lifted himself up and stood before Mrs. Freeman. "Well then ma'am, if it's OK with you I think it's about time I saw this eldritch fridge for myself."

"There," Mrs. Freeman announced in the voice of a prophet, indicating the dreaded kitchen appliance. "There is the Fridge."

For the source of such supernatural dread, the Fridge looked just like any other kitchen appliance in Frank's experience. It sat in the corner of the gloomy kitchen, small, squat and white. All in all it seemed to promise nothing more sinister than perhaps letting the milk go off.

Frank took a few tentative steps towards it, before he realized he was being unnecessarily cautious and changed his steps into the purposeful stride of an officer of Her Majesty's Police Service. The Fridge was surrounded by its own galaxy of candle flames, so Frank had to be careful not to crush any underfoot. He reached out and gripped the silver handle of its door.

"No!" There was an ungodly shriek behind him and Mrs. Freeman barreled forwards, scattering several candles in her panicked wake.

She yanked Frank's hand away and threw her back against the Fridge, pushing Frank away. The woman was breathing so heavily that Frank felt he should probably look away for decency's sake.

"You can't open it!" She shrieked at the police man. "Who knows what evil you would unleash upon the world!"

Frank blinked in surprise. "Mrs. Freeman, you mean to tell me that you haven't even opened this Fridge to check what's in there?"

"Of course not." She glared at the constable as though he had suggested they jump into a nuclear reactor.

"Then how do you know that something's in there?"

"Can't you feel it, man?"

"No ma'am, I'm afraid I can't." Frank put his hands deep into his pockets and rocked awkwardly on his heels. "Mrs.. Freeman, would you mind coming back to the station for a breath test?" He cursed himself for not bringing the breathalyzer with him. It would soon have told him just how much sherry this lady had sunk.

The woman's eyes narrowed. "You think that I am drunk?" She stepped away from the Fridge and strode towards Frank. "You think I am drunk? Me!? When I know for a fact," she jabbed an accusing finger at Frank's belly, "that you always have a bottle within easy reach. Even at the station!"

There was a sudden gurgling noise from the mass of pipes stretching out of the Fridge's back. It had been a long time since an attractive woman had flung herself at Frank and it was just a shame, he considered, that it was someone who was clearly off the deep end.

"Did you hear it?" She said. Her anger disappeared completely, replaced by wide-eyed panic. "It spoke to us."

"That was just some faulty pipes." Frank said, struggling to extricate himself from the frightened woman.

She shook her head. "No. It spoke to us."

"Really? Then what did it say?"

"I don't know." The lady turned from Frank to stare once again at the

Fridge. "Only my husband knows."

"O...K." Frank took her firmly by the arm and started leading her out of the kitchen. "Come on, let's get to the station. You'll be safe enough in our station, a nice cuppa tea will help, and you'll be far away from whatever it is in your fridge."

She struggled as he half dragged her back into the living room. They were almost at the door when from outside there was the sound of a car pulling up. Mrs...Freeman froze.

"He's back." She whispered.

There was the sound of footsteps steadily getting closer. Keys jingled and then the door swung slowly open. A tall, thin, slightly balding man stood silhouetted in the doorway.

"Oh, Constable Harrison isn't it?" The man stepped into the darkened room. "I wasn't expecting to see you here. Fancy a cup of tea?"

Behind the Mayor the door to the outside swung shut.

The spout of the tea pot chimed against the china cup. "I'm sorry about all this." The Mayor said, once his wife had finished pouring. "I am mortified that we ended up bothering the police."

He turned in his chair to face his wife who stood hovering behind them. "Could you please see if young David is ready for this evening? I believe he was playing 'mountain explorers' in the garden again."

Mrs.. Freeman nodded meekly and left without a word.

"Is your wife well, sir?" Frank asked before gulping back a mouthful of tea.

"Oh yes, quite well. You have no need to concern yourself about her Mr Harrison, I'm sure it's just all those magazines she's been reading." The Mayor flashed an electoral smile. "Now just what have she and my son been telling you?"

"Just that there's this great old thing inhabiting..."

"I think that you probably mean Great Old One." The Mayor cut in, his tone still genial.

"Er, yeah. Well something weird, living in your fridge."

The Mayor let out a hearty laugh. He had an infectious laugh and Frank soon found himself chuckling along with him. "Yes, it is rather ridiculous isn't it?"

"Oh, absolutely." The Mayor agreed.

"I mean, that anything monstrous, other than gone off cheese, might live in a fridge."

"Indeed," the Mayor agreed, "the fridge would be far too small for a Great Old One to live in."

Frank began to relax. He was relieved to find the Mayor to be a touchstone of sanity in a day which had been rapidly falling away from him.

"In actuality the fridge is simply a gateway behind which dread Cthulhu resides." The Mayor took a measured sip of tea. "You might want to close your mouth Mr Harrison, something might fly in."

Frank shut his mouth. Then he opened it again. His eyes searched around, as if he might find the appropriate diplomatic words written on the air that would let him keep his job.

"Sir," he said at last. "You cannot mean to tell me you really believe that there is an ancient evil in your fridge."

"Not in it exactly, Constable Harrison, I believe I just explained..."

"Damn well involved with your damn kitchen appliances then!"

"Of course." The Mayor calmly stirred in a sugar lump. "The evidence speaks for itself."

"What evidence?" Frank spluttered. "You have a boy with an over-active imagination, a distraught woman, and a fridge that gurgles! Where is the evidence?"

"All will become clear Constable." The Mayor got up and made his way over to a cupboard. "Actually it is fortunate you came this evening. You will be able to join us all for evening worship."

He pulled out a set of rich ceremonial robes and began pulling them on over his clothes. Last to go on was his mayoral chain of office. At its centre was a talisman which Frank hadn't noticed before. All tentacles and bat wings.

It was while he was considering this addition to the Mayor's ceremonial garb that Frank decided he'd had enough. He wasn't paid to deal with nutters. Well actually he was, he thought as he crept past the Mayor to the door, but he wasn't paid enough to deal with a whole family of them.

He was just reaching for the door handle when it swung open of its own accord. A hooded man stood framed in the entrance. Frank backed away, bringing his arms up to ward away this new loony.

"Frank?"

Frank lowered his hands. "Sergeant Walker?"

The hood was lowered to reveal the amiable face of his truant sergeant. "What are you doing here Frank?"

Frank just stared, shock turning to anger. "Forget me, just what are you doing here Sarge?"

The sergeant shrugged. "Well, it's something to do on a Thursday isn't it?"

"Worshipping a fridge?"

"It is not the fridge." A second hooded figure stepped up next to the sergeant. "It is the future it contains. We are its wards and its forbearers." The figure raised its arms high in exultation. "In his home in the Fridge dread Cthulhu lies dreaming."

"Ah, Mr Harrison." The Mayor had materialised at Frank's elbow. "I see you've met Dr Hamilton. And of course you know Sergeant Walker."

More hooded figures filed in and were introduced to him by the Mayor, many of whom he had known most of his life. There was even the church organist, for crying out loud! He stood there in a daze as robed cultists milled around him, greeting one another happily and exclaiming loudly about such mysterious, clandestine matters as the football match the other night.

"All right everyone," the Mayor's voice called out over the chatter, "if you all want to make your way into the kitchen."

Frank found himself jostled on all sides as they flowed through the small door which led to the Fridge's resting place. Unable to extricate himself, Frank was carried along in the crowd of hooded figures until he stood once more before the plain, white box.

Around the small room people began to take their places, forming a circle around the appliance. Frank spotted Mrs. Freeman standing in the corner of the kitchen. The woman was clutching her son tightly to her, keeping herself between him and the Fridge.

All around the police constable the hooded men began to chant. They swayed in time with their rhythmic gibberish, like seaweed swept by ocean tides.

Inexorably, Frank found himself turning to face the Fridge. The source of the afternoon's insanity sat squat before him, like a monolith placed in ancient days. From its network of piping there came another gurgling noise, the growls of some drowning creature reverberating over the strange chanting.

He reached out with trembling hand and grasped the handle of the

Fridge's door. Around him the chanting rose to a crescendo. Gathering his strength, Frank pulled. The door swung open.

The Fridge light never came on.

THE END

GOD DOES DAMN THE MIND
By Marc E. Fitch

There are three kinds of people who work third shift at a hospital psych ward; the socially awkward looking to avoid human contact, the grossly incompetent, or near-retirees just hoping to eke out the last couple of years without having to do anything difficult or deal with inconsiderate nuts. Ginny was all three; she rarely spoke, even with coworkers she had known for years, she was losing hair in her old age and wore coke-bottle glasses. Generally, she resembled the product of some kind of incestuous, drunken Kentucky fling that had long been hidden from society. However, at our hospital, the ability to breathe and occupy a time slot was generally enough to get and keep you employed, and thus Ginny had been working the unit for twenty-five years.

One night Ginny had a stroke. Actually, she had several, as they would find out later, but, at the time no one really knew what was going on, other than Ginny was acting amazingly strange (even for her) and some believed that she may have been drinking before the shift. She awkwardly stumbled around the unit, banging into doors, and generally making enough noise to wake both the dead and those who wished they were dead from their Ambien induced slumber. She made provocative gestures at Dave and started telling a story about her "first time," which was just enough information for the charge nurse to send her down the hall to a separate unit reserved specifically for schizophrenics, in order to regain a little peace for the night.

She shuffled down the hall and stayed behind a set of locked doors for the rest of the night. In the morning, she went home and slept. Later that afternoon, George McKay, a schizoaffective with a long history of hearing evil voices that urged him toward suicide, somehow obtained a straight razor and sliced through his carotid artery and bled out all over the floor.

A successful suicide on the floor is always a big deal. Generally it is referred to as a "sentinel event." There are investigations, everybody gets questioned, and the state comes in and makes asinine recommendations that won't help a damned bit but somehow makes them feel better. Like I said, suicide on the floor is always a big deal, at least with the hospital administration that is. With staff, however, it was a different story. None of us wanted to catch blame for the mishap, and really that was all we were concerned about. A patient killing himself is generally a relief. It sounds harsh, but the general public doesn't realize that there is no cure for these people, short of their death. Imagine if you were a medical doctor and someone came in with a broken arm. You fix the arm, cast it, send them home, and when it finally heals, they go and break the same arm again. And they do this dozens of times, over and over. You are continually setting and casting the arm, and they are continually breaking it, and every time you have to see them or set the arm, they tell you to go fuck yourself and spit in your face. Our patients, for the most part, preach constantly their wish to die and when we try to prevent it, they get angry but still expect us to be able to "fix" them as you would a broken arm. It's an impossible, Sisyphean task and generally you come to understand that the only cure for living is dying.

But still, you don't want your boss breathing down your ass because you didn't find the razor blade the patient had secreted under his ball sack. They determined that the patient had obtained the razor by sneaking into a room that was being remodeled and stole it from a toolbox. A big to-do was made and a whole-lotta-nothing was actually changed. But that's the way things are in the psych ward; people are dumped there by friends, family, and police and honest doctors want nothing to do with it, so it is, by and large, ignored.

Throughout all this, Ginny was acting more and more like a patient and less and less like staff. I didn't work the night shift because I didn't hate myself that much yet. Instead, I worked mornings, but it got to the point that Ginny stopped going home till much later in the day. I would walk off the unit through two sets of locked doors to our break room and there she would be sitting with a stupid grin on her face and just staring off into nothingness.

"Why are you still here?" I said.

She laughed.

"Just love it here that much, huh?" I tried to make light of it.

"Just love trouser snakes that much."

I found her disgusting even before the stroke and weird behavior. But now she was smiling at me and gyrating her hips in the seat and it was more than I could handle.

I shook my head and just left. She was only adding to my paranoia that the whole world was going insane, which is hard to avoid when you're constantly surrounded by the raving mad. But maybe that was part of the problem. We were so accustomed to seeing it that we barely noticed when one of our own turned the corner.

A week later, I pulled some over-time working the third shift. As long as you could tolerate not sleeping it was the easiest shift to pick up and I always got a lot of reading done. We had a patient on constant supervision, a borderline personality disorder who was constantly threatening to kill herself and cutting slash marks in her arm that would scare friends and family but would never actually kill her. Anyway, it was 3AM and I showed up the patient's bedroom with a paperback, one-liter of soda and the sneaking suspicion that I was going to probably fall asleep during my two-hour stint. The door was open but I didn't see Ginny, who I was replacing. I flicked on my flashlight and scanned the room real quick. Her face jumped out at me like some kind of vampire stalking out of the darkness. Her wrinkled face and pear-shaped body was huddled far too close to the patient's face and Ginny was whispering in her ear. I couldn't hear what she was saying. Her head snapped up and her eyes glared in the light. "What the fuck are you doing?" I said (no real need for professionalism around the insane).

She only stood up, visibly straining not to laugh or smile. Her head down like she was in on some kind of joke, and she brushed past me. I watched her go. I was really beginning to hate her. I turned the flashlight toward the patient. She had her eyes open, staring up at the ceiling. I said her name and her head turned and looked at me. Good. She was alive.

The next day the patient was dead. There was no visible cause of death; no bed-sheets wrapped around her neck, no slash marks on her arms, no sign of overdose, vomit and frothing at the mouth. Of course, there had been a staff member, including myself, with her every minute so she wouldn't have been able to do that anyway. Rather, she was sleeping and apparently just stopped breathing and died. Cured for life, another sentinel event.

Administration was having a shit-fit. I got questioned hard because the coroner put the time of death somewhere in the early morning hours and that just happened to be the time I was with her. So I was brought before a small tribunal of management and I told them without a shadow of a doubt in my mind that she was alive when I was there and when they asked if I had noticed anything strange I sure as shit told them about Ginny crouching over the girl like some kind of vampire, whispering to her.

Of course, no fault was found and the coroner could only conclude that her heart had simply given out in the middle night and there was probably no way an observer would be able to tell at that point. Maybe I was off the hook but I was pissed that I even had to put my face in front of management and offer any kind of explanation. Jobs were not easy to come by in this shit city I didn't want to be on anyone's radar when heads had to roll.

I found Ginny the next day during shift change. She was sitting at the end of the hallway. Just sitting there in a chair like a statue, not even watching anyone, not even on duty, just sitting in the chair grinning like a retard.

"What were you saying to Emily that night before she died?"

She was just grinning and then she started gyrating in her chair again.

"You were saying something to her. You were close enough to choke her to death if you wanted to and…stop fucking doing that!"

She was still gyrating and it was making me sick to my stomach. "I swear I'm going to report you to management and tell them that you've lost your goddamned mind."

She whispered but I couldn't hear her. I leaned closer and closer. She whispered again, just barely audible; "*God does damn the mind,*" she said. She smiled her big grin, but she had forgotten her dentures and there was nothing but a wet, sticky black maw. Then she stood quickly, with a hunched back and deftly moved down the hall as if carried on a breeze.

I hated it. I couldn't sit still that morning throughout the shift. I couldn't sleep when I got home. Her voice kept repeating that ugly whisper and her toothless mouth kept appearing in my mind and over and over I kept trying to decipher the meaning, God does damn the mind… what was that? A riddle? The woman could barely think, and I was trying to make sense of the senseless. But isn't that what I was supposed to be doing in the hospital for the past three years? Making sense of the senseless? Was it impossible or was I just out of practice?

Camus asked if suicide was the only answer in the *Myth of Sisyphus*. William Peter Blatty wrote that insanity is the only escape from the impossible questions and answers in *The Ninth Configuration*. Like I said, I got a lot of reading done at that job. Maybe Blatty was answering Camus, or maybe I was trying to stretch my mind around too much. Blatty had been trained as a Jesuit and his answer was far more disturbing than Camus', a French atheist that laughed at the absurdity of life and probably would have thought my unit the sanest place in the world. In the end, they were two writers who saw insanity as the natural state of mind. God damns the mind because it cannot perceive the face of reality. What was it that Shirley Jackson wrote? Nothing can remain sane in the face of absolute reality?

Her old wriggling hips and moistened toothless mouth danced in my mind. Maybe that was reality; the breakdown of everything in the onslaught of absolute reality. Ginny had never been married, had probably not even seen a man in decades. She could barely make conversation. Few people were probably as utterly and completely alone as she was and so she wiggled her hips now and made sexual comments, smacked her lips at everyone and everything that walked by. So she whispered deadly nothings in the ears of those who claimed to desire a cure for their ailment—their disease of reality, of life.

The third and last suicide was a doozy and the floor was shut down after that; patients shipped to other hospitals, staff put on leave, floor manager let go and a complete reorganization of the unit was on the docket. The state was laying down restrictions and families were lining up for lawsuits. People were saying that it was potentially the end of the entire hospital.

Willie Sanders jumped through a window and plunged down eight stories, landing in the parking lot of the emergency room. The windows were actually a form of heavy-duty tempered glass and should not have broken —at least that's what we were told—but Willie had generated enough force to smash through what experts thought was unbreakable.

I, for one, was through. There were other jobs in other hospitals around the state. I was taking my leave and not coming back. Before I left, however, I looked at the hall-check board, noting the initials next to every check of Willie that night. There she was: Ginny, working at the time of the jump, in the middle of the night.

I found her house on the outskirts of the city where urban tentacles stretched into dripping blue hills and spawned with the daughters of Eve. Her apartment was the second floor of a crumbling house that leaned against a steep hill. Frankly, I was amazed that she was able to handle climbing the catwalk stairs to the second floor all these years. People like Ginny amazed me to the point of envy sometimes; perfectly comfortable in never moving up the social ladder, never even trying to better her own lot in life. She was born in this kind of place and would stay there till death. I somehow envied that lack of drive, that ability to leave the rat-race to itself and wait to die, content with being as indistinguishable from everyone else as the next drone. Sometimes I wish I had that—what was it? —confidence? Or was it a kind of fatalism where she knew, better than anybody else, that none of it mattered, that it was all just a big, existential accident? There was Camus again, rattling in my brain.

I climbed the wet, metal stairs to the top and knocked on the door. No answer. I knocked again and, again, there was no answer...but I heard something. I heard a voice. I heard a voice whispering in the darkness. I put my ear to the door. I wanted to confront this bitch outside of the safety of the hospital; I wanted to tell her that I knew she had lost her mind and that she was somehow spreading it like contagion causing our patients to take the deep plunge into death; I wanted to tell her, face to face, to back the fuck off.

And so I heard that whispering behind the door. I heard the rocking of an old rocking chair on what were surely ancient wood floors of this ancient, remodeled farmhouse.

The door was open. It slid in with the sound of a toothless mouth sucking back saliva, and there she was, grinning, rocking in an old chair, whispering to herself while she stared out the window at the gray and wet day. She was alone. There was barely anything in the apartment. An old television was tuned to the 700 Club and a southern man with heavy makeup was talking to a Bonnie Bedelia look-a-like. She didn't even notice that I was walking into her apartment.

While I started out angry and aggressive, the fact that she didn't care or even notice, put me on edge. Now I crept toward her, somewhat afraid that The Exorcist was true and she would suddenly fall to the ground and crab walk at me and I would be defenseless out of pure fear. But she sat and she rocked. I squatted down next to her and said, "Ginny?"

She turned; her eyes rolled back in their sockets, and faced me. She smiled her toothless smile and her breath smelled of rot, as if she were dying from the inside. She started gyrating her hips and laughing at me and I suddenly snapped. I grabbed her by the throat and yanked her out of the rocking chair. She made no sound and I felt like I was outside my own body watching this all unfold before me with no control over my actions. I dragged her to her own bed, which was just a few feet away and put her on her back, still clasping her throat.

She didn't struggle. I choked the life out of her and she looked like she enjoyed it. The whole time she was whispering, whispering, whispering things in my ear. Things that I couldn't understand and sometimes in a language that must have been all her own; a demonic tongue. My hand had never left her throat. Her eyes were open and her toothless maw twisted into a hideous grin. But there was something else in that room that day. A shadow that hid just out of my range of vision and there was a sound—a dark, subtle, whispering sound—from behind me. My brain threw a thousand clots that bore black abyssal stars into my lobes and suddenly I saw the darkness, felt it inside me. I stared down at the thing that had been Ginny and a thick and terrible tongue slid heavy over my shoulder and lapped at my face.

It whispers. Dark and dangerous. I hear it constantly as if from Ginny's toothless mouth and it says the most awful things. Things about God abandoning the earth and mankind's rotting flesh and how our minds are designed to fail, to go insane because there is no other choice than insanity. It is the great flaw of humanity in the face of the abyss. Blatty was right; it is the finest option. Ginny's body wasn't found for days and when it was, no one particularly cared. No one investigated. No one mourned. She had been completely alone, except for me in our one dark, disgusting moment together when she whispered in her demonic tongue and said, "God does damn the mind." Then it says other things I cannot say out loud, demonic things that turn my stomach and exile me from this world. But I can whisper them. I can whisper them in secret, in the night, when I am completely alone or, even better, when I am sitting next to you on the train, standing behind you in line at a midnight mini-mart, near your children when I when I take a walk through a sunny park in hopes of spreading the new, good word. I whisper it but you are unsure that you heard anything at all. Maybe just a rustling of breeze or a slight wheeze on my fetid breath. But if you think back, if you strain to recall the echoes in your mind, then, you may find the black holes that my whispers are boring through your brain matter.

Can you hear me?

I SAW THE LIGHT
By Greg Stolze

I just wanted to get high.

Now I'm squatting in a dank cave with my eyes pressed shut, trying to think a way out of my goddamn dilemma. It feels like the only parts of me that aren't covered in ants are the ones where the icy water is dripping on my skin.

In a way, it's worse knowing I could just walk out. Open my eyes, flick my cheap green lighter and take three left turns and a right. I'd be out, in the sun, breathing fresh air, twenty shivering minutes to my car. The AC is a fond memory, but the heater works.

When the shivering gets bad—not just a teeth chatter when I move and accidentally touch the wet walls, but constant shuddering I can't control by clamping my teeth—I do it. I spin the wheel, push the plastic button and make that flickering orange flame. At first I just hold my fingers through it to get them less numb, but this won't do, this can't be sustained. I open my eyes.

And it's fine.

That's the hell of it, that usually it's perfectly OK. I leave the cave, I go into the light and it's just ordinary sunshine. After being underground, its warmth actually feels…nice.

But I still hesitate. My heart still speeds up when I see the bright entry crack. I'm instinctively scared because it could be the *other* light, the huitançi light.

The light that killed Jay.

Jay just wanted to get laid, which put me in an awkward spot. He didn't say "C'mon Carson, *bros before hoes*," because Jay's not that way.

Wasn't that way, I guess.

But when it came to Katherine Croft, he was close. What he *did* say was "Wingman, or cock-blocker?"

Katherine and I go back to high school. She was a junior when I was a pimply freshman, but her sister knew a guy who'd bought dope from my brother and, with one thing and another, both Croft sisters started buying from me.

I suppose I was their "pusher," if you want to be all After-School Special about it, but it wasn't a big…y'know…*thing*. I never got rich, never got busted, never got shot at, never had any hairy scary scenes. My older brother's weird friend Morten had a basement full of grow-lights and it just turned out that way.

Katherine's sister Kristin was the bigger smoker. They were twins, as you might guess from the names. Identical twins, but easy to tell apart. Even though they both had the headband-hippie-tie-dye look. Identical in the womb, but when they were seven or so, Kristin broke her leg. Like, bad broke, seven-pins broken. Then, when she was in the hospital she caught some virus that did a little dance on her nervous system and after that she had trouble keeping the weight on. So Katherine bloomed into this lush bouncy prom queen type while Kristin was her sad, scrawny, yawning shadow.

That said, Kristin was the smart one. You know that thing? "Are you the smart one or the pretty one?" The Croft girls were that, one hundred percent.

Their parents went to some Christian splinter sect and you could get either girl to pay you total attention at a party by talking about God after they'd had a couple bong hits.

Before you think I'm a turd—assuming it's not already too late—I'll say I was kind of interested. Their church said the Creator of All must have left some resonance in everything created, so if you could just tune out the static and imperfection of man-life, you'd hear God, like a radio transmission. Or you'd see it in everything, in sunrises and thunderstorms.

Now, mostly I was interested in seeing Katherine's big brown eyes and moistened lips, and in sneaking glances down at the intriguing movements underneath her dashiki every time she recrossed her legs—nope, no bra there!—but the whole thing turned into one big jumbled mess. Grass, religion and The Horny are a powerful blend for sophomores.

"What about pain though?" I asked, trying to draw her out and widen those long eyelashes and bring a little excited flush to her cheeks. It worked!

"If your view got *rilly rilly clear*," she said, leaning in, "You'd see how suffering is part of it! You'd be able to, like, perceive the hidden hand of God even in suffering, like you can see it in stars or hear it in music. But we're not perfect creatures," she said, while I privately thought she was close enough for me. "We can only perceive the *numinous* when it's aligned with beauty. But that's no reflection on God. It's a reflection on our weakness."

I didn't ask who'd made us weak. It wasn't that I was reluctant to pick a fight with her. (Though, shit, I was. Or saw no percentage in it.) I just didn't think of that until later. Even then, I never *got* it until a week later when I revisited the topic with Kristen (who did not have The Sexy but I couldn't think of a polite way to evade the conversation). Kristen said, "Sure, we'd rather be comfortable. But people at their most comfortable are rarely people at their best."

Like I said—the smart one.

At the end of my sophomore year, the Crofts graduated. While we hung out a couple times that summer, they were headed for higher education and I stuck around the ol' home town. They came back sometimes, but we drifted apart because they were going to college and it was more and more clear I was not.

I guess this is where I talk about Joanice, my junior and senior year girlfriend. Or would have been senior year if I hadn't dropped out.

You know how Katherine made you think sexy thoughts that were cute and sweet and fun? Like, you'd go on a picnic and make love on a blanket under a blue sky and eat strawberries?

Joanice wasn't that way.

She made you feel dirty and think about backseats and sweat and threeways. Joanice was punk rock hot and I did not ever understand her interest in me. She was out of my league; I never forgot that for a minute. After she relieved me of my virginity, I never forgot it for a second.

Joanice's affection for skipping class to exchange oral sex in Twin Oaks cave was starting to destroy my grades when Morten's house caught fire. His bathroom fan shorted out, and when the firetrucks showed, there was no way he could hide his basement pot crop. I don't even know if he's out of prison yet. We lost touch.

Anyhow, with Morten out of the picture, I lost my reliable reefer option but that was OK. Joanice knew a guy who slung heroin.

As soon as I mention H I'm sure you picture me in some squat, jabbing a collapsed vein, hollow-eyed, starving, with rats biting my nutsack and what have you. I won't deny, it messed me up. But just as my weed-dealin' never landed me in jail or a macho knife fight, I never got addicted. You probably figure I'm "in denial," but my bad experience was when I took it, not when I quit.

Look, if you don't smoke up—fine, good on you. You made a legitimate choice. But it's probably uninformed if you never *tried it*. Which may be OK! Kristin once said religion is necessary for some while others, if their lives are going well, can give it a miss.

Me, I have to believe. Not just in "seeing God in a sunrise," either. I wish I'd never seen God in a sunrise.

What I'm trying to say is, I'd been told marijuana was *super dangerous*. They said one huff off a Sharpie could kill you. All that seemed at odds with people I knew who did those very things and were fine. So I smoked and was fine. I figured I would, similarly, be fine snorting a little heroin, just like I was fine drinking beer but never got *desperate* when the supply wasn't there. I knew genuine addicts, but you have to believe my experience when I say I wasn't one. I really could take it or leave it.

But I got in over my head. I was with Joanice's friends and I drank more than usual and snorted more than usual because...I don't know. I don't know why. Because it was there. Because they were all fine. Because we were having fun.

It was the first time I mixed booze and heroin. Until that point H had been a "special occasion" thing. Like "a sometimes food." But heroin and booze, it turns out, don't play well together.

That's how I met Jay. When I woke up—I don't remember falling asleep, my memories of the night are pretty garbaged—he was knuckling my sternum and calling 911. The paramedics hit me with Narcan, I got arrested, plea bargained into treatment and, well, Joanice stopped coming around.

Jay and I decided to quit heroin and you know what? We never had any withdrawal. Not a single day, neither of us, none of that *Trainspotting* shit. I for sure know people who keep on a costly schedule of this or that because they are terrified—*terrified*—of getting dopesick. Drug rhetoric scores again.

Anyhow. You can see why, when Jay fell for Katherine, I couldn't tell him no.

The Croft girls moved home after college and I ran into Kristin at the local organic store. I cashiered there and was a mop-jockey at a bar on nights and weekends. Jay and I were sharing an apartment—my parents cut me off cold when I OD'd, thanks Mom. Jay's parents were dead by then.

Kristin scored a job for some religious charity with hungry kids and illiterate moms or whatever, writing grants. Katherine was repping for GlaxoSmithKline.

So Kristin asked which bars were still cool, I told her the one Joanice hated the most, and we arranged to meet there with the explicit understanding that it was old friends, not a date. When I arrived, she felt me out about whether I was holding.

When I said I was no longer on that scene, she didn't seem too disappointed. College was good for her. She still looked like she needed ten hours of sleep and a big omelet, but she was more composed. She'd softened the Hot Topic peace-sign look into something more "NPR, but funky."

"You've seen death, Carson. Haven't you?"

That made me jump. I mean, it came out of nowhere, right? But I eventually fessed up to, y'know, the whole near-fatal-heroin *thing*. She just nodded.

"People get a look," she said. "When I was young and so sick, I got it. And I felt like a freak because no one else in school did. But there was a girl at college who'd been in a car crash, the boy next to her...she saw it then. I suppose the older we get, the more common the look becomes."

"No offense Kristin, but you're kinda bumming me out."

That got a laugh, and we changed the subject.

So the next time I met Kristin at the bar, Katherine was there too. Not *quite* as scalding hot, but still turning heads. We caught up, my jokes about

GSK giving her free samples was pretty strained, but it was all right.

One night, Jay stopped by and that was the end of his free will. He met Katherine but—here's the thing—since I'd told Kristin about him saving my life, and she'd told Katherine, they took him seriously. Which is how, after a couple months, we agreed to go to New Mexico for huitançi.

Huitançi was—still is, I guess—this mushroom that grows out in the foothills. Looks like a pinkie finger poured out of concrete, smells like wet dog, supposed to make you feel like you're at the center of the cosmos kickin' it with God while everything around you goes twirl, twirl, twirl.

Kristin described it with a lot more dignity, saying it makes that radio in your head more sensitive. Instead of having to meditate under an icy waterfall, or starve and flagellate yourself on a pillar, you just take huitançi "with an open heart" and that part of your molecules that still remembers being forged by God in the Big Bang would grow three sizes that day and yeah, you can tell I didn't take it seriously.

I wish I had. I wish I had treated it as seriously as ass cancer and, moreover, had paid attention to the idea that the God of Everything is not just the God of puppies and rainbows but also the God of maggots and ODs and falling in love with women who can only make you miserable. Plus ass cancer.

I wish I'd reflected on what a fearful thing it is, to fall into the hands of a living God. But I wanted to get high.

After heroin, I was cautious, but at the same time, I can't deny that I missed it. I missed being chemically altered; I missed my little vacations from being Carson. I missed toking up and not caring that life was passing me by, missed finding everything profound, missed the sensation that maybe the whole point of me was to have things pass by, like some groovy parade. I missed snorting some Mexican brown and having the whole idea of "the point of _____" annihilated, I loved being unburdened and empty and blank.

Plus, maybe I wanted to see God? Kristin was smart, the smartest person who wouldn't ignore me, and she not only believed, her belief made things better for her. Or made her better at things. Or something.

Maybe I don't even know what I wanted. Maybe it's like drinking screwdrivers backstage and snorting again, other people were doing it and I did it too.

Jay borrowed his uncle's camper and we towed it to New Mexico behind Katherine's sport-ute, kind of vague about sleeping arrangements. Kristin took huitançi during her grad program (wish I could've read *that* grant application) and she talked about the effects of psilocybin, about Roland Griffiths and the Marsh Chapel experiment, about DMT and how people who smoked it not only reported seeing things, they reported the same weird silvery elves even when they hadn't read each other's reports. She talked about the Liao drug and the Huichol use of peyote and how this Dutch chemical NEXUS got adopted by South African natives because it let them hear their "singing ancestors."

She got our supply from this blank-faced old guy. He was Mexican or Native American or maybe a native from Mexico. He said maybe fifty words, wanted to make sure our hearts were pure. Sure dude. Pure something.

Huitançi isn't even illegal.

Kristin didn't want to have supper before we took it, saying we should be "purified" beforehand. She got outvoted, though. Hot dogs and s'mores, like in Boy Scouts, and then that desert sky that looks like a science fiction movie because you can see the whole smear of the Milky Way. No city lights, just star beams.

Looking up at that fabulous display, I think it would've been enough. If someone said, "Hey, maybe we can just have a nice time, enjoy the clean skies and not smack our brains into new shapes with entheogens," I probably would have nodded along.

But no one said that.

Once the fire burned down, Kristin gave us each one cement-colored dick-shroom and led us to a cave, maybe a half-mile from the camper. By the time we arrived, we were cramping and puking.

Kristin warned us that huitançi made you feel "a little ill" and really undersold it. I *never* puked so hard, and it felt *cold*. It was like barfing ice chips. When we got to dry heaves, Kristin beckoned us into the cave. That was about one in the morning.

We went in and, like Twin Oaks cave, you didn't have to go far to get to real, true, subterranean dark. The kind of underground where there isn't even a reflection of starlight bouncing off a damp corner to your eye.

Time started to get weird. Maybe blind, primal, dirt-dark would have made time stretch around in any event. I heard some rustling and people sounds too. Kristin was humming some church song I half-knew and then

Katherine said "Jay. No. It's not like that."

"What?" Kristin asked.

"Nothing," Katherine said.

Could be the huitançi, but those words sounded incredibly final. If I made a move on a woman and heard her say it was nothing, that kind of nothing? Don't know if I'd ever be able to try again with anyone.

Poor Jay. Would I feel better if he'd gotten somewhere with Katherine before he died? I honestly don't think I would.

Anyhow, at some point in weird time, Kristin said, "We should go out now. It's waiting for us. It's almost here." But we didn't turn on any lights. Kristin had been really particular about no cell phones or matches or glow-in-the-dark watches. I think she actually used the phrase "a womb of perfect darkness."

So we stumbled out and the stars were staring down at us. I could feel it. I could feel each star in the sky, its light, like a tiny pinprick on my skin, and it felt just like the OD. I'd had a terrible itch, then. Like I said, I don't remember much about it but that was unforgettable, itching everywhere and trying to scratch but being unable to make my hands rise or my arms move.

You know about skin mites? How there are millions and millions of tiny insects that live *on* you the way you live on Earth, and they eat your dead skin and (I'm sure) sometimes munch on living stuff too? When I OD'd, I swear I could feel every last one of them, every micro-parasite biting me, more than I could ever count, and it was just the same with the stars eating me in the desert. My teeth started to chatter and I looked at Jay.

The light was poking holes in him.

I could see it, tiny spears falling right through his skin, like when a spiderweb's invisible until it catches the light for just a moment. They hit him and his blood puffed out of the holes like smoke and he was whimpering.

"Oh no no no..." Someone said that, in this high horrible little-kid voice. Maybe it was me.

I looked at my hands and the same thing was happening, where the light touched it was *judging* me, punishing me, picking me apart cell by cell...

Then the dawn, all in a rush. Like I said, time got strange. The sun lurched up into the sky and the light...the light was *all* light, I mean everywhere in the universe, all of it was this thing, and it was *looking at us.*

Think about being one of those skin mites, on an eyelid, and the eye opens. The whole of everything gazes at you. You feel what the cosmos thinks about you.

Well. What do you think of your skin mites? Not much, I bet.

All of us screamed then, except Jay. There was…I didn't see him because I was looking at the sun, but he blew past us, a crimson cloud, turned into plasma. He left no stains on us, none on his clothes. His pants and shirt were just empty. He expanded, inflated by the light's regard, until he blew away like dust.

We ran back into the cave. Me and Katherine did, anyhow. I could tell it was her because she felt plump when we hugged each other, terrified and deranged. Holding her was the least sexy thing I've ever done. We were so scared it was beyond sex, beyond words, beyond being people. We were just failures of space to be empty.

Later, Kristin came in for us with a flashlight and we shrieked, but it was only light.

Kristin did not ever say Jay's heart was not pure. Didn't say anything about mine either, while wiping off the blood that speckled my skin like sweat. There weren't visible wounds or holes, but everything prickled, like putting on lotion when your skin's really dry. Or like a million insect feet walking on its underside.

On the drive back we decided to say Jay had returned to the apartment with me and gone to his day job at the normal time.

We all knew he was gone. His empty clothes, lying on the sand. Katherine was looking at him when he went. Said he got vaporized and lifted into the sun.

You may want to call this one big druggy freakout, but we all remember the same thing and saw it before we talked about it, like McKenna's silver DMT elves. Only deadly, big, and a million times worse.

"It never did that before," Kristin said, driving. "It wasn't like that last time."

"Is God angry?" Katherine asked.

"I think God doesn't give a shit," I replied.

It would be nice to think it was all chemical. Except when the light came back, it was more real than any drug. It was more real than what you see every day, more real than shoveling snow or stepping in gum or eating a chicken wing. One minute, light's just light, and the next it's Everything There Is staring at you.

When that light comes on me, the only way to get safe is to get somewhere dark and close my eyes. Even when I shut my eyes in the sun, there'd be a taste of it, breathing against my face like a hot acid wind, in the red light that seeps through my eyelids. The best place I've found was Twin Oaks cave—even the closet in our apartment was too light, it seeped in under the door like boiling water.

But Twin Oaks isn't a warm place to camp. It's public land, the cops and park district guys check it at closing time and they've started giving me the stink-eye. Maybe the light bouncing off me gives them a taste of that wrongness, of the universe's contempt. Or maybe I've let the ol' personal hygiene slide.

So now I'm back in my car. Safe and warm, rolling down the highway home, worried that, at any second, the bright blue-sky daylight is going to turn on me, prick my flesh, scald my eyes, knock me down with cosmic shame.

I'm going back to our apartment. Well, I guess it's now just my apartment.

I called Joanice again two nights ago, which wasn't much fun. But Jay had some money set by, and that smoothed things over. She set me up.

I've got an X-acto knife at home, I can sterilize that on the stove or using my good ol' green gas-station cigarette lighter. I can snort a third of the heroin Joanice sold me and find out if I can manage to blind myself.

I think I can, since I've seen the light.

After that, then, we'll find out if it's about me seeing it, or it seeing me. There's nowhere I can go with enough darkness to be safe, so if God can still find me blind, it's the rest of the junk and a bottle of whiskey.

One way or another, this has to end.

KICKSTARTER
By Richard Lee Byers

Wake Cthulhu!
Change the world!

4 backers
$37 pledged of $400,000 goal
11 days to go

    First off, sorry there's no video. Everybody says you should have one. But believe it or not, we're still on dialup here in Dunwich, MA (AKA the sticks!), and I can't get mine to upload.
    Anyway, hello! My name is Hezekiah Whateley, and I'm inviting you to join me on a quest I'm truly passionate about.
    Are you unhappy? Do you wish some mighty force would sweep away your dead-end job, your bills, your failed relationships, society's oppressive laws and institutions, and let you start over from scratch?
    Do you have nagging questions about the meaning of life and your place in the universe? Would it help if someone showed you the face of God? Or at least the tentacle-waving face of a "little g" god?
    Have you ever wished the world could be more like a Michael Bay movie?
    If any of that struck a chord with you, then this is the opportunity you've been waiting for!
    Because according to the wisdom of the ancients, my bestie Cthulhu is a "dead" god dreaming in the sunken city of R'lyeh on the bottom of the Pa-

cific Ocean. And with a little encouragement, he'll rise, smash human civilization, and reign over a blighted planet forever after.

Wow, Hezekiah, that does sound good! But how do I know you can really make it happen?

I come from a long line of cultists dedicated to putting Cthulhu (and entities like him) back in the driver's seat. My Grandpa Squamous, who is also my Uncle Squamous, (it's complicated) was reading the *Book of Eibon* and the rest of our family's collection of moldering tomes to me when I was still in diapers. (Well, if my family had believed in diapers.)

It made for a great start, but I haven't limited myself to what I could pick up hanging around the house. In high school, I made several B's in Latin (necessary for many incantations!), carried a 2.8 GPA overall, and scored 1525 on the SAT. Attending Miskatonic Community College online, I earned my Associate's degree in Eldritch Studies (AKA Shit We Know We Shouldn't Teach You, But Nobody Would Take Classes At This Podunk School If We Didn't).

Impressed? I thought so. But I'm just the tip of the cenotaph. I've put together a crack team to make this dream a reality.

Prior to her escape, Aggie Clyburn spent years in an asylum supposedly being treated for grand mal seizures, violent outbursts, delusions, hallucinations, and an annoying lisp. Her real problem was that she was in telepathic communication with an inhuman consciousness (exact identity TBD). Finally, the doctors did the sensible thing and tried experimental brain surgery. As it turned out, the operation enabled the emergence of several alternate personalities including June Bug, Mary Queen of Scots, Muffin, and A Boy Named Cthu, each with its own special insights into how to wake the Big Squid.

Before fleeing New York (something about child support), Moe Leibowitz bussed tables in Greek and Egyptian restaurants. There, he became fluent in those languages (also necessary for many incantations!) just like I'm fluent in Latin.

Jimmy Hawthorne has served time twice for Aggravated Assault and swears he's "just getting started." A survivalist, his proudest possessions are his 257 knives, his 403 guns, and his complete run of *Tiger Beat*. (I promised to also mention that he's single.)

You and your friends are obviously the real deal! But what exactly are you going to do with my money?

We're confident that together, we've got what it takes to function as Cthulhu's prancing, gibbering, hog-gutting living alarm clock. But the ritual is like Carrot Top's act. It's all about the props, and we still need three items:

The original manuscript of *Al Azif* (AKA the *Necronomicon*), which Grandpa Squamous is "65% sure" is locked in a secret vault under the Vatican.

An Atlantean athame forged of meteoric iron in the possession of a wealthy private collector (allegedly a drug cartel kingpin) in Bogota.

A ukulele constructed according to instructions left behind by the preternaturally gifted (and arguably cursed) musician Erich Zann at the time of his disappearance. Waiters at Fred's Luau Shack in Scranton strum it when they sing "Happy Birthday" to a customer. (Occasionally with gruesome results.)

Not being master thieves, we can't steal these articles ourselves. So we hired an expert, Larry Bosco (AKA "The Human Slim Jim"). Your donation will pay Larry's fee and cover his expenses as he jets around the globe swiping what we need.

Risks and Challenges

We honestly believe success is virtually guaranteed. We have a contingency plan to deal with the only thing we can imagine going wrong.

It's possible some busybody will decide to go all "occult detective"/Scooby Doo on us and try to interfere with the plan. It's happened before. (I'm looking at you, Armitage, Rice, and Morgan descendants.) But that's why Jimmy's on the team. I'd like to see some old professor throw pixie dust at him!

Stretch Goals

If we reach $450,000, we'll pop open a Gate and summon Cthugha, another Great Old One, to keep Cthulhu company. With all the volcanoes in the world erupting at once and flame creatures swarming in the sky, every day will be like the 4th of July!

If we make it to $500,000, we'll draw down Azathoth. He's the embodiment of primordial chaos, so his mere presence will pretty much shut down natural law and cause and effect. If (like me!) you loved "Anything Can Happen Day" on *The All-New Mickey Mouse Club*, then trust me, you really want us to hit this goal!

Backer Rewards

Pledge just $1 and I'll paint your name on the outside of my house in weather-resistant Glidden exterior paint. I admit, the place is kind of a dump, but even so, when Cthulhu returns, it's bound to be declared a shrine or a national monument or something.

Pledge $25 and receive a set of Essential Salte and Peppere Shakers hand-crafted of durable Chinese plastic. Even in the nightmare world to come, you'll need to eat, and condiments will keep your rations tasty.

Pledge $100 and we'll send you a pair of inflatable green "I Love Cthulhu!" water wings. When the god returns, you'll encounter flooding and his fierce aquatic minions, and this stylish accessory can protect you from both.

Pledge $1000 and our alien pals the Mi-Go will take you (well, part of you) on a fabulous vacation to Yuggoth and worlds beyond!

FAQ
How do you know this guy Larry won't just take your money and run off?

No worries there! We found Larry through his classified ad in the back of *Soldier of Fortune*. They wouldn't let him advertise there unless his credentials were solid, and besides, Muffin has a "good feeling" about him.

If Cthulhu makes a comeback, won't I probably die?

Look at it this way. If Cthulhu doesn't return, then sooner or later, you will *definitely* die. If he's on the scene, he just might confer some form of immortality on a chosen few, and who better than those who helped to wake him? It could be a sweet deal, especially if you like swimming!

I heard that Cthulhu will wake when the stars are right. Where do you factor into that?

At the moment, the stars are right*ish*. Cthulhu could wake soon, but he could also snooze for decades longer. Think how sad it will be if he doesn't get his ass up until after you're dead, and you miss all the excitement.

It doesn't have to be that way! My magic and your pledge can goose the process along.

So please, give what you can. It really will change the world, and it will get Grandpa Squamous off my back.

THE VINDICATION OF Y'HA-NTHLEI
By David Busboom

I didn't like his face and I told him so.

It was the spring of 1928 and I was sightseeing in New England. Newspapers were crying about a recent fire that wiped out most of the empty houses and buildings in some ancient waterfront town called Innsmouth, and about a simultaneous explosion that destroyed some reef a mile and a half out from shore. Most papers said arson, but nobody seemed to disapprove. In fact, the few folks who cared at all seemed more relieved than upset, talking about an old brick jewelry factory and some Hall of Dagon or something like that, and saying how good it was that they were gone. One or two papers said government raid, that Innsmouth was lousy with bootleggers and stills, and that the reef was torpedoed to keep smugglers from using it as a drop.

Anyway, I was at a shabby speak in Newburyport reading one of these papers when in walked this man, a damned drunken swine with small ears and bulging eyes and a narrow, balding head. He stank like fish. When he saw my paper he snorted irritably and muttered something to the effect that Innsmouth was nobody's damned business. There was something bizarre about his vocal timbre that made me uncomfortable. I told him I'd never even heard of the place until three days ago, and he cussed at me.

"You'll all get yours," he said. It was then I noticed the scabrousness of his skin and the loose wrinkled folds on his neck. I'd heard some locals call that the "Innsmouth Look." So he'd probably just lost his home, or his business, or both, and had every excuse to be mad—but just then I didn't care.

I'm a reasonable guy, most of the time, with the understanding that we're all God's children regardless of race, language, or appearance. But I'd had a few myself and this guy was funny-looking in a different way. Nobody would ever call him handsome, but, more than that, he seemed downright sinister. I could tell most of the people in the bar shared my unease just by looking around. There was an unnatural curve to the corner of his mouth, more pronounced now by the involuntary twitching of his upper lip; a warning that a man is carrying too much liquor and is getting to the stage where he'll slop over, which is his own business, of course, and not mine—except when that man decides to slop over on me.

"I don't like your face," I said, feeling mean and satisfied to get it off my chest. "In fact, I was going to drive to Rowley tomorrow, but I think I'll go tonight so I won't have to look at you any longer."

The Innsmouth man growled and cursed away to himself.

"Let him be, now," the bartender said. "His temper will work itself off."

"Miserable sluggard," I said.

"He's as the Lord created him," the bartender said. "But why He did it I don't know. Those damned Innsmouth fellers got it in their heads to spread all over New England now, except now they don't have that jewelry people were so mad to spend their money for. People will sure be keeping their eyes open for that stuff, now the factory's gone."

Here the Innsmouth man waved his hand and mumbled something indignant. The bartender went on: "I hear some Innsmouth folk are finding work on fishing boats, diving for pearl-oysters. Say what you want about their looks, they can dive more than fifty fathoms deep. Not entirely hopeless, if they don't mind a little adventure. I hear they're as comfortable in water as out, even the women."

The Innsmouth man blew into a sky-blue handkerchief and went on cursing to himself.

Suddenly he moved closer to me.

"You don't like my face, eh?" His pale-blue eyes stared, unblinking. The rough skin on his forehead contracted and formed little ridges all the way up to the wispy blackness of his receding hairline. The quivering lips turned into a sneer. There was something unnatural about that leering, threatening face. The stink of fish and booze was overwhelming.

I leaned back against the bar.

"Why don't you just crawl back into the water?" I said.

It occurred to me then that he might be carrying a gun. I can draw a little quicker than most men, but being quick on the draw's not much when your revolver's in the car outside.

So I moved down the bar, pretended that I didn't see him follow me, and also ignored the bartender's pantomime, which was to indicate to me that I was holding a Roman candle in my hand, with the wrong end up. Which was sound advice—but I didn't fancy the bartender butting into my affairs.

"You're a smart guy, ain't ya?" The Innsmouth man's elbow crooked on the bar and his uneven cheek went into his own coarse palm. "Private investigator? A dirty dick? And you don't like my face. Well—a lot of people don't like to see it. They've got cause to fear it." He paused a moment, licked at his lips, sort of smiled unpleasantly to himself—then his unblinking eyes glared at me like an animal, his lips slipping back.

"Well—it's ugly enough," I told him. "Why don't you take it downtown and use it to frighten policemen?"

"Yeah—yeah?" He didn't seem the sort of a guy who went in for light banter. "Yeah?" he said again, and then, "You read the papers. Wonder what they really found in Old Man Marsh's factory? And below Devil's Reef? Wasn't just sharks, by Hydra. Best be careful with us Innsmouth folk—you could die."

He'd been half-mumbling so far, but his voice was fairly loud now and others were listening. His hand shot up and fastened on the lapels of my coat. He jerked me straight—he was surprisingly strong. He kept talking, and his voice took on a slopping quality that gave me the shivers. "Your kind will pay for sticking their noses where they don't belong."

"If you don't want that face of yours even more mussed up, why, take your dirty hands off'a me!" People were gathering now. There was a chance for him to pull back, but he didn't take it.

"Face mussed up!" he repeated. He rather liked his twisted map, I guess. I tried to jerk free, but he held on tight—he was so strong—and threw open his coat with his free hand, let me see the gun beneath his armpit. "You'd like to think you have the guts to cross me?" A slight pause as he shoved his face closer, making me gag with his fish-and-booze reek. "Well—"

I pasted him. Maybe I lost my head. Maybe I didn't. Certainly, though, there was nothing definite in my mind when I let him have it. I had nothing in my mind but his glaring eyes and protruding chin and quivering lips. If I had any desire at all, it was to shut his foul mouth—and perhaps that's even stretching the truth a little. The desire, after all, was just to sock him.

He let go and stumbled back a step. He wasn't hurt—just surprised and drunk. I landed another punch right on his nose and he hit the floor.

I jumped over him and left before he could reach for his gun. "I'll kill you! I'll kill you," he shrieked after me, in a dazed sort of way. But I was already at my car.

I decided to cut my sightseeing short.

Three years later I was on a honeymoon cruise with my new wife, Anne, whom I'd met in Chicago after my return from Newburyport. It was eleven at night, and we were some thirty miles west of Cornwall aboard the ship Guinevere. The cruise had taken us on a tour of the Celtic Sea to Ireland, Wales, Devon, and Cornwall, and was now on its way back home to America. We were leaning on the rail, taking a breather. From the saloon came the sound of the dance continuing, and the crooner asking, "What is this thing called love?" The sea stretched in front of us like a silken plain in the moonlight. The ship sailed as smoothly as if she were on a river. We gazed out silently at the infinity of sea and sky. Behind us the crooner went on baying.

"I'm so glad I don't feel like him; it must be devastating," Anne said. "Why, do you suppose, do people keep on singing these dreary songs?"

I had no answer ready for that one, but I was saved the trouble of trying to find one when her attention was suddenly caught elsewhere.

"What's that?" she said.

I looked where she pointed at a small spot among the still, moonlit waters, and with some surprise. Something was sticking its head out above the surface to look at us.

"A fish?" I said.

We regarded the creature for some moments.

"It seems to be coming closer," Anne said.

We went on staring, and it came quite close. "There's another one," Anne said.

Sure enough there was: another head, a little smaller, a few yards to the right of the first. "*And* another," she said. "To the left. See?"

She was right about that, too, and by this time the first one was keeping pace with the ship in our slow wake.

"They might be some kind of dolphin," I said, and shrugged my shoulders as casually as possible, though I didn't believe it myself. I could see the thing's ugly mug now. It was a pale, grayish green and completely bald, with a narrow head that shined wetly in the bright moonlight and a wide, froglike mouth. But worst of all were its eyes—bulging, dark orbs that never seemed to blink.

I'd overheard some talk among the ship's crew about increased sightings of "sea devils" in recent years, but those half-remembered snippets were only secondary in my mind to a strange familiarity that both fascinated and repulsed me. These scaly monsters looked almost human, in their way.

We watched all three of them slowly getting closer, leaving little wakes of their own in the water as they approached ours.

"Five now," said Anne. "What are they?"

Others were leaning over the rail, and they appeared to have seen the creatures, too. Now there were eight of the things, nine, a dozen...

I shivered with sudden terror. The closest of the creatures had reached the edge of the ship, and now out of the water stretched an *arm*. Not a fin or a tentacle, but an all-too-human arm, ending with a long, webbed hand. With this it pawed at the side of the ship as though it intended to crawl up.

The rest of the things continued their approach. There was time for people to go back into the saloon and fetch their friends out to see, so that presently a line of us leaned all along the rail, looking at them and guessing:

"Did you ever see anything like that before?"

"Devils from the sea!"

"Man, there aren't any devils. And if there were, they would look like Europeans. Those things must be some kind of fish or something."

"A fish hasn't got any hands, sir. I went to school..."

"Didn't Beebe see something like that in his bathysphere?"

"Three fishing ships lost in the Pacific last year, two more off the coast of Iceland..."

They looked about man-sized, as far as we could judge; all we could be sure of was that they were crossing our wake and descending on the ship in a long, crooked line.

My wife looked from me to the creatures. It wasn't a memory that would linger pleasantly in her mind. I wondered if I should get my gun from our cabin.

Now the first creature pulled itself out of the water, anchoring itself to the side of the ship with claws or suckers or whatever was on those big hands. Then, swiftly, its companions spread out along the ship's sides and followed suit. They were indeed of the approximate size and shape of a man, with two arms and two legs and a total height or length of about two meters.

Then they spoke.

They were beginning to climb up when the croaking sound of their voices reached us. It was an articulate speech, but one I'd never heard the like of, full of frothy hisses and barks. They kept repeating something that sounded like someone half-belching the syllables *ee-ha-nith-lay.*

I decided we were in immediate danger. The crowd sort of fell back, and I took the opportunity to retrieve my gun. It was just a .22, and I had no idea if it'd prove deadly against these giant fish-frogs, but having it made me feel bigger, more in control, and it took the edge off my fear.

By the time I got back the passengers were scrambling all over the deck with desperate haste, and the first fish-beast was already clambering over the rail.

"Clear the way!" I yelled, and shot it in the face. It jerked back with a hiss like steam, but those huge, webbed hands clung tight to their perch. Another shot sent it tumbling back into the sea. The second of them came up, in just the same way, in almost the same spot. Five of them climbed up in total, one after another, only for me to send them back to the water with great whooshes. Then I was out of bullets.

And they were still coming, fast.

Bells clanged, the beat of the engines changed, and we started to change course. The crew turned out what few weapons there were to be had—fewer than a dozen firearms between them and the passengers, myself included, and not even a full spare load for each. Some men carried wrenches and other tools as makeshift clubs; one passenger even had a bayonet.

There wasn't time to organize all the able men. The monsters were boarding from all sides, and they didn't wait. Soon it was an all-out brawl. Some of them carried long knives that looked like whalebone.

One of them, clutching such a knife between its teeth like a pirate, stood out a bit from the rest. It was naked and bald, like the rest of them, but stood a bit more erect, with skin that was less scaly in patches. There was something familiar in its hard, cruel face, with its fishy lips and bulging eyes a little smaller than those of its brethren.

The Innsmouth Look.

The memory hit me like a brick. It was the man from the speak!

I think he saw me but I can't be sure. At least, he never looked straight at me. I stood back in the shadows while he went by to gut some poor sap, slicing the guy open like a calf in a slaughterhouse. I wanted to vomit.

Fingers fell upon my arm. I whirled, my pistol raised like a club.

It was Anne.

"Come on," she said. Her voice was soft, but her face betrayed her terror. "We have to hide!"

I nodded. She could see as well as I that it was useless to get mixed up here. The boys were fighting bravely, but the devils were still boarding and as soon as the bullets ran out the tide would turn fast. I followed Anne back through the narrow halls to our cabin. I don't think anyone saw us, but then being inconspicuous wasn't our highest priority just then.

We've been here all night. The fighting ended long ago, but we can still hear those croaking voices and the shuffling of webbed feet. I wonder if they intend to scuttle the ship. We can't be the only ones left. Someone else must've lasted this long, must've hid like we have. There were hundreds of people aboard. I only saw a few dozen of *them*—but who knows how many more crawled up since we abandoned the massacre?

Now I stand with my back against the cabin wall, Anne in my arms, and through our small porthole the sea looks placid and empty in the fuzzy morning daylight—but I know now what flounders beneath that unperturbed surface. If the captain radioed for help, it hasn't arrived. Perhaps our would-be rescuers met a similar fate.

Are we witnessing the beginning of humanity's end? I'd rather not think so. I'd rather wake up from this nightmare, finish my honeymoon, and eventually tell a kid with Anne's freckled looks and my unusual last name about the time Dad had a bad dream full of sea monsters.

It does no good to cry over what we never had, but I do anyway.

I hear a noise at the door, as of many slippery bodies lumbering against it.

"God," Anne screams. "The door! *The door!*"

It buckles, and creatures tumble in with a reek of fish and a chorus of gurgles, the Innsmouth man among them. Anne cries in my shirt and I hold her tight, unable to look away from my boogeyman. He looks straight at me this time, and I see recognition in his face as he raises his bloody whalebone knife and closes the gap between us.

"Get *yours*," he croaks.

ECHOES IN PORCELAIN
By Konstantine Paradias

For Gladys, it all started when the voices started whispering from her toilet bowl.

It took her a while before she realized it, as this problem began the way all great problems do: subtly, without warning and at the worst possible moment.

Gladys had been having bowel trouble, when she heard the first whispers. Distorted by the echo in the toilet bowl, they sounded like garbled transmissions (the kind she'd pick up in her car radio as she was crossing a tunnel). But later, as she was about to flush, the distortion faded, becoming a very clear and distinct sound that shook her to her core:

It was the sound of tiny voices, laughing hysterically.

Gladys flushed and shut the lid in one motion, staring at the toilet bowl as it gargled and roared. There was silence for a moment, which eased her mind. She was about to attribute the event to early onset of senility, when the noises began anew. Gathering her wits about her, Gladys kneeled closer to the porcelain bowl and stuck her ear to the lid, hoping against hope that she would hear nothing but the tumble of water and the gentle rumble of post-flushing.

What she heard instead, was:

"Scram, bitch!"

She did not go back to her bathroom for the rest of the day, no matter how loudly her stomach rumbled or how badly her gut ached. Instead, Gladys sat at her living room table, her eyes transfixed on the bathroom door, listening for any sounds.

Much to her dismay, they didn't cease for the entire day.

It was sometime around the afternoon, when Gladys was not having her scheduled nap and was instead pacing around her living room, when she came up with what could have been a rational explanation.

The sound proofing in her apartment building was wafer-thin, at best. The sounds could have been coming from the floor below her. Perhaps what had scared her out of her mind had, in fact, been nothing more than an insensitive prank that her downstairs neighbors were playing on her. But the prank had gone on long enough.

Without bothering to change out of her pajamas, Gladys put on her slippers, grabbed her sturdy oaken cane and made her way downstairs. Loud hip-hop music was blaring through the door. Without missing a beat, Gladys brought the solid bronze tip of her cane down on the door once, twice…

"Who the hell are you?" said the young man in the paint-stained overalls over the din of relatively modern music. Gladys clenched her teeth.

"My name is Gladys Montgomery and I'm here to tell you that this has gone on long enough!" she screamed.

The young man looked at the short, wrinkled woman that was staring up at him, seething with fury, motioned her to wait and turned off the music.

"Listen, if this is about the music, then I'll have you know I'm installing some proper sound proofing. You just need to be patient; it's just going to take me a couple hours, tops…"

"I'm not here to complain about the music, young man. I'm here to tell you that I'm on to your little game and that it needs to stop." Gladys stamped her cane on the floor.

"What needs to stop?"

"Young man, I am very much aware that I have been the victim of a cruel prank that has me scared witless and unable to enter my own bathroom since early this morning. Apparently, one of you residing in this house, perhaps even you, has been spewing profanities toward me by shouting through your bathroom ceiling."

"Excuse me?"

"You heard me! One of you, in fact, called me a…" the word came out with some effort "a bitch."

"Listen, Mrs…"

"It's Miss. The name's Montogomery. Gladys Montgomery" said Gladys, sounding downright tough.

"Miss Montgomery. There's no one else here and I have been very busy, trying to get this apartment ready. I've been here since last night, got the sound proofing almost set up, I've worked myself raw and, to be perfectly honest with you, I haven't had any time to prank you."

"Show me your sound proofing, then. If you're telling the truth, then you have nothing to hide." Gladys leaned on her cane, narrowing her eyes at the young man, who backed down at the sight.

"This way."

So he showed Gladys around the house (a one-bedroom apartment) and Gladys looked at the new paneling and the soundproofing foam and the cans of paint scattered all over. She took the time to inspect the boxes of his belongings (verifying his claims and sating her gossipy side at the same time) and at last, headed for the bathroom.

Much to her dismay, the bathroom had been covered in layers of thick plastic carpeting; the paint spatters on its surface reminiscent of early Jackson Pollock artwork, while the ceiling had already been layered with soundproofing foam.

"I haven't even been able to use my own bathroom." The young man explained. "I've had to go to the deli across the street."

Gladys felt her heart sink, as she turned to the young man and shook his hand, smiling apologetically.

"I'm so sorry for all this. You must think I'm losing my mind." Gladys said and hoped that this was the case.

"Not at all, Miss Montogmery. I'll keep the music down from now on, okay? Perhaps that'll help."

"Yes. Yes, I guess it will..." Gladys muttered, as she made her way back to her apartment. The whispers from her bathroom greeted her the minute she opened the door. With her knees shaking, Gladys sat back in her place on the living room table, staring at the bathroom door and wept.

By that afternoon, Gladys had mustered the courage to call an exterminator. She explained the problem, presenting a rational explanation that would retroactively translate horrible, human-like whispers into rat squeaks. The man on the phone was helpful and his voice was warm and consoling. Gladys would have felt much better after she put down the phone, if she hadn't heard the sound of her bathroom mirror shattering the very next moment.

By the time the exterminator came, Gladys had spent two hours locked inside her bedroom. Her gut was hurting fiercely now, making her eyes water. She ran to the door and tripped, nearly hitting her head on the fireplace's mantelpiece. Something from within her bathroom cackled maniacally.

When she opened the door, the exterminator noticed that she had been crying.

"Everything alright, Miss Montgomery?" he smiled at her and seemed like a knight in shining overalls, wreathed in a cloud of pesticide.

"Yes. Please kill them…" Gladys whimpered. Her knight in overalls shook her hand and smiled the way fairy tale princes smile, as they unsheathe their swords before they ride to battle.

"You'll never hear from them again."

Gladys left the house as her working class champion began to concoct his mix of chemical death, stirring and shaking his magical brew inside the canister on his back, muttering words of caution and exterminator-wisdom. Gladys left him to do his work, already feeling much better, with her gait lighter and her thoughts unburdened.

She thought of her bathroom and her peace and quiet. She thought of the whispers from her toilet bowl and rationalized them, turned them into squeaks and cries of rats, which made her feel uneasy, yet certain that the world was the way it should be. Her gut still hurt and her stomach still rumbled, but it was a matter that she could now cope with, tangible and easily resolved.

Her hopes were summarily crushed when she returned home. There was the scent of rusted copper and of something acrid and sinister, mixed with a touch of something foul that made her feel downright sick. There was silence in her home, a silence that was deep and tangible; the kind of silence one can only find in a wake.

The bathroom's door was open.

Gladys peeked in.

When the police came over, fifteen minutes later, Gladys was still screaming, trying to convince them of the sight she'd seen: the sight of the exterminator's leg, poking out from the toilet bowl's rim, dripping filth on the linoleum floor. It had been gone now, dragged inside the toilet bowl, leaving no trace.

All in all, the police officers were understanding. They did their absolute best to calm Gladys down and tried to get their forensics team in and out of the house as soon as possible. None of them burdened her with unnecessary questioning. None of them believed that something in her toilet bowl had also dragged a fully grown adult man through the s-bend, either.

A cynic might say that all they did was nod and smile and look around her bathroom and smashed mirror while pretending to do their job, before they left her to fend off on her own. Said cynic would not be far from the truth.

Gladys looked at her bathroom, the door now ajar. The voices had come back the second the forensics team left the house. She could hear them clearly now, reverberating though the sewage pipes and bathroom walls, words peppered with the sounds of tiny mouths, chewing:

"How'd you like that? How'd you like it, you crazy bitch?"

Schleck, schleck...

"Why don't you come over, then? You must be bursting!"

Click-hrr-click!

"Come on over, join us! We promise we'll make it quick!"

A tiny little head with ochre-colored eyes, dripping toilet water, poked out of the toilet bowl rim and winked at her.

Gladys ran down three whole floors, before she tripped over her oaken cane and tumbled down, nearly busting her hip. Swept up in pain, despair and terror she cried, her voice resounding through every floor in her apartment building.

It was fifteen minutes later when one of the doors burst open and a tired, old face of a man peeked out and shouted:

"Shut the hell up!"

She didn't give up all that easily, of course. Gladys tried calling an exorcist, first and foremost, believing that perhaps the word of God would make those creatures leave their haunt and leave her in peace.

The priest found nothing, of course. He didn't speak a word of it, but Gladys could read the look in his eyes plain as day, as he gathered his things and bid her farewell.

He never spoke a word of it, but they said:

Dear Lord, this woman's lost it.

He didn't show it in his eyes, but she knew he was thinking:

Her brain's rotted.

But religion wasn't Gladys' last resort, of course. Even though the pain in her gut had grown and she was feeling sicker every day, forced to sleep in hotel rooms for an entire week, she sought (and found) alternatives.

She tried calling animal specialists. She tried calling spiritualists. She got the phone number for a ghost-hunting agency. She paid a psychic to spend a night in her bathroom (and was not surprised in the slightest upon seeing her run screaming out of her house and into the street). She visited a psychiatrist, halfway convinced that this was all in her head. Through the psychiatrist, she met an elderly war veteran who had an affinity with weaponized flammable substances and asked him to give it a try.

After the fire department managed to put out the fire and the paramedics had safely escorted him to the hospital, Gladys finally made up her mind to try her very last resort.

When the time of countless prophecies came, and the multitude of stars overwhelmed the night sky, when the drowned city of R'lyeh did rise from the waves, revealing to the world its inhuman glory, it did not bring with it the eschaton or even the promise of disaster.

What it brought instead was multitudes of the poor and the suffering, who, having been trapped in their underwater enclosure for millennia-their natural resources long since depleted-rushed to the nearby shores and sought refuge. They were creatures of the deep, barely human in nature, which possessed the art of manipulating the arcane. They brought with them the knowledge of impossible geometries and unimaginable wonders, which they gave away in exchange for a place to live and three square meals a day.

In exchange for this, they were called "drownies" and were persecuted for giving mankind the gift of becoming more than what they could have ever dreamed.

Gladys always considered herself an open-minded person, with modern sensibilities, unfettered by the prejudices of people her age. She had a lot of colored friends and frequented establishments that were considered too "exotic" or "low-brow" for most in her social circle. Back in her day, people would have called her "tolerant" when she was around and "a dirty beatnik" behind her back. But Gladys' greatest weapon had, so far, been her ability to brush off those arguments and ways of thinking, choosing instead to enjoy the strangeness of the world she inhabited to the fullest.

Which is what gave Gladys the strength to walk into the drownie ghetto on a Sunday afternoon, into the very first store that seemed to possess a façade of what some people playfully called "spirituality".

The proprietor of the place, who eyed her over from his place behind her counter, the wood hidden under rows upon rows of unspeakable things floating in formaldehyde, eyed her over as she came in.

"Shtoresh's closhed." he spat, his thick lips slapping together.

"I'm…I'm not here to purchase anything." Gladys muttered, straightening her back, summoning every ounce of strength that she could muster, even as his huge eyes rolled in their sockets, transfixing her.

"We don't shell on Shunday. Inventory day."

"I have a problem. A very...peculiar problem. I need to find someone who can help me."

The owner of the place leaned over the bench. He seemed to stretch as he leaned closer, his face becoming elongated, distorted. Gladys did her absolute best not to turn tail and run away as fast and as far as her legs would take her.

"We do not deal with shplit-toe problemsh."

"Please. I have money, I can pay you. I just need someone who can help me…"

"Money? You think money will changhe my mind? You schplit-toesh come here in drowney town, treat ush like fish-filth and you think if you pay me I help you? You think drowney ish magic, don't you? You think drowney will shave you with mumbo-jumbo and juju? No. You schplit-toe sholve your own problemsh," the owner said, spraying salty, thick spit at Glady's face. His gills were flaring now, spraying water on each side of his face.

"No…" Gladys said, even as her eyes watered and her lip trembled. The strike of her oaken cane on the wood floor resounded in the store like the thundering of a great god's hammer, ceasing the store owner's ranting immediately. "I need someone's help because something lives inside my bathroom and it whispers to me every day and it's already killed another man that I sent there to drive it out!"

The store owner stood silent, contemplating Gladys' words, trying to make sense out of them.

"There's something in my house and every split-foot thing I've done so far has failed utterly. So please, I am imploring you, please help me or introduce me to someone who can…" Gladys said and there was a great weight in her chest that sagged once and then dissipated, never to return again.

The store owner reached to the unknown depths behind his counter and produced a chair, which he brought over to Gladys.

"Have a sheat. Tell me what'sh the matter."

So, Gladys told him about the tiny head with ochre-eyes and the terrible smile, the dead exterminator and the exorcism and every single failed attempt that had driven her near-mad with worry and fear. When she was done, the owner smacked his lips and said:

"One shecond."

Turning his waist in a way that seemed to Gladys downright obscene, the store owner twisted round until the top half of his body was facing the counter. She watched as he wiggled and waved his webbed fingers over the jars and then grabbed one, seemingly at random. He handed it over to her in one motion, a great jar made out of thick glass, filled with mud-brown fluid.

"Thish will make your problem go away."

Gladys looked into the jar, gently jiggling it, spying a black shape sloshing in the depths. She caught a glimpse of an eye the color of amber, the flash of something tombstone-white. The store owner's hand grabbed hers, ceased the motions. It felt wet and rubbery, like fish scales fresh out of the freezer that have only just thawed.

"Don't shakhe it. Jusht take it home, leave it there with your problem and it will make it dishappear."

"How…how much do I owe you?" Gladys asked, looking up at the great smiling face. In her heart of hearts, she wished that he'd look at her with eyes aglow with malice and speak with a voice that was rumbling, his spittle flicked with sulphur. She wished that perhaps he'd ask her for her soul, or the heart of a child. What she got instead was, somehow, even more alarming.

"For the good schplit-toe lady? No charge. Jusht come over one day, tell me how it went." he said. Gladys took the jar in her arms and left, barely containing her urge to break into a run.

When Gladys got back to her apartment, she was greeted by squeaking and squealing and cries from her living room. There was a riot in her kitchen as well; tiny voices screaming in unison, their every word a mockery of human language, accompanied by the crash of fine china and the clanking of kitchen utensils. It ceased the second she walked in. There was silence in her apartment suddenly, punctuated by scores of beady eyes.

She turned to look, suddenly numbed to horror, witnessing her tormentors:

Their faces were devoid of hair, their mouths overflowing with a multitude of teeth. They had long bodies, flabby and covered in coarse hairs the color of rotten pomegranates. They had arms, long and jointed, with tiny fingers and miniscule claws. They had feet like rat's feet and naked tails that trailed filth across every surface they touched.

The silence was broken as one among them (in Gladys' eyes the leader of the swarm by virtue of his girth) looked up into her eyes from his place inside her favorite coffee mug and said:

"Why if it isn't the lady of the house! Come to cry and beg some more?" his voice was greeted with tiny, shrieking cheers. Misshapen hands clapped and thin lips whistled.

"No. I've come here to ask you kindly to leave." Gladys responded and the jar with the brown liquid in her hand felt suddenly so much heavier, ridiculously heavy. Gritting her teeth, Gladys held it tighter, until her knuckles ached.

"Leave? Why would we leave? You're near mad and you fed us good meat on our very first day! You have plenty room, as well! If anyone should leave, it's you!" the lord of the swarm said. Had there not been such contempt and haughtiness in his voice, perhaps he would have turned Gladys away. Perhaps it would not have made her mad enough to want to squash him with the jar and even if it did, then maybe it would not have been thrown with enough force that it would have shattered.

But that is exactly what happened, as Gladys' rage grew and burst out and became of cry of wrath that gave her arms strength to toss the jar into the air. The lord of the swarm jumped out of his mug, narrowly avoiding it. He was splashed with the brown liquid but thought himself otherwise safe.

"You missed."

There was a growl from the black lump, no longer contained within the jar. There was the flash of hungry eyes and a flash of bone-white teeth. There was a screech that made every window in the house rumble in its frame. There was a cry of anguish among the rat-things, for they knew what it meant.

"Oh no" the rat-lord prayed, as the teeth came crashing down upon him.

When the drownies came to land, they brought with them more than just the secrets of non-standard physics. The fauna of R'lyeh and its intelligent pests that plagued them came right along with them. Mankind hated and feared those intelligent things that spoke their language and knew how to bypass their traps and means of containment. The pests, in turn, loved mankind for its inability to deal with them.

But the "drownies", who had lived with those pests for millennia, had known exactly how to deal with them. For a swarm of rat-things was intelligent, tenacious and malevolent. Therefore, the people of R'lyeh had been forced to breed a countermeasure that possessed ten times as much cruelty and three times their speed.

The fact that some of them had also cross-bred with regular household cats didn't hurt either.

Gladys watched in fascination, then shock and finally revulsion at the carnage that was taking place. She saw the creature that had popped out of the jar, a mass of flesh, fur and unimaginable appendages lash out at the swarm, running its claws and teeth over the mass, leaving behind only blood, shattered bone and severed limb. There were pools of blood and matted fur on her floor. There were stains that looked vaguely man-shaped on her flower wallpaper. There was a great green-red mess clogging up the sink.

It took the cat-thing an entire hour of running, slashing, biting and smashing before the noises ceased. Gladys caught sight of some swarm stragglers, as they climbed over the bodies of their comrades, seeking refuge in her toilet bowl, thinking themselves unseen. A second later, there was only a great black blur and a half-dozen voices, silenced in a flash.

When it was all over, Gladys watched the cat-thing that had curled itself up on her living room, table, chewing into the flesh of the lord of the swarm. She saw that it was still alive, bleeding out and very much aware of both the pain and its condition. It reached out its arm and mouthed:

"Please...kill me..."

Gladys walked away, gathered her mop, her broom, her duster and started cleaning up her house, silently muttering to herself, enjoying her newfound silence.

All in all, there were around two hundred of the swarm that Gladys placed in plastic bags and tossed in the garbage. One hundred and ninety nine tiny, mangled bodies accounted for, to be specific. Only one pleading little mess of bone blood and fur that squealed at her, halfway through being eaten alive inch by painful inch, remained:

"Don't do this! Don't let it eat meeee!"

Gladys smiled, walked into her bathroom and sat down to enjoy a moment's peace. The swarm-lord's cries went on for an entire hour, before they were finally silenced.

SHADOWS OF THE DARKEST JADE
By Sarah Hans

Satindra and I followed the Silk Road out of Gandhara and down into the plains of the Empire of Han, surrounded by merchants and travelers. The people we met along the Indus River, even many miles beyond prosperous Gandhara, recognized our saffron robes and gave generously to our alms bowls. We sat at their fires night after night, welcomed guests. In exchange for food and a warm place to sleep, Satindra told them of the *dharma*, mediated their disputes, and blessed them with his quiet strength. I knew, as I sat listening to him retell the tales I had heard a hundred times, the Guru had chosen wisely when he sent Satindra among the Han, for he had the calm charisma and sagely demeanor that befit a true disciple of Amitabha Buddha.

As we journeyed, the number of other travelers on the road began to dwindle. Eventually, we left the great Silk Road and walked into unknown territory. The road narrowed and wound its way through expanses of rice paddies, where stoop-shouldered peasants labored in the hot sun.

Unfortunately, the people of the Han Empire had rarely seen monks and, even more rarely, begging monks, and did not know what to make of us, especially as one of us was a foreigner and the other was barely a man, then unable to grow a beard. When we brought out our alms bowls, they scoffed, made offensive remarks about beggars, and some even spat on the ground at our feet. We ran out of our carefully preserved rice ration within a few days of leaving the Silk Road, and were so hungry our steps began to falter.

"Brother Satindra," I said reluctantly as we trudged through another hot, dusty day. "We must find food." I meant to imply we should steal what we could not beg, though I could not bring myself to suggest it outright.

Satindra nodded. "Amitabha will provide," he said, with perfect faith, never indicating whether he understood my hidden meaning. "The Guru sent us here to bring the *dharma*; Amitabha will provide."

I'm ashamed to say I lost faith, but Satindra never stopped believing. Even as we staggered up to a small, bamboo-and-mud hut, so exhausted we could barely stand, he drew his alms bowl from his robes and said the traditional words of blessing in a voice weak with hunger. The smell of the evening meal drifted out to us, a scent so tantalizing I moaned aloud.

The girl who came to the door of the hut could have been my sister. She was small and golden-skinned, her jet-black hair tied modestly at the nape of her neck. She wore the simple, cotton garments of all the Han peasants. Her narrow eyes — so like mine! — grew wide, and she turned and ran back into the house, calling to her elders in the local dialect.

I groaned again, this time sure of defeat, certain that we would be turned away and meet our deaths on the dusty road. Satindra turned and looked at me, a smile curving his chapped lips, and said, "Have faith, little Brother."

The girl returned with two women, one hugely pregnant, the other small and elderly with a round, plump face. Both women immediately ushered us into the hut, without any questions or explanations, and just like that, we were saved and Satindra's faith was proven.

The girl's name was Jun. The pregnant woman was her mother Bao-Yu and the elderly woman was Jun's grandmother, Grandmother Mei. The men of the household were off drinking rice wine and gambling, Grandmother Mei said, so the women could do what they liked, including feeding wandering monks. She explained all this while we eagerly devoured rice and what I can honestly say was the most delicious hot soup I've ever eaten. Grandmother Mei chattered throughout the meal, gesturing with her small, shriveled hands, squinting at us with her beady, black eyes and smiling a toothless grin. Unfamiliar with the local dialect, I only understood about half of what she said and poor Satindra, who spoke only the scholarly language of the Han and none of the rough dialects of the peasants, understood nothing. Nevertheless, we nodded enthusiastically and tried to be a good audience.

Finally, when our appetites were sated, Grandmother Mei asked us to tell our story.

"You will have to excuse Brother Satindra," I said. "He only speaks the scholar's tongue."

"Your accent is strange," Grandmother Mei said, squinting at me over her plum-like cheeks.

"I was raised in a village near here," I said, "but I have been away for many years. I remember very little."

She nodded, sitting back on her pillow, and repeated her request for our story.

I obliged as best I could, using words from the scholar's tongue and the dialect of my village interchangeably. This seemed surprisingly effective.

"We are monks from a monastery in the nation of Gandhara," I told her. "Satindra is gifted with languages and I was born in Han, so our Guru thought it would be wise to send us to spread the word of the *dharma* here. We have walked a long time, seeking the village where I was born. I don't remember the way, because I was very young when I left home."

Grandmother Mei snorted. "Why did your parents send you away? A healthy, strapping young boy?"

"I was told later, when I was older, that I was sent away because my family was so large my parents were unable to feed all of us."

The old woman nodded sagely, her head bobbing on her neck. "A few years ago, there was drought. I remember well, there were many families whose children starved." She clucked her tongue at the misfortune of it all. "Your parents were farmers, then?"

"Yes. My father and mother both worked in the rice fields. I remember four brothers and one sister, but there may be others, who were sent away like me, or who were born since I left."

"You should be grateful your mother sent you to live with the monks," Grandmother Mei chided me, perhaps hearing some sorrow in my voice when I spoke of my family. "She saved you from a life of backbreaking work, toil and sorrow. Instead, you have learned to read and write, haven't you? And now you travel the world!" She snorted. "It's a lucky thing for you. I only wish that little Jun were a boy so we could send her with you, away from this life."

I looked at Jun, who blushed and looked away. "Some say that the Amitabha Buddha's most dedicated disciples were his wife and consorts," Satindra volunteered, speaking slowly in the scholarly language of the Han nobles.

Grandmother Mei guffawed her skepticism. "The day women are allowed to become monks will be the day we learn to piss standing up!" She laughed wildly, slapping her small hand against her thigh. Bao-Yun and Jun looked uncomfortable, but smiled obediently at the old woman's coarse joke. Wheezing with laughter, Grandmother Mei requested tea and little Jun hopped up and began preparing tea for all of us.

"Tell me more about your Amitabha," Grandmother Mei demanded and, while Jun ground tea leaves and boiled water, Satindra and I did our best to explain the *dharma*.

While we talked, Jun placed an earthenware bowl of tea in her grandmother's hands, and the old woman sipped and made appreciative sounds. "It's too bad neither of you needs a wife; little Jun is an expert tea-maker, already, and she is barely ten years old! Think what a woman she will be in just a few years!"

Satindra and I blushed and looked at the floor. Some orders of Ambitabha's followers took consorts, but ours did not; we were humble monks dedicated to poverty and chastity. Grandmother Mei chuckled at our modest reaction to her words and said, "Did your mother make tea like this, Little Brother?"

"You should call me Wen, Grandmother Mei," I replied. "And yes, she did. I remember the scent of it." And it was true: the scent of the mint leaves crushed with the tea leaves brought back memories of my childhood and the bamboo house where I slept chest-to-back with my brothers.

"Then the village of your birth is near here, Brother Wen. You will always know what part of the Han Empire you're in by the taste of the tea, because the leaves taste different and are prepared differently wherever you go." She took another sip and sighed contentedly.

My memories stirred as Jun placed a bowl of tea in my own hands. The minty scent and warmth of the pottery clasped in my hands brought me back to that dark, warm bamboo hut with my family. "I don't remember much about the village, not even the name," I said softly. "But I do remember a festival, where we burned offerings of tea leaves like this...the festival of the Jade Crane."

Grandmother Mei threw up her hands so quickly her tea bowl dropped to the floor, spilling hot liquid across the dirt floor. She shrieked something unintelligible and the eyes she turned to me were no longer sparkling with kindness and amusement, but rather were full of fear and loathing. Her toothless mouth opened, a black cavern, and she made a loud keening sound that raised the hairs on my arms. The change was so abrupt I had no time to react; no one did. We all just stared at Grandmother Mei for a moment, baffled.

Then the little girl and her mother took action. Bao-Yun put her arms around her mother and began speaking calmly to her, so that gradually, the keening subsided to a low moan. It was still a terrible sound, like the squalling of an infant. Jun, meanwhile, collected the tea bowls from me and Satindra, and hustled us out of the house.

"What did you say?" Satindra asked, as Jun pushed us from the hut.

"I only said there was a festival in my village," I replied. "The festival of the Jade— "

I could not finish this thought, because Grandmother Mei began to shriek again, and little Jun pressed one small hand against my mouth. She shook her head fervently, her narrow eyes so wide I could see the whites all around her black irises. She pushed us both out of the hut and down the road a little ways, and then ran back into the house.

Satindra and I stood in the dark road for a few minutes, listening to Grandmother Mei's terrified wailing. It had all happened so quickly. We stared at each other numbly, then placed our alms bowls back into our robes and began to move down the road, away from the house.

Eventually, the wailing stopped and we heard the sound of footsteps. We turned to see Jun running toward us, a small bag of uncooked rice in her arms. Wordlessly, she pressed the bag into my hands. Her eyes were full of fear, but also compassion, and I thanked her for the generous donation. Then I said, "What did your grandmother say when I mentioned...the bird?"

Jun frowned, licked her lips, and glanced back at the hut, where the firelight spilled out of the open doorway and onto the road. "'Cursed'," she said, in a whisper, and the wind seemed to steal the word from her mouth, so it did not linger, but was whisked away into the night, so it almost seemed unreal. I wanted her to repeat it, so I could be sure of what she had said, but instead, she turned and ran back to the house.

"'Cursed'?" Satindra repeated. "Does that mean what I think it means?"

"Yes," I replied.

To my surprise, Satindra laughed, drawing one arm around my shoulders and patting my back. "Don't let a superstitious old woman frighten you, Little Brother. Cursed. Ha! If anything, we are blessed. Let's find a field where we can spend the night."

We slept under the stars that night and, though I glowered, Satindra remained in high spirits. He detailed the reasons we were lucky: before her fit, Grandmother Mei had blessed us with a generous meal and a chance to share the *dharma*; the evening was a pleasant temperature, and no storm clouds threatened to interrupt our sleep with rain; we had not been robbed or set upon by criminals; and we knew that soon, we would arrive in the village of my birth, and perhaps even find my family. Two wandering monks could hardly want for more, he said, as we bedded down in a cow field.

The following day, I was melancholic, having slept fitfully. Our morning meditation, where we chanted a mantra as we walked, brought me no comfort. During the hottest part of the day, we rested. Satindra cooked a little of the rice Jun had given us and we ate it slowly, savoring every grain. It tasted slightly of mint and the flavor brought me a confusing jumble of memories.

When we walked on the Silk Road, we passed many shrines to local gods. Some of the richest had been statues carved of jade or ivory, housed in pagodas and tended by priests. Travelers had laid offerings of milk, honey, rice, and even meat at these shrines. As we left the main road, the size of the altars became less impressive. Every day or so, we passed one of these little shrines, usually with a tiny, crude stone likeness of some god or another, or simply a collection of pebbles meant to be a marker. There were usually the remains of meager offerings at these smaller shrines, or no offerings at all, because so few travelers passed them.

Now, as we walked farther from the Silk Road and Grandmother Mei's house, the character of these shrines changed. Though we had ignored the altars previously, I now felt compelled to look at the small statues. The other shrines along this country road had been simple cairns or had little hand-carved animals made of a common stone or wood, something that would have no value to thieves. But the afternoon after our encounter with Grandmother Mei, we passed a shrine with a statuette, carved with great detail, out of what appeared to be some kind of jade.

I crouched in front of the shrine, staring at the dark statuette it housed in what might have been half of a huge, stone bowl, turned on its side. The little statue was black, and mostly in shadow, but when the sunlight hit it just right, it looked green, like the darkest jade. The details of the statue were difficult to discern, but the shape was not human, nor that of any animal I had seen before. I got the impression of bulbous eyes and an elongated head and many arms, like the Hindu goddess Kali, but no matter how I squinted, I could not determine the exact features of the statue. Finally, thinking that perhaps my fingers could make sense of what perplexed my eyes, I reached out and ran my fingers over the stone.

I expected the cool hardness of jade, but instead, the stone was warm, perhaps from the sunlight, and the texture was wet and slippery. I jerked my hand away and looked at my fingers, expecting them to be wet; they were dry, though the sensation of the oily stone remained. I didn't want to touch the thing again and couldn't stand looking at it, so I backed away from the shrine and hurried to catch up to Satindra, who squatted further down the road, waiting for me.

"What's wrong, Little Brother?" he asked as I joined him, still staring at my fingers. They felt tainted, somehow, as if I had touched something unclean. I had the urge to wipe them on my robes.

"There is something wrong with the statue in that shrine," I told him, scowling.

Satindra chuckled. "I think today you're determined to find something wrong with everything," he replied.

Thinking that perhaps he was correct, I sighed and resigned myself to our daily trudge.

We walked for several days more, each day passing more of the shrines with the black-green soapstone idols. The road became increasingly pitted and overgrown with weeds, narrowing down to almost nothing, but the shrines seemed only to grow larger, each statue taller than the last.

Even stranger, the number of people we saw along the road dwindled as the idols to the local god grew larger. The fields once full of workers were now empty, the rice overgrown and unkempt, as if the crops had simply been forgotten. The fields that had once gone on forever now ended in forest, and the forest was reclaiming those fields.

Eventually, we came upon some simple bamboo huts much like Grandmother Mei's, but these were empty and beyond them, the forest was dark and forbidding. The remains of cooking fires were still smoldering, in some cases, and half-finished cups of tea sat beside dirty rice bowls swarming with ants. After investigating one of these houses, I turned to Satindra and said, "It's as if everyone has just disappeared. This is unnatural. I don't like it."

Satindra tried to laugh off my fears with his usual grace, but failed. His laughter sounded hollow and misplaced in the silent, empty village. "Don't worry, Brother Wen. I'm sure there's some explanation. We should find a place to sleep."

Though we were not superstitious men, Satindra and I did not sleep in the village. We ate the last of our rice in a field nearby, where we could see the huts without being too close to them.

Every night since Grandmother Mei's, I had slept poorly, my dreams fraught with screaming old women and huge black birds with sharply curved beaks. Now the birds dripped oil and opened their mouths to shriek with Grandmother Mei's raspy voice, "Cursed! Cursed!" I woke in the night, sweating and tangled in my robes. I looked about for Satindra and found him crouched beside me, awake and alert despite the late hour. His eyes were so wide I could see the whites even in the darkness that shrouded us.

I followed his gaze to the abandoned village. There were lights moving among the previously empty huts. I started to say something to him, to suggest that we go speak with the villagers, but he silenced me with a hand squeezing my arm. Never had I seen him like this, with every nerve taut and straining, so I bit my tongue. After some time, the lights moved away and Satindra turned to me.

His eyes looked doubly huge with his face so dark. The night around us was eerily silent, not even the wind stirring the fallow rice fields. "I don't think those were people," he whispered.

"What do you mean?" I replied, squatting beside him in the dirt so we were almost at eye-level.

"I saw their faces. They didn't look right." He shook his head emphatically.

"What did you see?"

Satindra swallowed hard, as if something large and ill-tasting were caught in his throat. His huge eyes remained fixed on my face, unblinking and intense. "*Dakini*'."

Dakini is an ancient word that refers to an otherworldly, inhuman being: a god or a demon.

"We should go," I said.

To my horror, Satindra shook his head. "No," he said firmly. Though his hands were shaking, he stood, his eyes still fixed unswervingly on me. "This is why we were sent here, Brother Wen. Your people need to hear the *dharma*. The Guru sent us here to free your people."

I shook my head and stood up, too. Satindra was a full head taller than I, so I still stared up at him. "No, Brother Satindra! The Guru could not have foreseen this! We cannot go alone; it's too dangerous. We should return to the monastery..."

He interrupted me by gripping my arms hard and giving me a little shake, as one would a hysterical woman. "You would dare to question the enlightened Guru?" He released me abruptly and I staggered back.

Satindra whirled away from me and walked resolutely toward the village.

I watched him for a few moments, debating what to do. The night air seemed to rush into the space left by Satindra's quick departure, enveloping me in dark, cool silence. And then, beyond the quiet of the abandoned village and the overgrown fields, I heard a sound, faint but persistent. At first, I couldn't identify it. Then I thought it was the buzzing of insects. Finally, I realized that it was human voices, chanting a repetitive mantra.

I ran after Satindra.

The tracks of the *dakini* were easy to follow; they had not bothered to hide their movements, and we followed their trail of muddy footprints and broken branches deep into the dark, dense forest, where trees and bushes tugged at our robes and we tripped over huge roots. Here, we lost the trail, the darkness was too omnipresent, but now we could hear the chanting and the high-pitched, frantic notes of a zither.

The chanting people were in the center of a clearing, where they sang in the darkness without benefit of a fire. I couldn't see the zither-player in the darkness, but I knew he was off to the right somewhere, because I could hear the slithering, off-key notes. He played no tune, just as the chant seemed to have no rhythm. I had thought that perhaps, upon approaching the chanters, we'd be able to discern their words, but I realized, as we grew closer, the words were gibberish, meaningless, though they repeated them with conviction.

In the dim moonlight, we could see the villagers were mostly naked, though a few still wore shreds of clothing. They were turned away from us, kneeling on the ground, facing something at the center of the clearing. I had to peek around Satindra's bulk to get a glimpse of them - it was impossible to walk two abreast in the close forest - but I could see that a few were dancing ecstatically to the tuneless music. The din was horrible and I covered my ears to drown out what I could. It made me feel confused and hopeless, as if the veil between sanity and insanity could be breached by this combination of sounds.

There was a stench that made my eyes water. It smelled like rotten meat, sour milk, feces, and blood, all together. I fought the urge to vomit.

Satindra stopped in front of me and I ran into his back. He had stopped moving completely and I clawed at him, trying to make him move so I could see the people in the clearing, but he was frozen in place. Standing on my toes, gripping his shoulder, I was able to see a little around him, where the moonlight illuminated the dancers. For a moment, I saw with terrible clarity the twisted bodies, arms and limbs akimbo in unnatural positions, scattered on the ground. Among them were the tiny feet of children and the gnarled hands of the arthritic elderly. The dancers moved around and on top of these motionless forms, naked bodies gyrating horribly, eyes wide and mouths distorted.

Beyond the dancers was the thing they worshiped. It was so tall it blotted out the stars behind it, dwarfing the huge trees, and I squinted to make out its features. Was that a long, crane-like neck or arms? Was that a deformed head or a stooped back? Like the statues in the altars along the road, it was a thing that could not be seen completely, as if it undulated without moving.

Suddenly, Satindra turned and wrapped his arms around me, crushing me to his chest. His hand held my head against his shoulder. He mumbled something as he held me hard against his robes. I didn't struggle at first, thinking that perhaps he was frightened and hugging me against him in fear, but soon, I ran out of breath. Crushed against his chest, I could not inhale, so I fought him. Taller and stronger than I, Satindra won easily and, as I thrashed against him, he chanted softly in my ear, "Don't look, Little Brother. Don't look at it!"

I awoke some time later back in the village. Satindra sat beside me, guarding me from the possessed villagers lest they return, his eyes wide and unblinking as he stared into the darkness. When I asked him how long I had been unconscious, whether we should go back to the monastery, whether we had any food, his only reply was to repeat his bleak chant: "Don't look, Little Brother. Don't look at it!"

These were the only words Satindra spoke throughout our journey back to the monastery in Gandhara. The trek was dismal, now that Satindra was no longer an inspirational young monk, but instead, a mad, sorrowful man who sometimes screamed at strangers and other times, wept uncontrollably for hours. The weather turned foul and we trudged through mud up to our calves. We both grew pathetically scrawny, bones showing through our skin, but the other travelers shunned us because Satindra still moaned his disturbing mantra. We survived on will alone and the rare, meager donations of those truly generous followers of Amitabha who knew their duty, even if the monks to whom they gave alms were dirty and mad.

We barely survived that return journey and arrived on the Guru's doorstep shells of our former selves. The Guru could get nothing sensible out of Satindra, of course, so eventually, he came to me to ask what had befallen us in the terrible wilds of the Empire of Han. I could make no words in reply.

Now, knowing that death awaits me soon, I can write about the events that occurred, though they seem like a fever-dream after so many years. Even now, however, there are parts of the story I can't reveal, which I will take to the funeral pyre. These horrors destroyed poor Brother Satindra, who died muttering his cursed phrase to the last, mere days after our arrival in Gandhara. He left me alone to carry the burden of the horror and now, at last, I will be free of it, for perhaps in death, I will at last no longer see the jade crane when I close my eyes, blotting out the stars with its vastness, or hear the chanting of the mad acolytes dancing naked at its feet. There was a time when I sought the peace of enlightenment, but now I seek only the silence of death, where these terrors may be obliterated in nothingness.

THE DREADFUL MACHINE
By Martin James Hunter

1.

The moment I laid eyes on the new start I knew he wasn't going to last. Half of it was the look on his eyes, the other half was the look in everyone else's eyes when they watched him.

A lot of people don't make it in this line of work. Not many minds can cope with being planted this deep into the ground for long. The average new start does five days a week and the average worker does seven. I have been doing entire weeks devoid of fresh air and sunlight for longer than I remember. It has been a long time since I have seen my reflection. I imagine I am not a pretty sight.

The horrid gloom we work within helps no one. Even in my apathy I can taste it: the darkness that nestles within the oily depths of the shadows, the dull throb that resonates through the caverns, and the dreadful machine, always rumbling in the distance like an empty stomach. The heat too, emitted from its insides, made worse after twelve hours of working in the same suit collecting sweat and oil and dirt and sometimes piss. Then wearing it again the next day. Then for another year.

My suit smells terrible. Everyone's does. The tough leather is falling apart and the shoulder is torn. But we are used to it. Used to recycled uniforms and moribund tools. Used to safety equipment that is a hazard in itself. Used to the smell of ancient piss and shit. Hardly even notice it really. Only made aware of it when a new start comes down the cargo elevator twitching his nose and pretending the reek doesn't bother them. They all do that, then they either get used to it or lose their job. Back up the cargo elevator, or worse.

Workers with strong morals never last. Eventually they find out what the job really entails—the reason we are all sweating and bleeding and sometimes dying down here—and they can't take it. Through desperation they skip the part in their contract that warns them they won't like what they see, and often find they have made the wrong choice. Some of them are forced to remain in the caverns, they never last. Others have successful appeals and make it back onto the surface, but never really leave the machine behind.

It feels like aeons since I signed that contract. I used to work five days a week like all the other new starts. Every Friday night I would board the cargo elevator for fresh air, but nobody goes on like that. You can't look anyone in the face anymore knowing what you do down here. You find yourself paying for goods in shops with your eyes on your feet, ignoring your apartment door, drifting away from anyone you were ever close to. Then you take a little overtime. You work a few weekends. A few more. The next thing you know you join the hive. The beds are filthy but cheap and there is nothing special about the food, but they are free and you don't have to communicate with anyone to get it.

The caverns were not always like this. The conditions used to be good, the equipment worked, and the workers were fairly normal. The machine infected us from the top down; we never see the management anymore, we just seem to know what to do.

It is the end of my shift and I have just entered the sleeping quarters I share with twenty other workers. I tug at the leathers that encase me until they finally give. The flesh on my legs is bone white. No one notices my nudity.

A locker slams shut beside me. The sound of painkillers clinking together. Peter sits on the edge of his bed holding a novel. He has been on the same page for fifteen minutes now. The colour in his eyes has begun to go.

Last night I watched him shoot awake glistening and fighting for breath, scanning the beds around him until he came to me. We remained like that for a moment. His eyes hinting at the ineffable images of his dreams. I offered no help, just watched.

Today his eyes are pink and he seems a little dazed. He shares his dinner table with five empty seats. Above him a single bulb trembles from distant machinery. Other workers gather in groups and watch him poke at his breakfast.

The whole thing seems familiar. In fact I remember the same thing happening to me. The loss of appetite and the insomnia and the nightmares and the ceaseless glaring. It crossed my mind in the past that maybe everyone encounters these symptoms in their first few weeks. It is, however, what happens to you afterwards that counts. The change that takes place. You either pledge your loyalty to the machine, or become an opponent.

The penalty for speaking of the dreadful machine on the surface is either immediate conscription, or being hung in your home town. It's in the contract we all signed. When we were starving its words meant less than they do now. It's almost worth staying away from the surface just in case the wrong words roll from your tongue by mistake, and alcohol is best avoided.

These tunnels may be dark and cruel but it is not as though the surface of the Earth is without its problems. The world of love and charity and children and trust is also the world of disease and rape and murder and corruption and deceit. At least down here the unbearable truth is not kept from us.

Once on the surface an officer realized I had forgotten my ID card before I did. This is classed as having no official identity and I was almost conscripted to fight against Eastasia there and then. Somehow I managed to persuade the officer to come to my flat to rectify the mistake and offer compensation for the misunderstanding. After a thorough examination of my genuine identity card and the confiscating of a twenty year-old bottle of whisky, he left me alone.

The cargo elevator is only open to employees twice a week. Once on Friday night on its way to the surface, and once on Monday morning on its way back down. I stayed in my apartment for the rest of the weekend dying to be lowered into the ground again like a corpse, and to stay put like one.

2.

I have no idea what day it is. Weekdays and weekends are all the same now. There is no rush hour traffic or quiet nights anymore. There is no rain on glass or bar of sunlight as I pull myself from my bed. Nothing to suggest there is a natural world up there. Just the feeling of grubby leather as I drag my suit over my skin. Lockers slam shut and lungs are noisily cleared. Masks are pulled over expressionless faces. Together we start the march through the caverns to our designated working environment. Our feet move in unison. No one speaks.

We are all trained in most areas but assigned to only one. I operate the dreadful machine from a small cavern, thankfully nowhere near it. Every day I see a vile portion of the thing, a twisting and splicing knot of machinery through a panel on the floor. One of its main organs we call the heart. My job is to make sure the metal keeps screaming and splicing and battering and does not fail.

Today I am training Peter on how to work the heart. I did not hear him awaken last night, and he seems a little less disorientated than usual this morning. Perhaps there is hope for him yet. As I show him how to operate the control panel he is like a dog watching its master.

When I step aside he struggles to emulate me. I show him a second time but he still manages to almost break the thing. Three of the other workers watch him motionlessly from behind. Their silhouettes flicker and jerk under the torchlight like shapes tossed from a dying projector.

"Concentrate. Clear your head and try again."

"I'm trying."

"Not hard enough. You're distracted."

"I'm sorry. I don't mean to…"

"Clear your head and watch me again. Closer this time."

"Right."

I go through the procedure a third time. He watches closely before giving it another attempt. He struggles. Pulls at the lever, tugs at the valve, bashes the dial. There is a great moan of old metal as oil dribbles from above and quenches the machine's thirst. I nod and tell him to do it again.

Later he is trying to tell me about his wife and children but I pay no attention. He will soon learn small talk has no place in these tunnels. I also revoke my opinion on his progress. A man with so many connections to the surface has no place here. He does not belong amongst our dark ranks. I feel it will not be long until his replacement is standing in the same spot he is.

He asks me when I think the cargo elevator will be fixed since he has not seen the surface in over a week. I do not answer. He asks me about myself, my family, my life. I do not answer. My silence finally spreads to him. We continue working only in the company of our own thoughts.

I do not remember ever having anything to live for. My family was never there for me as I grew up, but I preferred it that way. My father was in the military and died before I reached fourteen. My mother was never the same. She would drink and ask me why I was nothing like my father. I never answered her. She eventually threw me out one summer and it was the last I ever saw of her. I felt as though I had just walked from a terrible job.

I have never had a lover. Never held a woman in my arms except one geriatric who collapsed on the train one morning. Never kissed or groped or made love to anyone. At first all I wanted was to meet someone, but never had the confidence to initiate conversation. My looks have never been on my side either. I eventually got used to the loneliness. Started to accept it. My libido drained from me and my emotions followed. I knew I was going to wind up dying alone and I realized I didn't mind. Then I found myself here.

I am torn from my thoughts by the wretched howling of a co-worker. I spin in time to see someone being dragged into the pneumatics as though they were a napkin. Oil spatters over the offending steel arms—the worker's last command—coating them in black as though covering up the murder. The others do not rush to help, nor do they deactivate the machine. They just watch for a moment in silence as the machine screams and clatters. The sound of knives being drawn across another. Then they resume their duties.

I turn back to the control panel. There is nothing I can do for the man now. Nothing anyone can do when someone serves the machine a final time. I grip a valve and turn to the rigid man glaring at the heart. I tell him to watch as I show him again.

3.

It comes as a surprise to me when I find out the worker claimed by the heart was in fact a woman. Everyone looks the same in their overalls and masks. Even without protective clothing I hardly bat an eyelid at the opposite sex. They are always walking naked in their sleeping quarters, unnoticed and unappreciated.

Occasionally two workers will fuck between shifts but no one ever pays any attention. It is only ever new workers that watch their female colleagues as the leather is peeled from their bodies. Another way to distinguish the new starts from the experienced.

I am woken by the approaching footsteps of a fellow worker. Soundlessly, he hands everyone a sheet of paper. My eyes are still aching as I scan over mine. It takes a moment for the words to make sense, and a few reads to fully process them.

I have been reassigned to feed the dreadful machine. For the first time in years I feel my heart jump. I feel the gastric juice in my stomach go cold and splash up its fleshy prison. I feel my spine jerk and tremble as though it is going to fall apart and leave me trembling and broken and helpless in this horrible place. The messenger holds out another sheet to Peter, daring him to take it.

Peter has been reassigned with me. He does not react to this news since he has not seen the machine yet. Does not realize what these words mean. Even I fear what awaits us in the great cavern, despite having already experienced it for a short period some time ago. This is coming from a man who has felt close to nothing in at least ten years. Distantly, I begin pulling my overalls over my body.

The great cavern is fervent and humid and foul-smelling and the noise is deafening, a thousand iron cogs and arms screaming in unison as they twist and turn and scrape and smash together, locked in eternal combat. I peer over the balcony and gasp as I behold the dreadful machine, a skirmish of metal and flesh, an orgy of machinery, a million scythes being sharpened at once. The dreadful sensation that any moment a spear may shoot out and pierce a worker and drag him back to its glimmering stomach. Amongst this even greater knot of metal and thick coral tissue and the occasional glimpse of ivory. Organic matter, nestled within the steel and iron. Fleshy orifices pulsating. Emanating heat and stench. Forever hungry.

And now it is time to feed it. I take one of the four valves at either side of the large gate. Ten others pull its chains like primitives restraining a behemoth. The gate comes down heavily, spilling bodies into the shimmering mouth. Mothers, children, infants. Hundreds of them fall like ragdolls poured from a toy box. Soundless figures toppling through the air to be crushed and devoured as they meet the machine. Torsos and skulls bursting and sinking amongst steel teeth, yanked into its depths, fed into its fleshy components. Limbs dance and jerk like obscure sock puppets before sinking into the steel.

Peter is staring over the chasm at the madness, his reaction invisible beneath the leathers. Now that I have seen the first batch of bodies being fed to the machine I feel better. The horror has passed and I am on my way to feeling nothing again. Obediently we continue.

Another bay is loaded up with the dead then spilled onto the pneumatics where they are burst and swallowed and rended. We repeat this a further four times until it is as easy as taking out the trash. So many bodies, dead from natural causes, diseases, murder, lethargy. All taken from their coffins and shipped down here along with scraps from battlefields. Splayed soldiers, hunks of torso, tattered limbs. Crammed in a container like pet food.

The worst has yet to come. I shake my head when I hear them in the next batch, trying to reject my surfacing anxiety. I start twisting my valve again, and watch as the other workers heave at the chains. The gate falls heavily like an iron flap and I can hear their panic as they are tipped towards the edge. Worried murmuring. Then screaming. A hundred Eastasians flailing helplessly as they fall towards the mechanics like birds too young to fly. Some of them still wearing their uniforms, some of them naked, some a mixture of both. Prisoners of war being torn up and spread across cogs and gears and pneumatics like machine grease. Their cries drowned out as they are drawn in. Open mouthed, they are swallowed, draining through the grille until there is nothing left. Relief returns as the last of their voices is silenced.

I don't know why we feed the machine, or what the fleshy thing is that huddles beneath the pneumatics. But I do know that it must be fed to keep the city alive. Without flesh it will starve. The machines and electricity and water will cease, and the population will begin to suffer.

Many years before I was born only animals were fed to the machine. However they say that one day an employee slipped and fell to his death, and that as he was crushed and split amongst the machinery the lightbulbs glowed a little brighter for a moment. A throb of excitement. An idea.

Peter is muttering to himself, attracting the attention of one of the older workers. He stares at Peter through his mask, his body impossibly still. A predator watching his prey. As he slowly approaches I lower my head. It is all I can do now.

Peter has lost it. He jerks into motion, taking off in the direction of the tunnels. Quickly and without effort the older worker has him in a headlock. The mannequins struggle with another but it is clear who has the upper hand. I can hear the panic in Peter's voice now that the physical boundaries have been broken. He now realizes that a different system of justice operates down here.

"You seem a little off, cherry!"

"Let me go!"

"Where were you heading?"

"Nowhere! Get off me!"

"Yeah? I don't think that at all. I think you were running off to squeal."

"No! I wouldn't do anything like that, I swear!"

"Convince me I'm wrong then. Go on."

"Where would I go? I swear to you on my mother's life! I swear to God!"

"God? I'll show you a real God, cherry!"

Others rush to help, but not to help Peter. They grab at him and haul his body into the air. They tear at the leathers and his mask until he is a wriggling knot of limbs. I watch as he is brought to the edge of the platform screaming and wide-eyed. His eyes meet mine and he pleads for me to make them stop. I continue watching in silence.

He is pleading with his assailants now, begging them to spare him. Promising to never speak of the great machine. But he is not amongst normal men. Not dealing with those who are familiar with pity. I cannot see their faces as they haul him over the balcony towards the machine, however I imagine their expressions are blank.

Peter leaves the world the way he came in, naked and screaming for his mother. The pneumatics assimilate his body as he meets them, silencing him in seconds. Having served the machine a final time, Peter is no more.

The gears and cogs groan for more meat. In silence, the workers resume their posts. Chains are pulled and valves are twisted. Then come the howls of anguish from yet more Chinese as the gate swings open and they are tipped towards the edge. As they spill like garbage across a landfill site their voices rise together in a dreadful chorus.

ABOUT THE AUTHORS

Michele Brittany

Michele Brittany is a popular culture scholar and is the editor of *James Bond and Popular Culture: Essays on the Influence of the Fictional Superspy* (2014) and the upcoming *Essays on Space Horror in Film, 1950s – 2000s*. She is a member of *H.P. Lovecast*, a monthly podcast analyzing stories by and inspired by H.P. Lovecraft.

A.C. Wise

A.C. Wise's fiction has appeared in *Apex, Shimmer, Uncanny, Whispers from the Abyss Vol. 1,* and *The Year's Best Dark Fantasy and Horror 2015,* among other places. Her collection of inter-linked short stories, *The Ultra Fabulous Glitter Squadron Saves the World Again,* will be published by Lethe Press in October 2015. In addition to her fiction, she co-edits *Unlikely Story*, and contributes a monthly *Women to Read: Where to Start* column to *SF Signal*. Find her online at www.acwise.net and on twitter as @ac_wise.

Laird Barron

Author of several books, including *The Croning, Occultation,* and *The Beautiful Thing That Awaits Us All*. His work has also appeared in many magazines and anthologies. An expatriate Alaskan, Barron currently resides in upstate New York.

Samuel Poots

Samuel Poots is a 24 year old English journalist and teacher, currently living in Nagoya, Japan. He studied literature at the University of Ulster, Coleraine, focusing on Victorian Gothic horror and American anti-war literature. Sam has worked as a journalist, editor and script-writer for the table top gaming website *Beasts of War* and has had stories published alongside two table top games, as well as by online publishers such as *The Bohemyth* and *Dead Beats*. "The Thing in the Fridge" was inspired by a run in with a fridge in China that had been left by his apartment's previous occupant. He never got up the courage to find out what horrors lurked within.

Richard Lee Byers

The author of over forty fantasy and horror novels including *Blind God's Bluff: A Billy Fox Novel* (Night Shade Books) and the *Black River Irregulars trilogy* (Privateer Press). His short fiction has appeared in such anthologies as Blackguards: Tales of Assassins, Mercenaries, and Rogues (Ragnarok Publications), The Fall of Cthulhu (Horrified Press), The Bard's Tale (Blackspoon Press), Cthulhu Fhtagn! (Word Horde), and Blood Sushi (Dirge Publications), and he has collected some of the best of it in the eBooks The Plague Night and Other Stories, The Q Word and Other Stories, and Zombies in Paradise. He writes an opinion column for the Airlock Alpha SF news site when the mood takes him and invites everyone to follow him on Facebook, Google+, Ello, and/or Twitter.

Chad Fifer

Chad Fifer co-hosts the *H.P. Lovecraft Literary Podcast* and works as a writer and musician in Los Angeles, where he lives with his wife Heather Klinke. He is the author of the coming-of-age novel *Children in Heat* as well as co-author of the Lovecraftian graphic novel *Deadbeats from Self-MadeHero*. His album *Sense Impacts*, an hour of soundtrack for the *Call of Cthulhu* roleplaying game, is now available from Chaosium, and more of his spooky tunes can be found at chadfifer.bandcamp.com.

Mike Hudson

He lives in Austin, Texas.

Konstantine Paradias

A jeweler by profession and a writer by choice. His short stories have been published in the *AE Canadian Science Fiction Review*, *World War Cthulhu* and the *Battle Royale Slam Book* by Haikasoru. His short story, "How You Ruined Everything" has been included in *Tangent Online*'s 2013 recommended SF reading list and his short story "The Grim" has been nominated for a Pushcart Prize. "Whispers in Porcelain" was originally read on Episode 33 of the *Bizarrocast* short story podcast.

Deborah Walker

Deborah Walker grew up in the most English town in the country, but she soon high-tailed it down to London, where she now lives with her partner,

Chris, and her two young children. Find Deborah in the British Museum trawling the past for future inspiration. Her stories have appeared in the 2015 *Young Explorer's Adventure Guide*, *Nature's Futures*, *Lady Churchill's Rosebud Wristlet* and *The Year's Best SF 18* and have been translated into over a dozen languages. "Baby Rhyme Time" was first published in *Innsmouth FreePress* in 2009.

Sarah Hans

An award-winning editor, author and teacher. Sarah's short stories have appeared in about twenty publications, but she's best known for her multicultural steampunk anthology *Steampunk World*, which appeared on *io9.com*, *Boing Boing*, *Entertainment Weekly Online*, and *Humble Bundle*. The anthology also won the 2015 *Steampunk Chronicle Reader's Choice Award for Best Fiction*. Sarah's next project is an anthology featuring characters with exceptionalities called Steampunk Universe. You can find Sarah online at www.sarahhans.com. "Shadows of the Darkest Jade" was originally published in *Historical Lovecraft: Tales of Terror Through Time*, edited by Silvia Moreno-Garcia and Paula R. Stiles, 2011.

Jonathan Sharp

Jonathan Sharp is an occasional writer, and full time maker of noise from the English Lake District. He doesn't get to write fiction anytime near as much as he'd like to.

Kevin Wetmore

The author of short stories published in such anthologies as *Enter at Your Own Risk: The End is the Beginning* (Firbolg), *Moonshadows* (Laurel Highlands), *Dark Tales of Elder Regions: New York* (Myth Ink) and *Midian Unmade* (Tor), among many others. A New England native, this now Los Angelino is also the author of *Post-9/11 Horror in American Cinema* (Continuum) and *Back from the Dead: Reading Remakes of Romero's Zombie Films as Markers of Their Time* (McFarland) as well as articles in *Rue Morgue*, *Horror Studies* and *Gothic Studies*. When not writing, he also acts, directs and is a stage combat choreographer.

Joel Enos

Joel Enos has written comics, graphic novels and books, published short fiction in *FLAPPERHOUSE* and *alphanumeric* and a comics adaptation of Anais Nin's *Under a Glass Bell* in *A Café in Space*. He's also edited many comics, books and manga including the best-selling series, *Tokyo Ghoul*.

Tom Pinchuk

Tom Pinchuk mysteriously emerged from the misty jungles of Southeast Asia and went on to ensnare the whole world in his tentacles. Like Nyarlahotep, he's assumed many guises as he's worked in a myriad of media – creating mind-bending comics like *Hybrid Bastards!* and *Unimaginable*, producing viral web videos to distract hundreds of thousands of anime fans from their schoolwork, and writing international animated TV series that are fun, sunny and not at all Lovecraftian. He hopes this journey into the darkest depths of the psyche has left you shaken, troubled and generally uncomfortable. Thanks for reading! Conjure him at www.tompinchuk.com

Greg Stolze

Greg Stolze is aging and cruel and bores easily. He's been writing horror stories since he was 16, and many of them can be found on his website at www.gregstolze.com/fiction_library. (Try "Locked Up", it's good times.) Lately he has been focusing on the horror games *DELTA GREEN* and *Unknown Armies*, when he's not grooming his brood for literacy and skill in martial arts. He's on Twitter as @GregStolze.

Robert Stahl

Unbeknownst to Robert Stahl, his body is an empty shell, telepathically controlled by a brain in a jar, which was buried long ago under the floorboard of his home in Dallas, Texas. Consequently, his days are filled with the urge to write: stories, letters, articles, whatever. At night, he listens to music, and when he drifts off to sleep, the brain laughs, a humorless, pitiful sound, as it jiggles alone in the dusty darkness. His work has been published at *Acidic Fiction*, *Urban Fantasist*, *Creepy Campfire Stories* (for Grownups), and Odd Tree Press. Contact him (if you dare) at RobertStahlWriter@gmail.com.

Nathan Wunner

Once tried to whisper something into the Abyss to no effect; proving beyond a shadow of a doubt that the Abyss's preferred method of contact is to whisper things to you. Nathan Wunner's work has been featured in magazines and anthologies from Insomnia Press, Surreal Grotesque, Sub-Verse,

01 Publishing, The Colored Lens, XNOYBIS, Ink & Coda, and Infernal Ink. If you'd like updates on future stories by Nathan, you can look up any of his long neglected social media accounts. But we'd recommend contacting him directly at nwunner@gmail.com

ORRIN GREY

A writer, editor, amateur film scholar, and monster expert who was born on the night before Halloween. His stories of monsters, ghosts, and sometimes the ghosts of monsters have appeared in dozens of anthologies, including Ellen Datlow's *Best Horror of the Year*, and been collected into two volumes, *Never Bet the Devil & Other Warnings* and *Painted Monsters & Other Strange Beasts*. You can find him online at www.orringrey.com. "The Labyrinth of Sleep" originally appeared in *Future Lovecraft*, published by Innsmouth Free Press in 2011.

MARC E. FITCH

The author of *Paranormal Nation: Why America Needs Ghosts, UFOs, and Bigfoot* and the novels *Old Boone Blood, Paradise Burns, and Dirty Water*, which is forth-coming from 280 Steps. His fiction has appeared in such publications as *ThugLit*, *The Big Click*, *Pulp Metal Magazine*, *Horror Society*, and *Massacre*. He currently lives in Harwinton, CT with his wife and four children and works in the field of mental health. www.marcfitch.com

JOHN C. FOSTER

John C. Foster was born in Sleepy Hollow, NY, and has been afraid of the dark for as long as he can remember. A writer of thrillers and dark fiction, Foster lives in New York City with his lady, Linda, and their dog, Coraline. He is the author of the novels *Dead Men* (Perpetual Motion Machine Publishing) and *Mister White* (Grey Matter Press). His short fiction has appeared in numerous magazines and anthologies. For more information, please visit www.johnfosterfiction.com.

DAVID BUSBOOM

David Busboom was raised in a castle that his father built in the woods of Champaign County, Illinois. He is a graduate of Eastern Illinois University, where he edited the student produced literary magazine, *The Vehicle*. His writing has appeared or is forthcoming in *Prospectus News*, *Shock Totem*, *Euphemism*, *Gonzo Today*, the *Providence Journal*, *Nameless Digest*, and the

Rogue Planet Press anthology *Swords against Cthulhu*. He lives in Central Illinois and can be reached on Facebook and Twitter.

Cody Goodfellow

Cody Goodfellow has five novels—his latest is *Repo Shark*—and has co-written three more with John Skipp. His collections *Silent Weapons for Quiet Wars* and *All-Monster Action* both received the *Wonderland Book Award*. He wrote, co-produced and scored the short Lovecraftian hygiene film *Stay At Home Dad*, which can be viewed on YouTube. As a bishop of the *Esoteric Order of Dagon* (San Pedro Chapter), he presides over several Cthulhu Prayer Breakfasts each year. He is also a director of the H.P. Lovecraft Film Festival in Los Angeles and cofounder of Perilous Press, a micropublisher of modern cosmic horror. He "lives" in Burbank, California.

Ferrett Steinmetz

Ferrett Steinmetz's debut urban fantasy *Flex* features a bureaucracy-obsessed magician who is in love with the DMV, a goth videogamemancer who tries not to go all *Grand Theft Auto* on people, and one of the weirder magic systems yet devised. He was nominated for the *Nebula* in 2012, for which he remains moderately stoked, and lives in Cleveland with his very clever wife, a small black dog of indeterminate origin, and a friendly ghost. (Oh, and the sequel, *The Flux*, should be out by now.) He Tweeters at @ferretthimself, and blogs entirely too much about puns, politics, and polyamory at www.theferrett.com. (Or, if your work has blocked his site, try it mirrored at theferrett.livejournal.com.)

Hunter James Martin

Hunter James Martin can be reached at hunterjamesmartin@gmail.com

Dennis Detwiller

Detwiller was a founding member *of Pagan Publishing* with John Tynes as art director where he co-created the Origins Award winning *Delta Green* in 1997 with Tynes and Adam Scott Glancy. He is known for his work in the collectible card game *Magic: The Gathering*, to which he was a regular contributor. In the gaming world, he created *Godlike: Superhero Roleplaying in a World on Fire*, *Wild Talents*, and the free horror setting game *NEMESIS*. He also participated in many other projects at Wizards of the Coast.

Patrick McEvoy

Patrick McEvoy draws, paints, animates, designs, podcasts, lives, breathes, and occupies space in the physical universe. His isthe co-creator of the hit mythos-noir graphic novel, *CASEFILE: Arkham*. In the non-physical universe, he can be found here: www.megaflowgraphics.com.

Kat Rocha

Kat Rocha began her career as a collaborating artist on such projects as *Utopiates*, a Catwoman story for *Batman: 80-Page Giant* for DC Comics and *Titanium Rain*. She produced numerous concept designs for Spartan Games and has had work featured in *Interzone* magazine. In 2011, Kat founded 01Publishing with the goal of producing the best in science fiction, fantasy, and horror of both prose and graphic storytelling. 01Publishing's catalog of books have received acclaim from *The Huffington Post*, *SF Signal*, *Kirkus Reviews*, *Innsmouth Free Press*, and *The Examiner*. She is also an Associate Editor with *Escape Artists* and *Pseudopod* and an active member of the *Horror Writer's Association*.

Melissa V. Hofelich

Melissa V. Hofelich is a freelance proofreader and copy editor. Born and raised in South Jersey, she now lives in Atlanta, Georgia with her husband Alex and their two cats. She is the copy editor for *Nightmare Magazine* and a former proofreader for *Lightspeed Magazine*. She has also contributed to several of the special *Destroy!* issues of *Nightmare* and *Lightspeed*. Melissa holds a BFA from The University of the Arts in Philadelphia and is a ravenous reader, gamer, and tikiphile. In her spare time, she is working for a mysterious benefactor, bringing the *Book of Eibon* and *Cultes de Goules* into compliance with the Chicago stylebook. You can find her on Twitter at @melissavh.

DEVOTED CULTISTS
"Celebrate the Cult!"

Nicholas Nafpliotis
William Finney
Jeremy D. Weinstein
Boebzial
Sivert Grindhaug
Justin Smith
Brett Daniel
Matthew Chilblain Willner
Lyman Tyndall
kbk
Lammassu Dam Ki Ag
D.L. Young
Karl Lembke
Cog Shoggoth
RiffTrax.com
E.S. Magill
William Rieder
Henry Case
Joseph Emmerth
Jonathan Sprague
Jeff Chapin
Robert Cougill
Haley McDonald

Mark the Encaffeinated ONE
David Linke
Strange Aeons Magazine
Jason Wilkes
Cisco
Jonathan "Munch" Keim
The A Store
Ricardo Arredondo Casso
David Raynaud
The Beetle
Kevin F. Wilson
Joseph Gustafson
Kerry Gisler
Charles Meyer
Paul Courtenay
Gary Roberts
John F.
Roger Corman
King in Yellow
Steven M
Robert H. Schneider
David A. Del Col
Joe Silvera

Darryll smith-walker	Tim Lonegan
Fabio Montenegro	Jessica Quezada
John W. Oliver	Bethany Scherbarth
Christopher B. Holm	Raven Daegmorgan
None.	George Lundin
Grubnash	William E. Hart
Chad M Smith	Daniel J. Wild
Marcus J Ellinger	Nicholas Diak
AmyA	Neal Kaplan
The Sex Machine	Karen Brigitta Goetz
Marco Piva	Yosef Maayan
Roger Strahl	Christopher 'Vulpine' Kalley
Dan Schwent	@drawnonglass
Laszlo Szidonya	Krisjan 'Top Cat' Cooper
lavvyan	Ed Kowalczewski
Lindsey Morse	Frances Rowat
eric priehs	Eric Andres
Finbarr Farragher	Patrick McGrath
Chuck Norris	Jmhesrn, of the third Oath of
Kent Nessa	Dagon
Scarlett Letter	Dick Jones
David Perlmutter	Alex "MonsterChef" Neilson
Petter Wäss	Kevin Lauderdale
The Amazing BabyPuncher	Derek Wentz
Ken Ringwald	David "Azzageddi" Farnell
Craig T.	Z. M. Wilmot
The Great Ghoul	Adam Kennedy
Jenna MacAulay	James Moss
Matthew Walker	Chris Duncan
Danny Secary	Vincent E. Hoffman
J. Michael Lanaghan	Shawn Marier
Carlos McReynolds	Todd ChicoineJosh King
Matthew Carpenter	Ian Welke
Katie Swanson	Edison Carter
Morgan Baikie	Russell Smeaton
Jean-François Boivin	Ian Welke
William Ide	Russel Dalenberg
Tim Moriarity	Joe Kontor

Ben W Bell
Paul Cardullo
Scott Maynard
Adam Alexander
Lewwy
Alexis Wolfe
Peggy Lee Carpenter
Christopher Hill
Chris Isberg
TrigglyPuff Kicker
Rebecca Fowler
Warpath
Ashley Knight
Claus Appel
Lochlan Sudarshan
Sheryl R. Hayes
Meg Taylor
Kristian A. Bjørkelo
Raymond Sturgess
Antti Luukkonen
Erin Hawley
H.G. Wells
LuciferIsMySavior
Paul Freelend
Chris Ganong
Temoore Baber
Asymptotic Binary
Michael Cieslak
Vertigo
Keelee von Cupcake
James Preston
Aaron T. Cole
John Bolton
Darin DuMetz
James Hardison
Alan Bundock
Mark Smothers
The Deadly Tranny

David Klein
Scott Sysol
William Lohman
Mitch keith
Chad Manning
Thomas Werner
John T. C. III
Callum Stoner
Ben Robitaille
Marine Sniper 99
Bret Burks
DeNaé Culp
J.R. Murdock
Frederick Foulds
@JamesFerguson

ACKNOWLEDGEMENTS

"Forward" © 2015 by Michele Brittany

"We Are Not These Bodies, Strung Between The Stars" © 2015 by A.C. Wise

"His Carnivorous Regard" © 2015 by John C. Foster

"The Labyrinth of Sleep" © 2011 by Orrin Grey

"Death May Die" © 2015 by Nathan Wunner

"Knot" © 2015 by Dennis Detwiller

"Skoptsy" © 2015 by Jonathan Sharp

"Red America" © 2015 by Cody Goodfellow

"Shadow Transit" © 2015 by Ferrett Steinmet

"Baby Rhyme Time" © 2009 by Deborah Walker

"Nyarlathotep's Way" © 2015 by Tom Pinchuk

"Strident Caller" © 2015 by Laird Barron

"Lucky Chuck Takes the Sunshine Express" © 2015 by John Palisano

"Notebook Concerning the Class Struggle in Dunwich, Found in the Ruins